IRON HAND

CHARLIE FLETCHER

Hodder
Children's
Books

a division of Hachette Children's Books

First published in Great Britain in 2007
by Hodder Children's Books

1

A Catalogue record for this book is available from the British Library

ISBN-13: 978 0 340 91164 8

Typeset in Perpetua by Avon DataSet Ltd,
Bidford on Avon, Warwickshire

Printed and bound in Great Britain by
Clays Ltd, St Ives plc

The paper used in this book is a natural recyclable product made from
wood grown in sustainable forests. The hard coverboard is recycled.

Hodder Children's Books
a division of Hachette Children's Books
338 Euston Road, London NW1 3BH
An Hachette Livre UK company

CONTENTS

Wounds are for the desperate, blows are for the strong.
Balm and oil for weary hearts all cut and bruised with
  wrong.
I forgive thy treason – I redeem thy fall –
For Iron – Cold Iron – must be master of men all!

'Cold Iron' – Rudyard Kipling

With all my love and thanks
to Domenica, without whom
none of this would be possible
or nearly as much fun.

THE STORY SO FAR . . .

On a school trip George breaks a carving of a dragon on the front of the Natural History Museum. This wakes an ancient force imprisoned in the Stone – a rough block, hidden deep in the City of London. As an immediate result a vengeful carving of a pterodactyl peels off the side of the building and begins chasing him. Just when all seems lost a statue of a World War One soldier, the Gunner, steps off a war memorial and saves him.

So begins George's ordeal – trapped in a layer of London, an *un*London, a city in which the two mutually hostile tribes of statues – the human-based spits and the inhuman taints – walk and talk and live in an uneasy truce, a truce that George's action has thrown into jeopardy.

1

The thing that makes his ordeal all the harder to endure is that no one else can see what is happening to him, except Edie Laemmel. Edie's a glint. Glints are women or girls with the ability to experience past events recorded in the stones they touch. The thing about Edie's gift is that nobody's ever explained it to her, so she just sees it as a curse and thinks she's mad. She's also on the run.

George, Edie and the Gunner set off on a journey to make amends, but unknown to them the Stone has alerted the Walker, one of its servants, who stalks them through the streets with the help of his own servant, the Raven.

On this journey, George discovers he has special powers that mark him out and make him a target for the enraged taints: one of the dragon statues that guards the City of London slashes a scar on to his hand that another statue, the smiling but sinister Black Friar, tells them is a Maker's Mark. It identifies George as a Maker, someone with a special gift for sculpting things from stone or metal. The Friar also tells them to find the 'Stone Heart' and put the broken dragon carving back to make amends for the damage George has done. Helped by benign spits and threatened by violent taints, they eventually find themselves at the Stone Heart of London, the London Stone.

But on the way the Gunner has sacrificed himself to try and save Edie, and ultimately falls into the clutches of the Walker. It is left to George to use his new found gifts as a Maker to rescue her.

And now the story continues . . .

1

DARKNESS FALLS

The Walker and the Gunner fell into the dark, pitched into a deep abyssal blackness beyond even the memory of light. But even though there was no possibility of seeing anything, the Gunner sensed they were plummeting through a succession of layers, as black seemed to flash an even deeper blackness in an unpleasant negative strobing that he felt rather than saw.

And then the horrible movement through the void stopped abruptly as they hit something solid.

The Gunner's knees crunched down into wet gravel, and his free hand instinctively palmed out to halt his fall, sending a jarring shock up his arm as it smacked into an unseen stone wall in front of him. He hung there, head low, angled between the wall and the ground, panting for breath. He felt wrong, more wrong than he'd ever felt, more wrong than he'd known it was possible to feel. He felt it in ways he couldn't begin to list or explain; it was as if an invisible hand had reached into the core of him and wrenched everything off-true and left it hanging there, twisted and broken.

He heard the birl of gravel beside him as the Walker moved his feet. Using the last of his strength he swiped a hand into the darkness, but his fingers only caught air and blackness.

He opened his mouth in an 'oof' of pain at the effort, instantly clenching it shut and cutting off the giveaway sound. Whatever was happening to him, he was damned if he was going to give the Walker the pleasure of knowing how much it was hurting.

And then the lights came on.

The first thing he saw was the upturned bowl of his tin helmet lying on the stones in front of his thick hobnailed army boots. Then he saw the protective legging buckled on his right calf like the residue of an ancient piece of armour. On a real soldier the legging would have been leather, but in this case, since he was of course a statue, it was made from bronze, like the rest of him. His left calf was unarmoured, tightly wound with bandage-like puttees instead. Above that he saw his hands, strong blunt fingers splayed on the knees of his army britches as he took his breath.

He scooped up the helmet, straightened up, smoothed the front of his uniform tunic, and adjusted the cape round his shoulders. It wasn't a real cape. It was the canvas ground-sheet from a one-man tent, hung round his shoulders to keep the weather off, tied in place with a piece of string through two grommet holes. He put on the helmet and then he stood up straight, every inch the battle-worn World War One veteran that he'd been sculpted to be.

And then his mouth, despite his best intentions, fell open again as his jaw dropped in shock.

They were in a large and ancient underground water tank. His feet stood on a small shelf of pea-gravel that sloped against one wall. This tiny beach took a bite out of a rough square of black water, about ten metres on each side. The irregular blocks of stone lining the walls of the tank were greasily mottled with age and tumoured with sickly blooms of fungus that hung around them at what looked like a high-water mark. Drips from the stone roof of the chamber plopped concentric circles into the dark surface below.

But it wasn't the claustrophobic dimensions of this doorless chamber with its dark water floor and half-moon gravel beach that made the Gunner gasp in surprise.

It was the lights.

Light blazed out from pieces of glass that someone had carefully arranged on each wall to make four gappy castle-shapes facing each other across the black water. A metal disk the size of a side-plate spun lazily on the end of a chain at the centre of the space, bouncing the light slowly around the room.

'What is this?'

The question croaked from his throat before he could stop it. He heard a sniff of contempt and focused on the gaunt figure up to its knees in the water at the edge of the gravel bar. The Walker wore a long green tweed overcoat with a hooded sweatshirt underneath it. He swept the hood back and ran his fingers through long rat-tailed hair brindled with grey. He had a skull-cap on the back of his head, and a jutting goatee framing a mouth twisted in a permanent half-open sneer. His hands held two small circular mirrors which he clipped together and stowed in his coat pocket. Then he bent and lifted a long dagger from the edge of the beach. He unpeeled a thin sour smile as he gestured around the water tank with the gleaming blade.

'This is a dream of four castles,' he replied, indicating the turret shapes on the walls around them. 'It is a vision that came to me, long ago, when I was a free man. It is a vision that I have made real. It is nothing that you could begin to understand.'

He shifted the blade in his hand and sliced angled

reflections of light around the room, revealing more of the edges of the subterranean tank.

'It was a void, and darkness was all it contained until I came across it. Now it is a place of power. My power.'

The Gunner felt burdened and squeezed by the great pressure of earth above him. He felt as lost as if he had been spirited into the bowels of the earth and pinned beneath a mountain. But he was damned if he was going to let the Walker enjoy his discomfort.

"Where are we? Where is this?"

The Walker spun slowly in full circle, sending the reflected beams of light around the dank edges of the chamber.

'We are under London. A city you will only ever see again in your memories.'

The Gunner would have swung a fist at the Walker, but the wrongness inside him seemed to have sapped his normal strength and left him needing all his energy just to stay on his feet. And besides, he had to know what was going on. He was nowhere he'd ever been, feeling like nothing he'd ever felt; and he could always try and flatten the Walker later, when he came within easier reach. Although he had a suspicion that escaping or even surviving whatever was happening to him was going to require more than swinging fists.

'Talk plainer.'

'This is where you stay. For ever, perhaps. Enjoy the light. When I leave, it goes too.'

The Walker looked at the Gunner with something like pleasure.

'You feel it, don't you, inside; the emptiness, the rising horror, the loss of strength, the sense that you're not master of yourself?'

The Gunner made himself stand straight.

'Don't you worry about me, chum. I'm right as a trivet.'

'Oh, I'm afraid you're not. You broke an oath sworn to me. You swore it by your Maker. You have to do what I say.'

'Not happening,' the Gunner snorted tersely.

'Oh, but it is. You're a proud man. I won't offend you by treating you like a lackey. After all, all I require of you is that you die. And all I have to do to effect that happy outcome is to forbid you to dig your way up out of here. And I do. I do order you not to try and dig up towards the light and the clean air. Simple isn't it? One instruction, and you're doomed. Midnight will come, your plinth will be empty and whatever animates you dies; you'll be nothing more than scrap for the smelter.'

The Walker's eyes burned bright with banked up malice.

'Do you still feel master of yourself?'

The Gunner tried to lift his hands, determined to wrench one of the ceiling slabs down into the water to show the Walker he was wrong. But his arms wouldn't move to do it. He shook his head in frustration.

'I think I'm gonna grab you and shove your mirrors where the monkey put its nuts, that's what I think.'

He lurched towards the Walker, but he was much too slow, and the Walker danced back out of his reach. The Gunner stumbled back against the wall, horrified by how weak he'd become, and as he reached back to stop himself falling he dislodged one of the bright pieces of glass.

It fell at his feet and he stared at it, at the opaque surface, at the rounded, sea-tumbled edges of it. And as he stared, his memory fired on reflex – and he saw a similar piece of tumbled glass in Edie's hand. Then it fired again – and he remembered the first time he'd seen her smile, like sunlight breaking cleanly across her face, and he relived the surprise he'd felt when he realized that all it had taken to kindle that blaze was to smile at her and call her by her real name, and he remembered strongly how that realization had made him feel suddenly fiercely protective about this strange and outwardly flinty girl. And that surge of paternal protectiveness collided with the dreadful realization slowly spreading across his mind like a dark stain and made something shift uncomfortably inside him.

He bent and picked the sea-glass up between thumb and forefinger.

'These are heart stones.'

He heard a dry humourless chuckle and looked up into the sour slash of the Walker's smile.

The Gunner heard the horror in his own voice as the question gritted out of his mouth, unbidden.

'What have you done, Walker?'

The gaunt figure above him just kept smiling like a wolf airing its teeth.

'The glints, Walker. What the hell have you been doing to them?'

2

STICKS AND STONES

Edie and George hurried away from Cannon Street, happy to leave the London Stone behind them. They were both shocked and footsore and because both kept their eyes on the hard road in front of them, neither noticed the leaden cloudscape darkening the sky above, or indeed anything that was happening overhead.

Which was a shame. Because what was above was definitely noticing them.

The stone gargoyle on the roof didn't have to look up to see the storm-clouds. It felt the rain even before it started to fall. It felt it as a kind of itchy premonition right in the middle of its back, high between the spiked shoulder blades, in a place it couldn't have scratched even if it had had normal arms instead of the talon and wing arrangement its sculptor had given it. Feeling rain coming in was part of who it was. When rain came it normally had a job to do, spouting water on the roof of St Pancras Station a mile or so to the north. This was not that roof. On this roof it was hiding and watching.

It was hiding because it was in the grip of a new and dangerous sensation: it was feeling curiosity. It bared its savagely curved fangs and stretched its head over the guttering to scan the street beneath. For the first time in its existence it knew that it had something more important to do than respond to the rain-drops now inbound from the clouds above.

It was far more interested in the boy and girl hurrying along the pavement below. And as they moved west up the street, it stalked the parapet, keeping down, bat-like wings folded behind it, stony tendons quivering in anticipation – ready to pounce.

At first glance George and Edie looked like any tired kids after a day at school, hopefully heading back to secure, reasonably normal homes where hot teas waited and a long day would come to a happy ending.

But at a second, closer look it was clear that these children belonged to quite a different story.

Look deeper and you could see the marks of that story all over them.

George seemed about thirteen, shoulders starting

to fill out, bones beginning to lengthen into early maturity, muscles stretching to keep up with the growth spurt. His hair was unkempt and just long enough for him to have to keep sweeping it untidily behind his ears. His jacket was torn at the shoulder and all scuffed up as if he'd been rolling on a very dirty floor. His knee flashed white through a tear in his dark trousers as he walked, and a smudge of dirt smeared along the upper curve of his left cheekbone. The dishevelled look was, however, at odds with the steady and determined set to his eyes.

The look in Edie's eyes was different. She was walking with her head bent down, a long swathe of aubergine-dark hair keeping them in shadow, but in the glimpses of them that George was occasionally getting, he could see that they were troubled, and he could also see that whatever her eyes were seeing it wasn't only what was actually in front of her. Her normally pale skin seemed even whiter, as if all the blood had drained from it, the skin stretched taut with exhaustion. She tripped on a kerb and only his hand whipping out to catch her stopped her hitting the ground.

'Edie!' he said. 'Watch where you're going!'

He saw himself swimming into focus in her eyes as she returned from wherever she had been in her head.

'You ever think you're cursed, George?' she asked

abruptly. George took a second to absorb what she was saying, and why.

'You think you're cursed?' he responded.

She shook her head in irritation, as if he wasn't keeping up.

'Not like by a witch or something, not like turned into a frog; but you know, like you done something bad once, so bad that bad stuff happens to you because of it?'

George rolled his eyes.

'Um. What, like break a statue by mistake and end up being chased through London for a day and a half by gargoyles and Minotaurs and all that? Er . . . yes.'

She shook her head again.

'No, I don't mean that either, I mean before that. Your whole life, like something bigger, something that made you break the statue in the first place, something that screwed up your luck for ever, that sort of thing . . .'

He had a brutal flash of memory: he was shouting something vile at his dad. He was shouting so loud that snot and tears were flying from his face. He saw the answering tears start in his father's eyes. He saw the door he had slammed on his father. And he saw that same door opening later that night, revealing the policeman and woman who had come to tell his mother that there had been a car accident, that his father would never walk back through that door, any door, ever again.

'No,' he said.

The tough spark in her eyes kindled a little as she cocked her head at him.

'Been that peachy and perfect, your life, has it?'

It was his turn to shake his head.

'Edie. We don't have time for this. We need to come up with a plan. We have to rescue the Gunner. If we don't find him and get him back on his plinth by turn o'day, by midnight—'

'I know. He's a dead statue. He'll never move again. I know, George. I'm not stupid.'

'I didn't say you w—'

'I want him back as much as you, you know. I mean, it's not just because he saved us and we owe him—'

'We *do* owe him,' George cut in, emphatically.

'I know. But it's more than that.' She took a deep breath. 'The Gunner made me feel safe.'

'Me too.'

The first few fat drops of rain flecked the pavement, followed by a lot more right behind them. In no time rain was falling so hard that it bounced back upwards off the slick paving-stones beneath them. George instinctively stepped sideways under the cover of a café front, pulling Edie in after him. They had the wall at their back, and the meagre protection of a thin awning overhead.

Seven floors above them the gargoyle on the roof

17

snarled in frustration and leant out, trying to keep them in sight, but all it could see was the pigeon-splattered plastic canopy above their heads. It hissed with fury and scuttled back, trying for another angle. It stopped when it could see Edie's feet. It was pleased they hadn't gone inside the building. That would have been complicated, and it had enough novelty in its head right now without it needing more company.

'What are we doing?' she asked.

'I have to think. We might as well stay dry while I do.'

'OK. But you're right. Time's ticking away. It's getting dark already. Think fast.'

They stood there, watching the deluge. George tried to come up with a plan. The problem was that first he had to conquer the sick fear that kept telling him that finding the Gunner, who had been spirited into thin air and now could be anywhere in the vast city or indeed outside it, was just too big a task for him. He knew he really didn't know enough to make a plan. His mind just kept spinning, and returning to her question about whether he felt cursed.

A young dad walked past with his toddler in a backpack. The backpack had a clear plastic rain-hood on it, and the toddler was laughing and reaching out of the protection of the hood and tapping his father on the head with a series of gurgling laughs as the dad reached back and squeezed his thigh, tickling him. They didn't seem to mind the rain.

He watched them walk past until he became aware of Edie watching him watching them.

'Do you remember when you were a kid and it all seemed safe because your dad was there?' he said.

It was her turn to shake her head.

'Not really.'

He took a deep breath. The only way to rid himself of her question was going to be to answer it honestly. Maybe then he could stop his mind sliding about on the how-to-rescue-the-Gunner problem.

'OK. I do. Before he . . .'

He realized this was probably going to be hard to say.

'Before he died?'

'No. Before I messed it all up. Between him and me. I said stuff.'

'Everybody says stuff.'

He took a deep breath.

'Yeah, but not everybody has their dad die before they get a chance to say they didn't mean it.'

He was surprised. Saying it wasn't as hard as he'd feared. Time passed. More rain fell. Then Edie spoiled the moment by snorting derisively.

'That's the *sooooo* terrible thing you did? That's why you think you're cursed?'

19

He didn't like her tone much.

'What?'

'So you said something nasty. That's nothing.'

He didn't like her tone at all.

'Yeah well, it doesn't feel like nothing.'

'*Yeah well,*' she mimicked. 'It's peanuts.'

He hated her tone. Maybe it was the way she spat the 'P' in peanuts. When you expose a private part of yourself you really don't want people to snort in derision. He pulled his dignity back round himself like a protective cloak.

'Oh and I suppose you've got a deeper darker secret, right?'

'Yeah.'

'Great.'

There was no way he was going to give her the satisfaction of asking what it was. She always had to have the last word. There was no way he was going to ask.

Then she said:

'Sticks and stones.'

And because it made no sense he almost said 'What?', but then he remembered he wasn't going to give her the satisfaction, not after she'd snorted at him and made as if her big secret was *sooooo* much darker and more important than his. So he didn't.

And then she looked at him with eyes as shiny and

tough as the rain-slick street behind her.

'It wasn't just words with me and my dad.'

And George suddenly knew she was telling him about why she felt cursed, and although he also knew the answer was going to be bad he knew she needed to say it. So he asked.

'What does that mean?'

And she said:

'I killed him.'

3

BLACK BIRD

Something was wrong. The Raven felt it in its bones and feathers as it overflew the green space of Regent's Park. It looked down and caught sight of its own shape, doubled in the reflection of a pond below.

For a moment it was distracted from the feeling of wrongness as it saw itself as others must see it. It made, it noted with grim satisfaction, an ominous sight – an elemental winged silhouette starkly outlined against the bruised cloudbase above. In the past it knew people would have looked up from their campfires or plough-handles and shuddered at the black bird-shaped hole it cut across the sky, casting a baleful shadow over their lives as it did so. They would have seen it and thought it was an omen – and not a good one at that. Not that the

Raven put much store in what people thought. Against the scale of time that it had to measure things against, most of them were scarcely here before they died and were forgotten.

It flew on. The cause of the wrong feeling was this: it didn't know where the Walker was. Most of the time the Walker's presence exerted a magnetic pull on the ancient bird who had spent the last four centuries or so in his control.

It circled over the sharp-edged hump of the British Library, slowing its flight as it came in to hover over the front courtyard, where the white and brick-pink grid design on the ground was broken by a perfectly circular sunken area. It was here that the Raven felt it had the best chance of finding the Walker, but the circle was empty.

It needed to find the Walker, and it needed to find the children the Walker had sent it to hunt. And because the Raven had an infinitely retentive brain but only one pair of eyes, it decided it needed help looking. And with that in mind it flew south into the tree-crammed space of Tavistock Square. At the centre of the square was a statue of an emaciated man, half naked and cross-legged, sitting on top of a plinth that had a small arched shrine cut into it. The shrine held a couple of crumpled beer cans and a jam-jar full of bright marigolds. The cross-legged statue had his lap filled with flowers in varying stages between fresh-cut and compost. And opposite him, on one of the park benches, sat a tramp with plastic bags over his shoes and a hank of dreadlocked hair hanging off the back of his head like a dead badger. He leant back to up-end a beer can, blue, alcohol-washed eyes staring at the sky.

As he satisfied himself that he'd shaken the last drop of beer from the can, he belched and adjusted himself more comfortably on the bench, deep within a parka so greasy it looked as if it'd been dipped in engine oil at some time in the distant past.

The Raven dropped on to the back of the bench on which the tramp was sitting. It waited until the man completed a complicated spasm of coughing by spitting up a small green gob of phlegm on to the ground between his shopping-bagged feet.

The Raven hopped on to the tramp's shoulder and gripped hard. The tramp stiffened, but showed no surprise. His voice slurred and rumbled in a deep, partially gargled bass.

'What would you be wanting, bird? What would you be wanting with the Tallyman?'

The bird ducked in closer to the side of his head. The tramp began to judder imperceptibly. His eyes closed and his lower lip disappeared under his upper teeth as he bit down, for all the world like a child concentrating. And what he appeared to be concentrating on was the disjointed clacking of the Raven's beak next to his ear. He nodded slowly.

'We'll see what we can see.'

The tramp opened his eyes and stood up, abruptly, tossing the empty beer can to join its mates in the shallow arch beneath the statue of the cross-legged man.

The Raven hopped into the air and hung there, watching. The tramp still juddered but now his eyes had changed. Where once they had been pale and booze bleached, they were now black, black eyes with no whites, a black as sharp as the eyes of the Raven itself.

Which was, of course, exactly what they'd become.

And all over London, under bridges and on park benches, in back alleyways and in hostels that smelt of old soup and new disinfectant, eyes that had been rheumy and bloodshot, blurred with drink or just simple hopelessness, suddenly changed. Men who had closed normal eyes as they went to sleep in the shelter of vacant shop doors woke up with raven eyes and walked out into the street, scanning the roadway. Lonely women shuffling flatfooted under the weight of a life boiled down into what could be carried in old carrier bags stopped avoiding people's eyes and straightened their necks, also scouring the streetscape.

The Raven had spoken, and all over the city the eyes of the Tallyman had opened.

4

SMILER WITH
A KNIFE

Edie was staring at the downpour beyond the awning, face unreadable as she hugged herself against the cold. George was still absorbing what she'd just told him.

'You killed your dad?'

'Well yeah . . . no, not as such.'

He looked at her in outrage.

'Edie! That's not funny—'

'No. I mean he wasn't really my dad. My real dad. He was a step-dad sort of thing.'

George deflated a little.

'Oh.'

'No, don't worry, I killed him all right.'

George nodded slowly. Keeping up with Edie was

sometimes exhausting, and this was not only exhausting but distinctly disturbing, *and* confusing.

'Right.'

'No. It was all wrong.'

A stream of water from a broken gutter changed direction in the breeze and splattered them. The awning wasn't much cover. In fact it seemed to be doing a better job of channelling water on to them than actually offering protection. She pulled her clothes tight round her and ducked into the alleyway beside them. George was still trying to get used to the fact that she had just claimed to be a killer, so a couple of seconds passed before he realized she had gone and hurried after her into the rain.

The alley was empty.

'Edie!' he shouted, suddenly panicked. There was nothing in the alley but a dead end and a parked and dented Japanese car by a builder's skip.

'EDIE!'

He ran into the narrow space, checking the car as he went, looking for a hidden way out. He couldn't believe it was starting again.

'It shouldn't have happened,' said a small voice from knee level. 'I just belted him.'

He looked down. Edie squatted in the dry area provided by the angled lip of the skip and its overhanging tarpaulin, looking up at him. She shuffled sideways, making a space.

He exhaled in relief and ducked out of the rain next to her. Once more he couldn't make eye contact because she seemed to be looking at something beyond the wet traffic hissing past at the end of the alley.

'Don't do that again.'

She might as well not have heard him for all the reaction she had to his words. She just carried on with her train of thought.

'I just hit him. Didn't know how else to stop him. See, he kept coming after me. With a knife. It was on a beach. I just hit him. I didn't mean to kill him. I just hit him.'

'You killed him by just hitting him?'

'Well. I had a big rock in my hand. He . . .'

She pulled her legs up to her chin and rested it on top of them. George waited for her to go on.

She chinned herself hard on the knees, as if punishing herself for the momentary catch in her voice.

'. . . he was a boozer, drunk all the time. When the pubs were closed he'd go fishing. That's what he called it, but he just went to this beach hut he had and drank more, that's what my mum said. And then, later, when my mum went, when she was taken away and never came back, and it was just me and him, he took me down to the beach. It was the first time I'd seen his hut. It wasn't much. It was one of half a dozen, sort of set into the cliff, next to each other. I'd always thought it'd be wooden, a cool shack kind of thing, but they were more like concrete bunkers set into the rock and when he unlocked his and I looked through the door I saw something and I knew I was in the wrong place and . . .'

She ground her chin harder into the tops of her knees, jamming her mouth shut to help keep something inside.

'What did you see, Edie?'

She shook her head and exhaled.

'Doesn't matter. It wasn't something that was really there anyway. It was something that had been there. Once upon a time. When I touched the wall I saw it, and I knew I should never ever go in that hut and I ran.'

He thought of her gift for touching stone and metal and experiencing the memories of highly charged past events recorded in them.

'You glinted it? You saw the past?'

'Yeah.'

She wasn't going to tell him what she'd seen. She'd made a deal with herself that what she'd glinted in the beach hut was one of the things she just wouldn't ever talk about.

So instead she turned and looked at George and told him the rest of it, the other stuff: she explained how she had just run, and when her step-father had tried to grab her and ask what was wrong she'd hit him in the middle of his smile and sprinted off along the pebble beach.

She told him of how tired she had got, running on pebbles, and how calmly he'd followed her, climbing over the wooden groynes that divided the deserted beach, one after another, the smile on his face wholly at odds with the open knife he held in his hand.

She told George how she'd run up a final steep hill of pebbles and found her way blocked by a deep chasm between her and the new wooden wall being built to contain the stones in high storms.

And then she explained the worst bit, how he had caught up with her on the lip of this man-made ravine. She didn't tell him what he'd said, or how unnaturally bright his smile had been. She did tell him about the knife, and how she had felt the smooth flint pebble under her hand, and how when he had lunged she had hit him with it.

He had gone down like a tree, tumbling into the dark pit at the bottom of the chasm, dislodging an avalanche of stones that land-slid down in his wake. When things stopped moving he was more than half hidden by pebbles. She hadn't known what to do. She had looked at the heavy stone in her hand, and when she saw something wet glistening on it she'd tossed it in after him.

And then she'd walked back into town and got on a train and come to London.

George nodded slowly. Making sense of what she was telling him and realizing he was never going to ask her about the things she wasn't.

'So it was an accident?' he said slowly.

'No,' she said flatly. He saw the doors closing in her eyes, locking whatever heavy burden she was carrying back inside.

'Look, Edie—' he began.

'Have you thought where we're going?' She dropped the question in front of him like a roadblock. It took him a moment to mentally slam on the brakes and change gear.

'I thought that's why we stopped,' she continued. 'So you could think.'

He was aware that she was staring at the side of his face. When he turned, she turned away faster as if she hadn't been. But he knew she had. Her jaw worked. 'So what's the plan?'

'Stay alive. Rescue the Gunner.'

'How?'

'No idea. Start by asking for help seems like a good first step.'

She thought of the things that had helped them before, things and people who hadn't really given them straight answers, only riddles and obscure clues. Still. He was right. They had helped, after a fashion. But there was a problem.

'We can't go to the Sphinxes or Dictionary, because of the City Dragons. We're on the wrong side of the boundary, aren't we? They'll still be guarding it, on the lookout for you.'

'We could go to the Black Friar.'

She stared at him.

'The Black Friar? Are you mad? You said you didn't trust him!'

'I don't. Not entirely. Not as such. But he did show us the way to the Stone, didn't he? I mean, he dressed it up and made it all flowery, but the information was good. He just—'

'He just smiled too much and seemed too eager to get his hands on that broken dragon's head of yours, right?'

He felt the now familiar heft of the dragon's head in his pocket. She went on.

'And the Walker, he was awfully keen to get his hands on it too.'

He nodded slowly, and then shook his head. She was right, but she was wrong too. She had to be wrong, otherwise they really didn't have a place to start.

'I think he might be dodgy, but I don't think he's evil. Not like the Walker. I think he's just out for himself a bit more than the Gunner or Dictionary, you know. I think he'd be open for a deal.'

'A deal? What have we got to deal?'

He pulled out the broken dragon's head and looked at it. As he looked he realized that though he'd been sure it was a dragon's head, when he looked closer it was beakier. More like a gryphon kind of dragon . . .

'This. He wanted it. I didn't give it to him because I wanted to make my own amends by putting it on the stone, but in the end I decided not to, didn't I? So maybe we can give it to him in exchange for help. Yeah?'

In the absence of a plan, and in the presence of fear and danger, sometimes all you need to feel better is forward movement. Edie couldn't argue with his thinking. So she nodded.

'The Black Friar it is.'

He saw she was still shivering. He took off his jacket and handed it to her.

'Go on. I'm warm enough.'

'I'm OK.' She tried to push it back towards him.

'Edie. You're shaking. Put the coat on and let's get moving. We're not going to save the Gunner just sitting here shivering.'

After a long beat she gave in and draped the coat over her shoulders.

And then she stopped and pointed.

'George. Your hand.'

'It's fine.'

His eyes followed her look. He suddenly felt sick.

'OK.' He swallowed. 'It's not.'

5

DEATH OF GLINTS

Something was very, very wrong. The Gunner could feel it like a kind of cold heat filling the whole underground space.

'The glints, Walker? What the hell have you been doing to them?'

His voice echoed round the watery chamber. In the beat of silence that followed the only sound was the gravel crunching under the Walker's feet as he paced the half circumference of the small beach. His tufted beard split lopsidedly to reveal a cruel smirk.

'Oh, I have done much and more than you could begin to understand. And when I have the boy in my power, I shall do more still.'

'I'm not talking about the boy,' grunted the Gunner,

putting the thought of George away in his head for later. Right now the blazing pieces of glass on the walls were the things that had his attention.

'The glints. The wise women, the sharp girls. You've been hunting them. All these centuries. The reason we all thought they was dying out as a breed – it wasn't dying out, it was you. Picking them off. It was *you* . . .'

The enormity of it robbed him of words for a moment. It was as if a great puzzle had been revealed to be the simplest of things, as if a fool should have seen it. The horror of it made his voice raw.

'Wasn't it? How else could you get these heart stones?'

The Gunner held up the glass in his hand, like an accusation. The threadbare shoulders of the Walker's coat rose and fell in an irritable shrug.

'Heart stones? Pah! Baubles. When a man is doomed to walk the world beyond the natural span of his days, he needs a . . . hobby. Mine has been to collect a few dainties and eye-brighteners that give me pleasure.'

It was the pause as the Walker chose the word to describe his actions that confirmed the Gunner's fears and triggered an explosion of outrage.

'You been killing them and stealing their warning stones for a bloody *hobby*!'

The Walker waved a bored hand at him.

'You exaggerate. I don't kill all of them. Killing them

is superfluous, after all. I may kill some, but it's far from a habit and entirely not the point. After all, without their heart stones they're lost and spinning in the wind anyway. Their minds unspool and they're fit for little but chattering and mowing like senseless apes, squatting in their own filth and dribbling into a cup.'

The Gunner shook his head.

'Why, Walker? Why've you been doing this? Why would the Stone want it?'

The Walker almost spat his reply.

'The Stone? The Stone wants none of it. This is *my* doing. The Stone has me cursed and in thrall to it, so I must do all its bidding; but not all I do is at its beck and call. I was a great man, centuries before you were anything – when you were just ore at the bottom of a mine that hadn't even yet been dug – and I will be a man of power again!'

Spittle flecked his beard as his voice rose and the light blazing out from the sea-glass mosaics reflected wildly from his eyes.

The Gunner overrode the rising wave of despair in his gut and twisted his face into a dismissive grin.

'Man of power my Aunt Fanny. I seen blokes with gibbering shell-shock make more sense than you . . . Only reason you're still around is you got on the wrong side of the Stone, and now you're one of its servants.'

The Walker's eyes blazed angrily back at him.

'And what are you, pray? A lump of bronze in man-shape who has broken his word and is himself now doomed to die alone and in the dark.'

He waved his hands at the glass shapes on the walls.

'These warning glasses light up when I'm here because that's what they do when a Stone servant or a taint is near. When I'm gone . . .'

He waved his hand like a magician.

'Abracadabra, out go the lights.'

'Wait,' said the Gunner, appalled at the desperation he heard cracking through his words. 'Those kids . . . don't . . .'

'Oh, the children? The boy who thwarted me? Don't worry about the boy. I shall turn him to my will.'

'I doubt it. You saw how he chose the Hard Way. He's got grit, more grit than I gave him credit for.'

The Walker snorted in irritation.

'He's wilful, Gunner, that's all. He's shot through with the stupid impetuosity of youth.'

'It's grit,' insisted the Gunner. 'He may not have known exactly what 'e was signing up for, but 'e knew it'd be rough. And he did it for the girl. He wouldn't leave her in the lurch, and good on him I say.'

Dark humour danced in the Walker's eyes.

'Yes, *good on him*, as you say, good on him for

protecting the girl, good on him for caring, good on him most of all for showing me what he cares about, because if you find out what a man cares about, then you can take it and threaten it, and then you have a lever. And with a lever and the right place to put it you can move the world. And I shall move the world. I shall change everything.'

'Leave the kids be, Walker. Don't mess with them.'

'Sorry. Can't oblige. I have a job for the boy if he is the maker he seems. Once, many years ago, I had two black stone mirrors, darker than the blackness you will be left to die in when I leave.'

He reached into his pocket, unsnapped two small circular silver mirrors from each other and held one in each hand.

'Compared to the stone mirrors these little glass mirrors are like a baby's toys. A thief and a cheat took one of my black mirrors from me, afraid of the power they would give when used together. One stone mirror – a mirror made of the right stone – one mirror is a thing of some power, but two together . . .?'

His eyes blazed with an intensity that matched the heart stones on the walls.

'Two together can open portals where there are vast powers that make even the might of the Stone pale into insignificance. And it is that power I shall harness to free myself. The boy will make it for me, the girl will choose the stone he should shape—'

'No, Walker, the boy, and the glint, are j—'

The Walker cut across him with a dismissive wave of his hand.

'The boy, the unmade maker and the plucky little glint? The poor dears. Poor, poor dears . . . Strange word, "dear". Say it one way it's something you love, spell it another way and it conjures up stags and antlers and the thrill of the chase. I love the chase – but you know what, Gunner? You know what part of it I really enjoy?'

His smile widened, red and wet.

'The killing,' said the Gunner hollowly.

'Not just the kill . . .' smiled the Walker. 'It's the moment just before, when you know you can either kill or choose not to, and the prey knows it too. That's the best part. When life or death are in your gift. Because that's where the real power is . . .'

And he lifted his foot and with an eye-twisting pop, gently and impossibly stepped into one of the mirrors he was holding. And then he was gone, and the lights on the walls faded and in the afterglow, before the blackness descended, the two mirrors hung there in the air, facing each other, and the last sound the Gunner heard was the Walker's voice, diminishing and very far off. And it sounded like he was saying:

'Whoso list to hunt . . . I know where there is an hind . . .'

And because the Gunner knew a hind was another word for a female deer, he knew exactly who the Walker was talking about, and he was filled with another surge of unbearably helpless fear for her.

6

THE FLAWED HAND

Edie stared at George's hand, eyes wide in shock at what was happening to it. She tore her eyes off it and saw that George had gone very pale as he examined the changes. He was staring so intently that he had completely stopped blinking.

'What's happening to it?' she asked, quietly.

He had no idea. From the scar that the Dragon had slashed on it, three distinct lines had begun to emerge, dark veins colouring the pale skin of his hand as they spiralled down and round his wrist like tendrils on a briar.

'Is it blood poisoning?' Edie asked, tentatively.

He examined the three lines closely, although everything inside him made him want to pull his eyes away from what they were seeing.

'No,' he said, mouth drying up, 'it's something worse.'

Each twisting vein was a different colour and texture from the others. All three were slightly indented into his skin, like flaws in a rock.

'George. We should get you to casualty or something . . .'

He shook his head, fighting the waves of nausea rising inside him.

'I don't think this is something a hospital's going to be able to help with.'

Edie bent in to examine the triple skein of veins more closely.

'They're all different.'

'Yeah . . . And they're not me. I mean, they're not made of me.'

He couldn't keep the revulsion out of his voice, though he tried to.

'Can I?' She reached a hand hesitantly forward.

He turned his head away. Not wanting to see.

'This one's smooth. Like metal.'

He decided he couldn't duck this. He swallowed hard and turned back.

'It *is* metal,' she went on. 'I think it's bronze or brass.'

He moved her hand out of the way and made himself trace the mottled bluey-green channel twisting next to it. It was cool to the touch.

'This one's not so smooth.'

'It's like marble.'

That left the last, pale flaw, twining down to his wrist. He rubbed it, feeling the rough shaley texture of limestone. As his thumb skated along the channel, tracing its course, he could feel a piece of grit detach from the surface and stick to it.

'OK,' he said, clenching his teeth before managing to cloak them in a grin. 'This *is* scary-ish.'

'Does it hurt?'

He flexed the arm. The veins of bronze and stone seemed to flex with it. He shook his head.

'No. But you know when they say something makes your flesh crawl?'

She nodded. He pointed to his arm.

'It's crawling. It's like I've got something inside my arm that isn't me. I mean, if I think about it, it's definitely going to creep me out.'

'So what are we going to do?'

She stared back into his tight smile. Seeing the concern in her eyes somehow triggered the opposite reaction in him – he found himself once more determined to erase that look in her by making sure she was OK. It wasn't necessarily a rational thought, but it was one thing, in their almost entirely ungraspable predicament, that he could hold on to and work with.

'Not think about it.'

He stood up. The rain was easing. He reached down and pulled her to her feet. He didn't really know what to say, so he dragged up things he'd heard other people say on TV and in films.

'Edie. We're going to be OK. We're going to do this together. I'll be right there with you. Anything, anyone trying to get you, they're going to have to get past me first.'

As he said it he was pretty sure he wasn't as convincing as the actors he was trying to copy had been. Maybe you had to be an adult to sound macho. Edie swept the hair out of her eyes and gave him a long, appraising look.

'What? All seven stone of you?'

He grinned back at her. At least she hadn't laughed. Not outright. He curled his lip and mugged at her, making a caricature of a tough guy.

'Yeah. All seven stone of me. Until we get out of this, I've got your back. Look round any time, I'm there.'

He waited for her to join in the joke. Instead she nodded slowly.

'That's . . .' she struggled for the word, then levelled her eyes right into his, '. . . that's good.'

And because the earnestness of her belief in him was

so unexpected and so sharp, he immediately felt like he wanted to escape the moment.

'Come on then. Let's go see the Friar.'

And because she felt buoyed by his confidence and strangely comfortable with the fact he'd got her back, she straightened, walked ahead of him out into the dwindling rain shower and pointed down the road.

'Blackfriars is down this way.'

And because she was ahead of him, she never saw the stone gargoyle take a headfirst leap off the guttering along the top edge of the alley, falling like the half-ton of rock that it was, before its bat-like wings snapped open at the last moment and it swooped upwards again, one foot-talon neatly hitting George in between his shoulder blades while the other closed round his ankle like a gin-trap.

And because a half-ton of wet airborne sandstone packs quite a punch, she never heard George yell. He couldn't. All the air was knocked out of him as the gargoyle carried him looping up and away into the darkening sky.

Instead she turned round to see what was taking George so long, and saw nothing. No George, where an instant before there had been, and no friendly face in the stream of wet pedestrians hurrying along the pavement behind her. No one watching her back. It was as if someone had thrown a switch and George had simply been turned off.

And Edie was alone.

7

THE ICARUS

There was a pop, and unseen by anyone hurrying through the rain-spattered fastness of Old Change Court, the Walker stepped out of his portable mirror, and looked around. There were only a few young office workers chattering and laughing their way to the pub on the way to the bus stop. He slotted in behind them and followed them across the square.

Their talk withered as he trailed them, becoming less and less cheery – dying off into an uncomfortable silence. He stopped and let them carry on into the street, plans for a convivial beer before going home having become significantly less appealing in all their minds, but for no reason that any of them could have put a finger on.

He stopped by a pinch-waisted bronze plinth, on the top of which stood a grotesquely distorted winged figure. From the back he was naked, attached to chopped-off wings by a harness that looked more like an instrument of punishment than a means of flight. His head was jammed uncomfortably backwards, and his torso was bound inside an open-work breast-plate device that curved round the front, hiding his face and trapping his arms within.

It was a monument to agony, not flight.

And it whimpered as the Walker came round to the front where the only human pieces visible were the legs, buckling under the weight of the painful apparatus.

'Icarus. I thought you might like to know. Your brother is dead.'

The Icarus flinched, and started to twitch. After a moment, low, stifled moans began to emerge from the brutal constriction of the cage hiding the face and torso.

'Yes. Your brother, the Minotaur. The Minotaur that was sculpted by the same Maker as yours. Your brother is dead.'

The Icarus screamed, a deep man's scream, horrifying and raw, though muffled, as though the mouth hidden inside the apparatus was sewn shut.

'Yes. He died badly. I could do nothing to stop it.'

The scream changed tempo, and was punctuated by

panting sobs as the man or the creature within absorbed the news.

'I thought you might like to help me find the people who did it. Two children. I have a use for them, but if you bring them to me, I will give them to you when I am done. You have my word.'

The Icarus screamed more deeply – as if some of the stitches in his lips had ripped out with the force of his previous cries – and then hopped grotesquely, awkwardly, off the plinth and landed in a kind of hunched squat, his chopped-off wingtips clapping together above his head in furious eagerness.

8

AIRBORNE

Everybody wants to fly. At some stage in their lives, everyone looks up in the sky and sees the seeming effortlessness of a bird in the gulf of air overhead and thinks: I wish, just one time, that could be me.

Nobody wants to fly like George was flying.

He was upside down, back arched, staring at the ground below, winded by the sledgehammer blow between his shoulder-blades, gagging soundlessly for a breath that just wouldn't come.

All he could do was reach a despairing hand back towards the rapidly diminishing figure of Edie as she spun the wrong way on the crowded pavement, trying to see where he'd gone. She was turning like a leaf caught in a whirlpool in a fast moving stream, looking everywhere but the right way, which was up.

And then just as his vision started to spot and dim through lack of oxygen, he found a breath and took a deep hooping lungful of air, then another and then yelled – at the very moment the gargoyle crested a building and she was lost to his sight.

'Edie!'

He shouted his throat raw in one ragged word that tore out of him like the death of hope but his yell was lost in the greater noise of the city below.

Above him he heard the gargoyle hiss in disapproval, and felt its grip on his leg tighten. In a couple of thunderous wing-flaps they had cleared the next block of buildings and were flying across the Thames.

George looked at the water beneath, then he glanced up just in time to see the stone creature taking a quick look down at him. In the microsecond where they were face to face he recognized the snarling cat-head. He gaped in disbelief.

'Spout?'

There was no doubt in his mind. This was the gargoyle he'd called Spout, the gargoyle who had tried to kill him at the Monument that morning – the gargoyle he had seen shot to smithereens by the Gunner. The taint that was definitely dead.

'But you're dead.'

And then the gargoyle hissed again and George turned and saw the brick face of the industrial chimney above the Tate Modern building coming closer and closer, and though he was sure that Spout now meant to dash him against it, he just stared at it, without even the energy to put out a futile hand to ward off the inevitable. But at the last instant Spout twisted in the air, and jerked the talon at the end of one wing over the lip of the chimney and brought them to a sudden halt.

George hung there, nose to the brickwork, head pounding with blood, filling his lungs and wondering whether his heart was going to actually manage to pound its way out of his chest like it was trying to.

9

RED QUEEN

The Black Friar walked purposefully east, past the end of Westminster Bridge through the thin flow of pedestrians, none of whom, of course, could see him, or if they could they had strong rational brains that wouldn't believe the evidence of those irrational and untrustworthy eyes, telling him a statue walked amongst them.

The Thames was to his right, and the great clock-tower of Big Ben soared overhead, the illuminated clock-face shining out into the gathering dark.

His eyes flicked sideways as he passed an impressive double equestrian statue. A regal woman in a simple shift dress, flowing cloak and a small spiky crown stood in a chariot, her right hand holding a business-like spear, and the other hand languidly urging her two surging chargers forward.

She was flanked in the light chariot by her two daughters, crouched for balance over the brutally curved blades sticking out from the centre of the chariot's wheels. The whole group seemed on the very point of careering off the plinth and into Parliament Square.

The Friar nodded as he walked past. When it was clear he had no intention of stopping, the Queen spoke.

'Friar.'

He paused, waited a beat, then turned, not entirely hiding the fact he didn't want to do so by the polite smile he erected in front of his face.

'Queen.'

'You do not bow.'

His smile deepened.

'Indeed.'

'You never bow.'

He spread his arms wide, the gesture of a man with nothing to hide, nor a care in the world.

'I am friend of all men, equal to all, subject to none. I mean no offence by it.'

Irritation ticked across the royal brow.

'You mean no offence, and yet you give it.'

'Not by intent. It is my way, the way of my calling.'

'Priests bow to kings.'

He exhaled in the long, drawn-out way that people do when they wish to make it clear how long-suffering they are.

'Not *good* priests, dear lady. Not ones *I* should value, at any rate. But by "calling" I was not talking about my priesthood. I was talking about my profession. As a publican. Why, as a host and a tavern-keeper all men are equal in my sight.'

'And women,' she interjected sharply.

A shadow of a smile passed over his face, gone as soon as it appeared.

'Women, in my experience, are perfectly equal, as long as they keep to the lounge side of the bar.'

She bristled and gripped her spear tightly. Behind her the two daughters exchanged a look.

'You find this amusing? This is how you preach, fat man?'

The Friar raised an eyebrow at her. He smoothed the cassock over his belly.

'You crave a sermon, lady? Why, upon my word, I thought war was more your pleasure . . . but certainly, I'm sure I can conjure an improving text for you to consider. Let me see, yes: it goes like this:

"When Adam delved and Eve span, who was then the gentleman?"'

She glared at him, as if trying hard to work out both

where and how deep the insult hidden in the words was. Eventually she waved it off as too much trouble.

'Blowhard words – beyond my understanding. Perhaps they make more sense in an alehouse.'

He smiled his unimpeachable smile.

'Well, I can see they wouldn't make sense in a palace, where queens imagine themselves better than ordinary people.'

The spear shook in her hand as she spoke, the huskiness of anger building within.

'You are purposely insolent!'

His face broke into a perfect grin of good humour, like a great round cheese splitting. He chuckled apologetically.

'No ma'am, I beg your pardon. It is a childish pleasure in me to tease a fine, fiery redheaded woman such as yourself, for as the woodsman knows, no tinder is quicker to kindle than the red-barked.'

The daughters gasped and immediately looked away.

'You take me for a redhead, priest?'

'Why certainly. Why else would they call you the Red Queen?'

She finally exploded, eyes flashing and jerking the sharp end of the spear at him as she did.

'Not for my hair, fat man – not for my hair! They call me red because I swept down on this city in vengeance for the wrong to my daughters, and when I and my army turned our backs on the smoking ruins and hied us homewards, my arms were red to the elbows with the blood of London and its insolent—'

'Mother,' said the daughter on her left, taking her arm, trying to slow her down. The other one took her right arm and attempted to stop the tirade by redirecting her attention.

'Mother. The glint . . .'

She controlled herself with a visible effort. The Friar's eyes were all innocent good humour, much too innocent – enjoying the fall-out of the detonation he had provoked. She spoke as calmly as she could.

'Yes. Of course. The glint. A glint, Friar. Last night we saw a glint run past us. With a boy.'

His eyebrows rose skywards in a show of surprise belied by the entirely uninterested face below them.

'Oh. And you're sure it was a glint?'

'You know as well as I that we sense them as strongly as they sense what is in stone. She was young. She was strong. And she was brave. But she ran. We wish to know what has happened to her.'

'And why is that? Pardon my impertinence, but what business of yours are glints?'

She gripped her spear and banged the haft on the floor of her chariot.

'They are strong girls and they live at a peril beyond bearing. We have not seen one in years.'

'Perhaps you are mistaken.' He shrugged.

'Not about that, Friar. And *any* woman in peril is my charge and care.'

'And why is that, pray?'

She slammed the spear down even harder, making her daughters jump.

'Because I will it so. I have ALWAYS willed it so!'

The fire seemed to blaze from her eyes. The Friar had been right about how quick she was to kindle.

'And why do you ask me this, madam?'

'Because she was running along the river, and sooner or later the river passes your door.'

He passed a hand over his face and wiped all mirth off it as he did so. He inclined his head again, but not far enough for the gesture to be considered a bow of any kind.

'The river passes many doors. I saw no one. Good night, ladies.'

And with a nod of his head he strode off eastwards.

The Queen watched him go. She took several deep breaths, then turned to the daughter on the right side of the chariot.

'He lied. There is a glint abroad. We must ride. If this feeling I have in my bowels is true, there is a girl in peril.'

10

EDIE ALONE

One minute he was there. Then he was gone. It was that simple, that horrible, that brutal. She stepped into the street from the alley, looked right and left, turned to say she thought they might as well run if he was up for it – and he just wasn't there any more. It was so sudden and so shocking that Edie's mind wouldn't let her see the truth of it. Her first reaction was to be annoyed that George was playing games with her. She was tired, bone tired, and trying as hard as she knew how not to let him see how close to the end of her rope she was feeling. Now here he was playing hide and seek or something.

'Come on, George,' she said tightly. 'I'm not in the mood—'

Then a nastier thought hit her – maybe he was hiding

because he'd seen a taint or the Walker coming for them. So she spun and checked the view behind her again. There was nothing. An old homeless woman pushed a rattling shopping cart full of plastic bags and newspaper past on the other side of the street. She was too far away for Edie to notice that her eyes were entirely black, and looking at her. And whatever she was mumbling to herself was drowned in the sound of the passing traffic. Edie, seeing nothing threatening, let a half grunt of relief escape, then stepped back into the alley, looking for him.

'George!'

He wasn't there. She checked the skip and beside the car. There was no mistake. He was gone as cleanly and brutally as if he'd never been there in the first place. Panic swelled in her gut and swirled up into her chest, tightening round it, making her heart beat faster. Again she whirled around, looking for the hiding place she must have missed, fist already bunching so she could punch him when he jumped out and laughed at her. But she hadn't missed a hiding place. George was not there.

All there was was the city and the street and the people hurrying past in the rain. And then just for a treacherous instant she was sure she heard George calling her name, impossibly far off and desperate, but when she spun in the direction she thought it had come from there was nothing to see, and she knew her mind had betrayed her, making her hear things that weren't there, just because she wanted them to be.

And as she spun slowly on the edge of the street, she felt her connection to it, and to everything around her slowly begin to unravel, as her mind finally allowed her to start believing that George had just vanished from her world. The hard fist at the end of her arm unknotted itself, the bony bunch of white knuckles and taut sinew slackening into an open hand whose limp fingers trailed in the air, making a lifeless circle around her as she turned, beginning to wonder if she was going mad . . .

. . . and then her foot stumbled over something and she looked down. And though she kept slowly turning, her knees bent and straightened as the limp fingers flexed and came back to life and scooped up the thing that had caused her to stumble.

A shoe. George's shoe.

It was wet and scuffed but when she put her hand inside it, it was still warm. Then a piece of normality reasserted itself and she realized she had voluntarily reached inside the shoe of a boy who had spent the last twenty-four hours or so doing little else except running, and she quickly pulled her hand back out of the clammy interior into fresh air. Her nose wrinkled into a momentary disgust that flattened out into a stiff little smile as her hand clenched tightly round the shoe, drawing life from the concrete proof it gave that George had been there, was real, and that she was not going mad.

And holding the shoe made her stop spinning round, and she knew that was good too, because she was suddenly aware that she had momentarily lost her grip and had been slowly unspooling herself on the pavement.

She was done with that.

She banished the weasel voice back into the shadows by thwacking the heel of George's shoe on to the palm of her other hand, insistently beating toughness back into herself. The shoe, with its trailing laces, reminded her of the Gunner's tightly-cinched army boots and the reassuring clatter of hobnails that they made when he walked or ran. And thinking of the Gunner seemed to help too. She knew instinctively what he would say if he was there now, if he'd been able to be inside her, listening to the doubts rising in her head.

He'd have dismissed them and sent them away. She knew exactly what he'd do, and so she did it.

'Right. Enough of that. Job to do. Get going,' she gritted. 'Go mad later.'

And because she had thought of him and drawn strength from that thought, in a way the Gunner was there with her, riding inside her head. And maybe that was the thing that put the iron back into her eyes and made her stride off with her back straight, heading for the river.

11

HUNG AT
THE TATE

All the blood in George's body was obeying the call of gravity as he hung upside down, nose to the brickwork of the high chimney. He could feel his heart slamming as it fought a losing battle trying to pump blood out of his head and circulate it normally, back up round his body. His ears pounded with a percussive swoosh and thud that got louder and louder until he was sure his head was going to burst with the pressure. He hadn't been held upside down since he was a toddler. He had a sharp memory of his laughing mother stopping his father dangling him over a pile of leaves, and he remembered the relief as his dad had turned him the right way round, and how they'd all tumbled into the pile and had a leaf fight. He must have been about six, and those were the happy days, when his mother's laughter was just laughter, not a means of hiding something. The thought of her seemed to come from another life. He wondered if she was back in the country yet, if she knew he was missing. She must. Somewhere out there she must be looking for him. She had to be.

He tried to think what he should do, and then just at the point where he was beginning to see little dancing spots of black unconsciousness whirling in from the edge of his vision, the gargoyle's other leg-talon closed around his neck – not hard – and he found himself being turned the right way up and brought face to face with the great feral cat-head.

Spout's stone eyes seemed to bore into him as the pressure that had built up in his head drained away and the black flecks whirled back out of sight. His heart was still jack-hammering in his chest, but the noise in his ears quietened to a background bass thump.

One feline eyebrow rose higher than the other, signalling a question. The stone mouth worked, trying to get a word out from behind the great teeth, with the awkwardness of someone attempting to dislodge a fishbone without using their hands.

'Gack?' it said, and paused, as if waiting for a reply. When none came it grimaced and appeared to try again. 'Gowk?'

Somehow the strangest thing, stranger than hanging off the top of a tall industrial chimney in the grip of a flying gargoyle, was the fact that the gargoyle appeared to be trying to talk to him.

George knew there was something wrong with this. He knew it in his guts.

'Why aren't you dead?' he asked, voice raw as the wind whipping round the top of the stack. As he said it he realized he also wanted to know why *he* wasn't dead, why the thing hadn't ripped him limb from limb or dropped him to shatter on the stone below.

Spout looked at him, and though it said nothing, George was shocked to see that it shrugged. When something with a seven-metre wingspan shrugs, it's about as big as a shrug can get.

By all the rules about spits and taints that George had learnt since he had fallen into this layer of unLondon where statues walked and talked and flew and fought, Spout should have been dead, back on its perch, never to move again. He'd seen the Gunner smithereen it with some of the last bullets from his gun. It was a taint. That meant it was dead. When taints were damaged like that they were finished. On the other hand spits – like the Gunner – had a stronger animating spirit holding them together. Even if they were badly damaged, as long as they could find their way back to their plinth by midnight

– the time the Gunner had called 'turn o'day' – they were revived. Taints didn't have the same strong animating spirit to hold them together. They had a void at their core. Instead of a personality they had malice and envy.

And Spout was a taint, and Spout had been blasted to shards in front of his eyes. That meant it should never walk the city or swoop over its rooftops again. That meant it should no longer be a threat.

Except it had swooped. It had swooped and grabbed him. And it was looking at him expectantly. And he had no idea why. Unless . . .

With a jolt he suddenly thought he knew what Spout wanted. It wasn't complicated. Spout wanted what the Walker had wanted. He wanted the broken dragon's head in his pocket.

The jolt he felt was elation: a moment ago George had had no hope and a strong conviction that there was no way out other than a long drop or a short – hopefully – nasty encounter with Spout's ripping talons. Now he had something to exchange for his life. He didn't mind giving the gargoyle the broken piece of statuary, not if it bought him his life, not if it bought him the time to rescue the Gunner and find Edie again.

'Look!' he blurted. 'Look, I know what you want. Here. I've got it. Put me down and you can have it. Oh.'

Until his scrabbling hand found nothing where his

coat pocket should be, and his mouth hit the 'Oh', his plan had been almost instant and great.

He'd bargain with Spout by threatening to toss the broken dragon's head into the deep river below unless the thing put him on the ground in one piece. Only what his hand had discovered, an instant before his mind remembered, was the now presumably lethal fact that he had given his coat to Edie when the rain set in. The coat in whose pocket he'd put the dragon's head.

'Oh,' he repeated. 'Bugger.'

'Gugger?' echoed Spout nastily, head still cocked.

'Exactly.' George's voice sounded as defeated as he felt.

'Gackly?'

'Yes,' said George. 'Gackly.'

He was getting hysterical. He must be. There was a big sound rising like a tide inside him, and it wasn't a scream or a yell. It was laughter, and there was nothing funny about any of this.

And then he couldn't stop the laughter, not even as Spout adjusted his grip and launched himself off the top of the chimney into the great gulf of air below. Tears of mirth streamed into his eyes as he flew through the air, so he saw the white metal blade of the Millenium Footbridge below him through a blur as the gargoyle swooped low over the river, heading north.

'Gackly,' he choked, as the first chunk of laughter burst out of his nose in a convulsive snort and the great white dome of St Paul's loomed straight ahead.

'I'm guggered . . .'

12

THE KILLING BULL

The Walker emerged with a pop from the small glass mirrors in his hands and looked up at the classical front portico of Tate Britain, and then turned around. There was no one to be seen except for people waiting for a bus on the other side of the road.

He approached the grey steps and hurried up the left hand side of the wide stairway. He kept his hood pulled over the right hand side of his face, in a gesture that seemed to have an unaccustomed air of furtiveness for a being who was, by the very nature of his curse, so good at not being seen.

The truth is that he had come to visit one new statue, but was very keen not to see or be seen by another one.

The statue he wanted to see was round the left-hand

side of the entrance, on a little adjunct balcony space beside the double-columned edge of the portico. The one he particularly didn't want to see was on the other side.

As soon as he was round the corner he relaxed and resumed his normal arrogant strut.

He looked at the group of statues he had come to see. It was a hybrid, because not all statues are either spits or taints. This was both – or rather the human statues were spits, two muscular men like Greek wrestlers, struggling with a taint, a huge and murderous bull, on whose back was tied a naked woman.

It was not a happy group. It was a monument to the fact that the Ancient Greeks had had much too much fun thinking up ways to execute people.

The Walker cleared his throat.

'I want to talk to the Bull.'

No one moved. The frozen moment of struggle remained paralysed in midair. The Walker sighed.

'It's the Minotaur.'

The Bull's eye swivelled and looked at him.

'He has been killed.'

The Bull convulsed and threw the two men into the corner of the balcony. The woman tied to its back screamed.

'Yes,' said the Walker, unmoved. 'Yes. It's distressing.'

The Bull stood there, snorting angrily through its

nostrils as the woman struggled to free herself.

'I wondered if you'd like to help me punish the ones responsible.'

And then the woman screamed louder as the Bull tossed its head and horns back, and then drowned her noise in the primal bellowing it blasted up into the darkening sky.

And the Walker looked up and smiled as a darker shape dropped out of the night and landed gently on his shoulder.

'Ah. There you are.'

The Raven clacked its beak in his ear. He nodded.

'Good. If they are to be found, the Tallyman will do it quicker than anything else. Now come. We must go east.'

13

THE TALLYMAN

Edie was stuck at the kerb, waiting for the crossing lights to change from red to green. She was on the edge of a knot of pedestrians, all of them impatient for the traffic to stop so that they could continue on their way towards Blackfriars station. Everyone was in their own world, listening to music on their earphones, talking into mobiles or just staring vacantly ahead, lost in their own London. No one paid her any attention.

'One glint. Topper Puddleduck.'

Her ear caught the words right on the edge of her hearing. The voice was a man's, lumpy with phlegm, flat and uninflected as a machine talking. She turned, half sure that she'd misheard, half certain that she was getting jumpy and starting to imagine things. Nobody was looking at her. She must have imagined it. The words didn't make sense anyway. 'Topper Puddleduck' was just gibberish. She'd obviously just caught a snatch of conversation that she couldn't really hear properly, and her mind had filled in gaps in the sentence with sounds that made semi-coherent nonsense out of them.

'Puddleduck' was a word from her childhood, not this present London. She had a flash of memory – real memory, not a glint's vision – of pale little drawings of a white duck in a pink shawl and a blue bonnet, the exact blue of the frosted glass earrings her mother always wore, and her mother's fingers tracing the words beside the picture and conjuring a story out of them. The memory was a happy one and therefore treacherous and not to be kept in the mind too long in case it started to hurt too much.

The lights changed, the obstruction cleared and the tight little knot of humanity that had been blocked at the kerb started moving again, thinning out as people walked on at their own different speeds.

Edie angled down towards the river, and as she did so she caught sight of the street name bolted to the building on the corner, clearly outlined in black and white. She was walking down Puddle Dock. And just as she was turning Puddle Dock into Puddleduck and back again, she heard the phlegmy voice once more, very clearly.

'One glint. Top of Puddle Dock. Walking down to the river.'

This time when she turned she saw him, and for a stomach jolting instant she knew it was the Walker, and then an equally strong wash of relief hit her as she realized it wasn't. It was just a tramp, wearing a long coat that gave him a silhouette like the Walker's. Instead of the Walker's hood he had a cowl of matted hair framing his head in rough-sleepers' dreadlocks. He was squinting, eyes slitted, jaw hanging slack as he mouth-breathed at her in lumpy gurgles through gappy black and orange teeth. He stared back as if waiting for her to do something. Then a tiny shudder twitched through him and he shrugged.

'One glint. Top of Puddle Dock. Standing still in the middle of the road . . .'

His voice was still uninvolved, almost disembodied. He had the look of a man who had zombified himself beneath relentless waves of alcohol. She decided he was deeply drunk.

The other pedestrians had moved on. Just the two of them faced each other in the middle of the road.

Edie should have run, she later decided, but he was a street-crazy, and street-crazies and drunks were things that didn't frighten her. Firstly, because she felt somewhere deep inside that she was a street-crazy herself, and secondly because she knew all about drunks and the different levels of zombification into which they fell. And it wasn't just because she was not frightened by the tramp – she was also intrigued by what he seemed to be saying. So, keeping out of the reach of any sudden lunge that he might make, she took a couple of steps towards him.

'What did you say?'

'One glint. Top of Puddle Dock. Standing still in the middle of the road . . .' His voice repeated itself, a flat and exact replica of the previous sentence he'd uttered.

'Why d'you call me a glint?' she asked, mouth drying as she tried to anticipate the answer.

'Because you are a glint,' he said, without either interest or taking his squinting eyes from her. The lack of interest was somehow more disturbing than the fact he seemed to see what she was. She jutted her chin forward, determined not to betray the unease and intimidation beginning to rise around her.

'Who are you?'

His tongue roiled wetly in the stump-scattered ruin of his mouth.

'We are the Tallyman.'

'You're the *what*?'

'We are the Tallyman.'

Again the inflection was identical to the first time

he'd said it – flat, uninterested, lifeless. Like a recording. Like a computer speaking.

'We?' she said, looking round. She was relieved to see he was alone. The cars now passing them on both sides weren't relieved. They were irritated, and a couple of them used their horns to communicate the fact.

'You're a "we" are you? Royal like the Queen, are you?'

'We are the Tallyman,' he said, echoing himself, uninterested, immovable, eyes locked on her.

This flat repetition was annoying as well as unnerving.

'What are you doing?' she asked as a truck rumbled past her right shoulder.

'Counting you.'

'Counting me?'

'Counting you. One glint. Top of Puddle Dock. Standing still in the middle of the road . . .'

'Why?' she asked, confused. 'Why are you counting me?'

As the high-sided lorry paused in the traffic behind Edie it threw the Tallyman into shadow and he stopped squinting.

'We are the Tallyman.'

Again his flat answer came back as if he was explaining the obvious. It wasn't his tone that made her feet suddenly feel like they were glued to the tarmac. It was his eyes, no longer squinting. Because they weren't man's eyes, not the bloodshot whites she would have imagined; they were entirely black eyes, eyes with no whites at all — they were dark and beady and inhuman as a raven's eyes. And she was filled with the sudden and horrible conviction that more than just the tramp was staring at her out of them. She wrenched her feet into motion and darted between a car and a shrieking despatch rider and sprinted towards the river.

The Tallyman didn't run after her. He just spoke calmly as he waited for a hole in the traffic.

'One glint. Running down Puddle Dock. Towards the river.'

14

GUNNER IN
THE DARK

'Whoso list to hunt . . . I know where there is an hind . . .'

The Walker's words seemed to hang in the dank air long after he had left the Gunner alone in the darkness. And he was sick with the certainty that the Walker would hunt Edie and get her. There had been just too many heart stones belonging to other glints arranged like grisly trophies, on the walls of the water tank, to leave any room for doubt about it. The Walker clearly knew what he was doing. Each of those worn pieces of sea-glass had been the precious possession of a woman or girl, the kind of possession none of them would have given up without a fierce fight. The Gunner wondered how many of the heart stones had been pried from cold, dead fingers.

He felt weak at the thought.

'Right,' he said to himself. 'Smoke break.'

And he felt for the wall behind him and slid down to a sitting position, hunched against the damp stone at his back. He reached under the tarpaulin cape he wore round his shoulders and fumbled something out of a pocket. There was a scrape and then a match flared into light, and the red end of a cigarette was ignited.

He held the match out at the end of his arm, not wanting to waste a moment of its illumination as he sucked hungrily at the cigarette between his lips. He used the fleeting light to orient himself in the space: he saw the castle-shaped outlines of the sea-glass fragments, and he noted the disc hung in the centre of the room, reflecting the tiny flame in his hand. And then it guttered out and he was in the dark again.

The only sound was his breathing, interspersed with his inhaling and exhaling the tobacco smoke. Each time he inhaled, the tiny red dot at the end of the cigarette glowed brighter, like a tiny heart pulsing.

He took an inventory of how he felt, and what his options were. He seemed wrong inside, still twisted and hanging by a thread, which he realized was the result of having broken his oath in order to try and save Edie. He imagined this wrongness was going to get worse. It certainly made him weak, and it seemed to be making it hard for him to think as straight as he normally did. The thing he was most worried about, after what was going to happen to Edie and then George without him there to help them, was what was going to happen at midnight.

Midnight, or turn o'day, was the time when the statues based on real people – the spits – had to be on their plinths. It wasn't optional, it was part of who they were and how they were. An empty plinth at turn o'day meant the death of a spit. When it returned or was returned to its plinth it never walked again, and became no more than a human-shaped lump of metal or stone. Since he was now paying the penalty for breaking an oath sworn by the Stone and the hand that made him, he imagined midnight might mean, if not the end of him, then the start of an eternity of wandering like the Walker, in thrall to the dark powers pent in the Stone.

He didn't seem to have much chance of leaving this subterranean cell before midnight unless the Walker got him out the way they'd come in, and there just didn't seem much likelihood of that. Even if he had his normal strength he didn't know how deep underground he was, and he certainly didn't think he could claw his way to the surface given the fact that the last time he had tried to lift his arms to do so he had failed so badly. The Walker's power over him seemed to be working. He wondered if the Walker would be back before turn o'day, before midnight came and brought his death.

He wasn't looking forward to his return, if only because his sneering boastfulness was hard to bear on top of all the bad things that were happening to him. And then he thought of a way to stop having to see the Walker's face at least, and that gave him a plan.

'Come on, you dozy beggar,' he said to himself as he grunted and heaved himself back on to his feet.

If the glint's glasses blazed into life because of their power to warn when a taint or a Stone-Servant like the Walker came near, and that was the perverse way the Walker provided light for himself in his subterranean lair, there *was* something he could do. And the fact that it involved disassembling the Walker's carefully made castle shapes only increased his desire to do it.

He unhooked his tarpaulin cape and felt for the mural on the wall behind him.

By sucking hard on his cigarette he caught a pale reflection in some pieces of glass on the wall. He carefully laid his cape on the gravel beneath the castle outline, and reached high and wide, using both hands to brush the glass pieces off the wall and on to the tarpaulin.

'Abracadabra to you too, mate,' he muttered in grim satisfaction.

Once he'd convinced himself that he'd cleared the first wall of heart stones he bundled up the tarpaulin and turned 180 degrees to the wall and walked in a straight line off the gravel spit and into the water. As he passed the centre-point of the space he stopped and cast around with his hands in the air, until they clattered into the spinning disk on the chain. He tugged hard and there was a percussive 'spang' noise as the chain parted and the disc came free. He reached into his pocket and pulled out his matches. He lit one and stood there, hip deep in the water, looking at the disk in the light of the small flame.

It was an old pewter plate: on it someone had scratched a series of concentric circles with turreted castles round the edge, as if marking the points of the compass. A road led from an arch in the base of each castle, and they made a cross where they met in the centre of the plate, joined by another series of circles like the central boss of a shield. There was writing all over the design, but all the Gunner had time to read was *The King and his Princes* . . . and *Occidens* before the match guttered out. He carefully stowed the plate inside his jacket and headed for the glass castle on the wall facing him.

'King, my eye,' he snorted. 'You won't need all this

malarkey, because when you pop back in here with the lights out, I'll bloody crown you for nothing.'

And though there was no one to see it, he grinned as he reached for the first piece of sea-glass on the wall ahead of him.

15

PATERNOSTER

At the same time Edie was running south towards the river, George had just recrossed it heading north. Spout held him firmly round the chest as he flapped towards the great dome of St Paul's Cathedral. It was a jerky passage through the air as the gargoyle grunted and flexed its muscles on each downbeat, swaying so precariously from stroke to stroke that flying was more a matter of will than aerodynamics for the bulky stone creature. There was a strong sense that he might plummet to the ground at any moment. One improvement was that he wasn't carrying George upside down any more, so his head no longer pounded with blood.

The flash of a camera caught his eyes as they overflew a gaggle of tourists taking pictures in the dwindling light in front of the Cathedral. He shouted 'Help!' more for the form of it than from any real hope, trying to throw a verbal grappling hook back into a safer reality that he barely remembered.

Just as he'd expected, not a single tourist looked up. They couldn't see him in his layer of London. The unconscious, instinctive part of their brains stepped in and erased him, protecting their consciousness from the shock of seeing the impossible: a boy being flown through the city beneath a gargoyle, like a mouse being taken by an owl. The last day or so had been so full of terror and running and people not seeing or helping him that he'd got used to it.

Because he gave up expecting anyone to notice him, he missed the wiry old broken-toothed man in the mismatched grimy suit, sitting on the ground in a doorway. He didn't see him put down the cider bottle and squint into the sky at George. He didn't see the unwashed hair or the broken veins crimsoning the man's face in a drinker's blush. And he neither saw the jet-black eyes nor heard the lifeless voice saying:

'One boy inna sky. Carried by a gargoyle. Flying round St Paul's, heading nor'-nor'-east.'

Spout suddenly stood on one wing and turned an abrupt ungainly right-angle in the sky, diving low round the side of the dome, across the radiating white sunburst design inlaid on the surface of Paternoster Square.

Now it was clear that the gargoyle wasn't going to kill him immediately, there was room on top of the fear for anger too: he desperately needed to rescue the Gunner, but he could do nothing about it because he'd been grabbed and was being taken wherever the gargoyle felt like going. He thought of the Gunner and how relieved he'd been when he'd reappeared as if back from the dead at the Monument. In the pit of his stomach George nursed the conviction that you really only get to come back from the dead once, and that was only if you were very lucky. And the Gunner had done something fatal to his luck, by sacrificing himself for George and Edie. And George knew that if they didn't get the Gunner free and back on his pedestal by midnight, he'd have no need of luck at all, because he'd be finished.

He caught a smeared vision of a strangely familiar arched gatehouse, its Georgian elegance at odds with the modern piazza beyond, and then unaccountably he heard a noise so out of place that he looked wildly around for the source of it: it was the sound of sheep, bleating plaintively in the middle of this windblown stone piazza.

It was a peaceful sound of grass and hills and summertime, and for all its alien-ness, it flowed into his overheated brain like cool water after a long dry spell.

For some unaccountable reason the sound of innocent animal noise in the midst of all this turmoil made him lighten inside.

Then, as if he really had become less heavy, they suddenly lifted higher and climbed up and over the office building ahead of them, too quickly to be certain, but just slowly enough for George to be almost convinced that he heard a voice amid the sheep shout after him:

'Hold on, my son!'

He twisted and wriggled in Spout's clasp, desperately trying to see the sheep or the man whose voice he was sure, heartbreakingly sure, that he'd both heard and recognized – but the gargoyle flew on over the rooftops, and the square was lost to his view.

It had only been a snatch of sound, but it had gone through him like a burst of adrenaline. He felt invigorated, as if he'd just had a night's sleep. He didn't feel any less scared or confused by what was happening to him – he just suddenly felt a lot more able to cope with it.

The zigzag scar on his hand twinged sharply, but it wasn't an unbearable pain, and it didn't stop the unaccountable surge of well-being he felt coursing round him. He snatched a look at the three lines twining down to his wrist. Unless he was mistaken they'd travelled further, one of them actually crossing his wrist and starting a curving fissure on to his forearm. Somehow looking at these flaws that seemed to be spiralling through his flesh made him feel more nauseous than all the swerving through the sky.

'Gaven,' croaked Spout suddenly, and there was another swooping heave and the world tilted alarmingly.

If you can trip up in the sky, one hundred metres above any possible obstruction, that's what this felt like. George concentrated on keeping whatever was in his stomach on the inside, and then, once he'd gulped it back into place, he looked upwards to see what was troubling the gargoyle and saw that Spout's neck was craned backwards.

Then the world bucked and rollercoastered once more and George's stomach popped up to say hello to his tonsils again, and he realized that Spout was taking evasive action, diving down between two skyscrapers to get below the roof level – as if trying to put them between him and something else in the evening sky. He craned round and followed the direction of the gargoyle's eyes, but saw nothing but the city as the lights came on and the colours drained from the day. The sky was empty apart from a large crow or some such bird, flapping slowly north in the distance. There was nothing obviously threatening. George couldn't see why Spout was acting so strangely.

'Gaven!' panted the gargoyle, this time more intently.

And then the early night sky disappeared and they swooped over the rooftops of a large older building that seemed to take up an entire city block to itself. He caught a glimpse of the pillared frontage of the Royal Exchange building to the right, and realized they must be flying directly over the Bank of England on Threadneedle Street.

He looked down and saw the dark hollow made by the central courtyard of the building, and then he heard someone singing.

It was only a snatch of song, but it cut through the rumbling snarl of the city and came as cleanly to his ears as the sound of the sheep had in Paternoster Square. It was a clear girl's voice and it had a lightness and a clarity to it that spoke of sunshine and light spring breezes. It was the happy sound of someone singing solely for their own enjoyment, drawing out the trilling rhyme at the end of each line with a joyfulness that had something unmistakably pure and elemental to it.

'Where the bee sucks, there suck I

In a cowslip's bell I li-i-i-ie;

There I couch when owls do cry.

On the bat's back I do fl-y-y-y . . .'

The singing was coming from the top of a small domed cupola on the sharp angle of the building to the north. The singer was a bright splash of gold against the grey of the building and the darker shadows of the narrow street beyond. She was balanced like a ballet dancer on the toes of one slender foot, while her other leg stuck out behind, in the beginnings of a dainty arabesque. Golden drapery shimmered around her legs and torso, as if blown and held on by an invisible breeze that ruffled her gilded hair as she sang, her throat arched back in joyful abandon, singing to the sky and the moon that had just started to rise.

For an instant she was a vision of poise and grace and happiness – and then, just as George saw her, she saw him, and though her mouth stayed open, she stopped singing and stared at him in unfeigned surprise as Spout flapped past.

And it seemed to George that her face shone, more than just because it was gold. It shone because her eyes were bright and full of hope and something that made him uncomfortable – though not in a necessarily bad way.

'A boy?' she said in a voice running clean as a mountain stream. 'Hello, boy.'

And then, as Spout kept on flying away from her, her smile changed to a small sad pout and she traced a half-wave with her hand.

'Goodbye, boy.'

'Help?' he shouted awkwardly.

Spout hissed in disapproval. George twisted to see her getting smaller in their wake.

'No, really!' he shouted with more conviction. 'HELP!'

And then she was lost to sight behind the angle of the next building they flew over. Spout was looking back too, and something it saw didn't please it at all, because it suddenly hissed even louder, dropped a shoulder and curved in and down behind a tall office building with the sudden jerking swoosh of a skier abruptly swerving to a halt.

Its talon reached out and grabbed the parapet and it neatly pinwheeled itself to a stop, flattened against a sloping roof of greasy greenish-grey tiles. Its wings were spread out like a partial umbrella, and George was stuck between them and the angle of the roof.

For a long minute they stayed there, unmoving. The only sound was Spout panting and George's heart hammering. He looked down and saw that his feet were braced on a slippery gutter above a lethal drop to the street below. He noticed that he had only one shoe on, because his sock immediately became soaked. Then Spout did something terrifying.

He let go of George.

George scrabbled with his hands and then realized the

only way not to fall was to flatten himself on the sheer angle of the roof and hope the guttering didn't give way.

He stopped scrabbling and pressed forward. Spout kept his eyes on him and nodded slowly. He pointed one claw warningly at George. And then he reached above himself and slowly began to crawl to the edge of the roof above. His ears were flattened back on his head, like some great hunting cat. George could see the spines that ran up his backbone quivering, like the hair on a dog's back when it's alarmed. He wondered what it was that was frightening the gargoyle. It gave him a treacherous spark of hope: perhaps there was someone out there looking for him. Perhaps the Gunner had got free and was coming to his rescue, perhaps having enlisted some flying . . .

And here hope dwindled as he realized that the only statues he could think of that could fly were taints, not spits. He saw Spout cat-crawl to the roof ridge and slowly slide halfway over. He paused in that position, only one leg and the edge of a wing still visible to George, ready to duck back into hiding if his search of the sky revealed anything alarming.

George concentrated on keeping a grip on the distressingly sheer slope of the roof. He thought he'd be OK if he didn't make any sudden movements. He was pretty sure he could be still, especially since the consequences of *not* being still were going to be moving very quickly downwards and then being still for ever. He concentrated on sticking to the roof. He was going to be able to do this.

He felt his hands splayed against the slates. He saw the greenish flecks on the grey surface in front of his nose. He felt the stone under his fingertips. Maybe because he was concentrating so hard on staying stuck to them he somehow felt that he could feel the structure of the stone itself, the tight grain, the compressed layers running parallel with the face, the layers that made it possible to split it into the thin roof tiles. He even felt a magnetic tingling, as if those green flecks were not stone but little flecks of iron embedded in the slate.

He was so taken by the immediacy and intensity of what he was feeling beneath his hand that he forgot to be scared.

Then something tapped him on the ankle.

He jerked away on reflex and nearly tumbled into the street. He flattened against the tiles, trying to become part of the roof, hoping that every extra bit of him that he could press against the surface would help him stick there. Even his face was squidged against the cold slate.

'Are you perchance trying to hold on with your nose?' said a tiny whisper behind him.

He looked down and saw the golden girl looking back

up at him, both elbows perched on the gutter, chin cupped in her hands, as nonchalant as if leaning on a bar – despite the fact there was nothing but a lethal gulf of air beneath her feet.

His eyes automatically flicked upwards, to see if Spout had heard her. All he could see was the one talon on the ridge and the bit of wing. Spout was still on lookout.

The girl pushed herself off from the gutter and held on with her hands, arms at full stretch, still looking up at him.

'Come,' she said simply, and she held out one hand.

'Who are you?' George whispered, trying to put off the moment when he might have to reach away from the comfort of the wet tiles and find out if her ability to hang in the air included being able to carry him too.

'I am minister of your Fate,' she said with a heartbreaking smile. He returned the smile. It seemed the polite thing to do, even though he hadn't a clue what she was talking about.

And then she tugged his ankle off the gutter.

He didn't even have time to yell or grab a handhold. He just fell, snatching handfuls of air–

– and then she caught him.

'Wha'?'

'Shhh,' she whispered, mouth pressed close to his ear,

breath warm on the back of his neck. One finger pointed at Spout's back on the ridgeline above them. He shushed and nodded.

'Hold on, boy,' she breathed. His hands locked on her arm, which wasn't hard and metallic, but as warm and soft as her breath.

'What do we do now?' he asked very quietly, eyes locked on Spout's back view.

He could hear the smile in her voice as she answered. 'I fly.'

And then she let go of the building edge and fell slowly backwards with the clean grace of an Olympic high-diver, pivoting on her toes as her head described a perfect 180-degree arc, and George went along with her as upright changed to upside down, and they were suddenly diving face-first for the paving stones beneath.

He opened his mouth to shout but her free hand clapped over it and stifled the yell, and all he could see racing towards his bulging eyes was granite oblivion.

16

CARELESS TALK
COSTS LIVES

Edie hit the pavement at the end of the pedestrian crossing and trotted downhill, turning right and heading under the dark railway overpass at the bottom of the slope. She saw the white triangular shape of The Black Friar pub beyond, jutting towards the Thames like the prow of a land-locked ship.

She stopped as a taxi slowed and turned across her, heading up the hill. When it had passed she didn't continue crossing the road. She just stood there, staring at the pub façade, not at what was on it, but rather at what wasn't. The clock below was still stuck at five to seven, but above it, where the statue of the Black Friar normally stood like a figurehead, was a blank plinth.

The Friar was gone, and the empty space stared back at Edie like a threat.

She'd been running all the questions she wanted to ask him through her head, trying so hard to imagine what he'd say, how he might help, how she might have to cajole him into doing so, that the one scenario she hadn't catered for was that he might not be there to ask in the first place. She also hadn't thought how she might get into the pub if he wasn't there to let her in, with his jovial laugh and jangling keys. Another car turned in front of her and splashed the kerbside puddle across her ankles, jolting her out of her frozen state.

'Right,' she said, smacking her palm with the heel of George's shoe again. 'Right.'

She jogged across the road and under the railway bridge as a train rumbled ominously overhead. She rounded the point of the building and slowed, suddenly wary.

The door to the pub stood open, but the lights were off. As she approached it she saw two builders carry out a stack of planks and load them into the back of a white van fly-parked on the kerb. She flattened herself against the side of the building and went very still, concentrating on not being seen. Not being seen was a skill she had realized she was good at very early on in her life. Sometimes she'd thought people were just ignoring her, but she'd later decided that they just found it hard to see her a lot of the time, and this was because she could, when she concentrated, be very still and unnoticeable. Once she'd understood that this was something that she could do, she did it more and more, really putting a lot of mental effort into making herself invisible. She knew she wasn't *actually* invisible, but she also knew that she had something that made people's eyes slide off her as if she was covered in non-stick coating.

She waited for the men to go back inside the pub, then slid quickly up to the open door and pressed her back against the outside wall. She slipped the frosted circle of sea-glass out of her pocket and checked it. It was dull and unthreatening, no inner fire kindling within to warn of the closeness of danger. She slipped it back into her coat, and as she did so she felt the heavy lump of the dragon's head in the pocket of George's coat bump against her thigh. She knew then that whatever had happened to make him disappear was bad, because he'd said that he'd stay with her, and his word was good – and even if it wasn't he'd never have run off and left her wearing a coat that contained such a precious object.

Before she could think more about this, the builders came back out, knees buckling under the weight of a second, bigger stack of planks. They walked it right past her as she stood there, not breathing. As soon as the second man had passed her she pivoted neatly and slipped inside the door, into the gloom.

The bar interior was much the same as it had been the last time she'd been there, still shrouded with drop-cloths and littered with builder's jumble. She heard the rear door of the van slam and feet heading back towards her. She lifted the edge of a drop-cloth and bent double beneath a low pub table, flicking the cloth back into place to hide her. She held her breath again and listened as one man walked back into the room, picked up something that clanked like a tool-box, switched off the lights and then walked out again. She heard the door shut with the finality of a church door slamming – keys turning in the lock. And then as she relaxed a fraction and breathed in quiet shallow breaths, she heard the hollow thump of a van's side-door closing and the noise of it driving off into the traffic noise in the main road beyond.

She still didn't move for about five minutes, just crouched there in the darkening room, behind the grubby canvas of the drop-cloth, listening for noises made by anyone or anything locked in there with her. When the complete absence of sound or movement from anywhere in the locked building had told its incontrovertible story of emptiness and abandonment, she rolled out from under the table and walked purposefully towards the bar. The room was fuggy and overheated. It smelt of workmen and wet plaster.

She shrugged out of George's jacket and put it on the counter-top as she boosted herself up on to it, swivelled her legs over, and dropped on to the barman's side in one decisive movement. She bent down and examined the cardboard boxes stacked neatly along the foot of the bar, then plunged her hand into the torn hole in the side of the one with pink writing on it and fished out a pair of prawn cocktail crisp packets.

She was so hungry that she'd torn the first one open and was munching a mouthful of tangy potato shards into starchy shrapnel by the time she stood up again.

She closed her eyes and allowed herself the momentary pleasure of enjoying the taste and the feeling of eating. Then she got down to business.

'OK,' she lisped through a full mouth. 'Come down here. We need to talk . . .'

Nothing but silence answered her.

She opened her eyes and tipped the other half of the packet straight into her mouth, chomping happily for a moment, clearing a passageway for her next words.

'Seriously. Don't make me come in there after you . . .'

Silence. She reached under the bar and came out with a bottle of ginger beer. She stuck it in the opener screwed to the inner wall of the counter and popped the cap without looking. She chugged a couple of mouthfuls and swilled the impacted potato wodge from the spaces between her teeth. Then she burped and smacked the heavy glass bottle on to the bar-top.

'Oi. Tragedy. I need some straight answers.'

She made a point of not looking into the dark alcove beyond the three low arches to her right. To the trained ear it was entirely clear that this was where all the silence was coming from.

'I know you're there.'

Silence. And then, just as she was opening her mouth to speak again, another voice dodged quietly out from under the arches.

'No I ain't.'

It was a cockney voice. Edie hid a smile by popping the second bag of crisps and pouring some of them into her mouth.

'Where's the Friar?'

Now it had leaked a voice, the silence seemed much more eloquent. It spoke of someone trying to find a way to avoid a straight answer, she thought. A small throat cleared itself.

' 'E's not here, an' all.'

'You're both not here?'

'No. Yes. Er. Yes . . . only 'e's more not 'ere than what I am. See?'

A tousled head of bronze hair poked into view at the

top of one of the arches, hanging upside down, and then a face dropped into view, the impish face of a street cherub carrying a mask which the sculptor had carved into the distinctive features of Tragedy. The face was grinning and mischievous.

'I do now,' she said drily.

'You're in a pickle.'

'Am I?'

'Biggest pickle in the barrel is wot I 'eard.'

'Heard from who?'

'Dunno.' He dropped to the ground and looked at her. Then he looked at the mask he held in his hand. He put it in front of his face and then took it away, grimace giving way to smile.

'You get all sorts in a pub. Keep your ears open, you pick up a lot of stuff.'

'What kind of stuff?'

He hid behind the mask again, and then half took it off, winking with the one visible eye.

'Careless talk costs lives.'

She had no idea what he was talking about.

'What do you mean?'

'Careless talk costs lives. You know.'

'No. I wouldn't ask if I knew.'

'It's what they say. What they used to say.'

'Who?'

'I dunno, do I? Them. Everyone. There was posters. We had one over there.'

'When?'

'In the war. You know. When they was dropping bombs and all that. In the wossname. The Blitz. You remember.'

She realized he was talking about the Second World War.

'The Blitz?'

He looked pleased. His little chest swelled in front of her and he nodded enthusiastically.

'There you go. You remember. We had the poster over there. You liked it.'

'I wasn't alive during the war. Not that war.'

His eyes flicked left and right and then centered on her, beneath a newly wrinkled brow.

'Wasn't you?'

She shook her head.

'My *mum* wasn't even alive in that war.'

'I thought you . . .'

'I'm twelve.'

'Well that don't mean nothing. That's older than me. I think. I mean I *think* I'm not twelve. Not yet.'

He began to look confused.

'You look about ten. But then you'll always be ten, won't you?'

'Will I?'

'You will. Statues don't get old. You'll have been ten in the war like you're ten now. But I wasn't born, my mum wasn't born. I don't even think *her* mum was born . . .'

The furrows on his brow curved and deepened.

'But you liked the poster. I'm sure I remember.'

She shook her head. This was getting ridiculous. 'I never saw any poster.'

He held her gaze for a couple of beats longer.

'I thought you did. I—'

'I didn't.' She cut him off hard. She didn't have time to waste. He looked offended and suddenly deflated. He twirled the mask in his hands and examined his feet.

'OK.'

His toe traced a pattern in the carpet.

'It's just that I been seeing so many things for so long that I get it all in a ball, you know? Like knots. It all gets tangled. Like I think I remember stuff I ain't supposed to have seen, and I seen things I ain't supposed to remember. And that's not even counting the stuff I definitely ain't seen, don't remember and can't forget. You know what I mean?'

'No.'

'I got so much stuff in my head, I can't keep it all apart. It gets jumbled. It's one of the things makes me feel like I'm made wrong, you know?'

There was a small gust of wind from behind her. It rustled a newspaper left on a stool beside him. He reached out and caught the top sheet as it lifted off the pile. He held it as if surprised to find it there. Then he scowled intently at it and crumpled it into a ball that he kept bunched tight in his hand, and smiled hopefully at her.

The last time Edie had met Little Tragedy he had been keen that she use her power, her ability to glint – to suck the past from rock and metal – to touch him and see if she could sense if there was something wrong with him. She hadn't touched him, but she could see there was something not right. She didn't know if he was made wrong, or made to be wrong, but his eagerness to be glinted when every other statue shied away from the pain and distress caused when she touched them had been one of the things that she and George had mistrusted about the whole set-up of the pub and its threateningly cheery landlord. She thought Little Tragedy was a spit. The suspicion was creeping up on her that he might have a dual nature like the half-human/half-fantastical sphinxes. Maybe he was taintish when he had the mask on, spit-like when he didn't. So she didn't answer his question directly. Instead she changed the subject back to the reason she'd returned to the pub.

'Look. I haven't got time to talk. I need to find the

Gunner. And I need to find George. I don't even know where to start except with this one thing: what's in the mirrors?'

He looked perplexed again.

'What mirrors?'

She pointed to the two mirrors on either side of the arch he was standing in. They faced each other on the inside pilasters of the arch, and standing between them and looking sideways gave the impression that the reflections in the mirrors not only framed each other, but repeated themselves into infinity.

'Those mirrors. I need to know about the mirrors.'

He scratched the back of his head with the hand that still held the balled newspaper and shifted his weight from one foot to the other, avoiding her eyes.

'Nothing. They're just mirrors, yeah?'

Edie stepped towards him. He raised his eyes and smiled brightly, as if seeing her for the first time. Whatever look she had parked on her face clearly wasn't returning fire on the smile, because his faded fast, dimming to a grin before curdling into a grimace and an awkward rise and fall of his shoulders.

'Just mirrors. Straight up, no messing. That's all they are . . .'

Edie cleared her throat. The question she was about to ask was going to be so outlandish that she didn't want to give it the chance of catching on something before it even got out of her mouth.

'Are they the kind of mirrors you can step into?'

'Do what?'

His head suddenly tilted and bobbed from one side to the other as he squinted up at her like a blue-tit eyeing a particularly complex bird feeder.

'There are mirrors you can step into aren't there? You said there were other places, other "heres". You said you could show me how to get to them . . .'

'Oooh, I never! What a whopper!'

She turned on him, hand clenched into a fierce and knobby fist.

'The only whopper you're going to get is when I lay one on you if you don't straighten up and start telling me the truth. I want to know about the mirrors, because I think it's to do with them, isn't it? When we left here I looked in and it was all like this, hundreds of reflections of the same thing snaking off into the distance, all copies of each other – except for one thing.'

Her finger stabbed at the mirror. He flinched as her hand passed his shoulder, but his eyes followed the direction she was indicating.

'It's not there now. I hoped it might be, but it isn't. But it was. There was one slice that was different to all the others, and you know why?' asked Edie.

'No. I don't want to know, an' all . . .'

He was backing into the shadows again. She could hear him nervously crumpling the newspaper ball in his fist. Her voice cracked like a whip, and he stopped dead.

'Tragedy! Stay there.'

She followed him into the gloomy nook.

'The rest of the slices were identical to each other, just getting smaller, but there was this one slice with a bowl and a knife lying on the ground. Only that's what I *thought* they were. Until I saw them again, later.'

Little Tragedy's Adam's apple bobbled up and down twice. His eyes slid around the room, looking for an exit. Or help.

'You saw them later? This bowl and knife whatsit?'

His Adam's apple came up for the third time, like it was drowning.

She nodded grimly. She knew from the unmissable awkwardness of his body language that she was on the threshold of something new, something powerful.

'I saw them again just after this evil bloke called the Walker pulled two little round mirrors out of his pocket and stepped into one of them. I saw them just after he disappeared into the mirror, taking our friend with him. Only it wasn't a bowl and a knife. It was the Walker's dagger and the Gunner's tin helmet. And they lay there on the ground, and these two little mirrors hung there in the air on either side of them for a moment, like a magic trick, with no one holding them. Then there was a little pop and the mirrors and the hat and the dagger just sort of disappeared. So what I want to know, what I need to know is: are these the kind of mirrors you can step into? And if they are, how come I saw the hat and dagger lying there before it happened?'

'Er,' said Little Tragedy. 'Well. Ah.'

His eyes were sliding all over the room.

'You should ask himself. He's got the words. I only see stuff really. Ask old Black.'

'I'm asking you.'

'Ask him.'

'He's not here.'

Tragedy looked at the newspaper crumpled in his hand. Then placed it delicately on a table-top. She flashed the memory of him catching the paper as it lifted off the pile in the gust of wind from the door, and only then remembered that the door was shut. Had been shut. Locked. Tight enough to keep draughts out.

Little Tragedy grimaced again as if knowing what she was belatedly realizing.

'Er . . .'

The hairs on the back of her neck went up. Her hand reached instinctively for the warning glass in her pocket. The deep booming voice behind her froze her hand.

'The little imp is trying to say "Yes, he is", '

She turned, knowing what she was going to see.

She was nose to belly with the Friar himself, towering over her like a dark cliff-face. And as her eyes travelled upwards she couldn't help but notice that the previously jolly face was now as cheery and welcoming as a black thundercloud in a cold, dark sky.

17

ARIEL RISING

George plummeted towards the ground, held in the tight embrace of the golden girl. He knew he was dead. In one short second his head would pile-drive into the pavement. And the Gunner would be dead too, and Edie would never know he hadn't deserted her by choice, and his mother – his mother would never know how much he . . .

He threw his hands out reflexively, and two things happened at once: the girl batted them down with the arm that wasn't wrapped round his chest and clamped them tightly to his side.

And she swooped.

There was no other word for it. At the very last moment she defied all the laws of aerodynamics and flattened out her dive, acrobatically swooping left in a ninety-degree barrel-roll, so that instead of splatting into the stone pavement she flew along it at an altitude of about half a metre.

'Keep your arms in or you'll hurt yourself,' she said calmly. George just stared at the paving stones whipping past his nose and got used to being alive again. He nodded and then made the mistake of looking ahead.

Not only were they running out of pavement; the intersection ahead was busy and in motion. Buses and lorries sped through in opposite directions, and the girl seemed to be leaving it too late – suddenly, much much too late, if she hoped to gain altitude and fly over the vehicles powering across their path at right angles.

A big high-sided lorry hurtled in from the left on a certain collision course, much too close to miss or avoid, and once more he knew he was dead, and once more he refused to close his eyes – and then he wished he had, because instead of hitting the lorry she dinked even lower and underflew it, between the moving wheels.

And he heard her laughter gurgle in his ear, and she banked left and up and where before George had been terrified he realized that his mouth wasn't shrieking but smiling.

And the reason was this: she flew.

Just as she had said she did.

And when she flew, she *really* flew.

Spout, by comparison, had not really flown. Spout, by comparison, had dragged himself painfully through the sky by grabbing great untidy chunks of air and forcing them under his wings as he desperately snatched for the next one. Spout had propelled himself through the sky in a constant battle against the air and the pull of gravity. The girl didn't fight the air. She flew in it as if she was a part of it.

And he realized that this was why she laughed. She loved the simple freedom and exhilaration of flying.

As if she had read his thoughts, she slalomed between three lampposts and then down into a tunnel under a modern building that quickly opened up into a small square in front of an ancient stone church. She cut a wide arc around the right hand side of the building at gargoyle height, close enough for George to see with relief that the only gargoyles on this church were grotesque mediaeval heads pulling ugly faces.

Then she tightened the radius of the arc and circled in to the pavement at the foot of a bulging gherkin-shaped skyscraper that was as modern as the church at its base was old.

She daintily released George and stepped back, running her fingers through her hair to restore some order to the wind-blown golden locks. They were both panting and took a moment to get their breath back. As they did so he could see her eyes were bright with exhilaration.

'I guarantee we lost him,' she said.

He looked upwards and was pleased to see no sign of Spout. He nodded.

'Thank you.'

'It was nothing more than a pleasure, boy,' she smiled.

'My name's George,' he said. And he held his hand out because he didn't know what to do, and shaking hands always seemed to be part of a good introduction. She looked at him oddly, and then took his hand. But instead of shaking it, she turned it over and examined it. He saw she was looking at the scar, the dragon's wound, his Maker's Mark.

'Oh,' he said. 'That's a—'

'I know what it is, boy,' she laughed. 'Being one of the "made", how would I not?' And she gave him his hand back.

'Who are you?' he asked.

'I am Ariel.'

George nodded, smiling, then glanced up to keep a wary eye on the darkening sky in case any Spouts suddenly appeared out of it.

'I'll hear him coming,' she said. 'He punches great holes in the sky as he drags his ungainly bulk through it.

I will catch the vibrations. I am after all a spirit of the air.'

And George remembered who Ariel was, because his school had been to see a play in the park two summers ago.

'Er, no offence, but I thought Ariel was a boy.'

Her head came up and she looked at him with an expression that was half hurt, half outraged pride. He swallowed and hurried on, before the insult could take root.

'No, I mean, when we saw it in school. The play. That's when I thought Ariel was a boy. In the play, right?'

He was burbling. He knew he was burbling. He definitely wasn't making it better.

'Do I look like a boy to you, boy?'

It was a disconcerting question and she had a disconcerting way of asking it. It wasn't just her voice which, for all its disapproval, was rather low and quite velvety. It wasn't the sense that she was always on the point of laughing at him either, although that was quite irritating. It was that there was something unnerving about her clothes. It wasn't that they were golden or filmy, or even that they were covering – just – a body that the sculptor had made distractingly lithe and curvy. It was that they were, he realized, not really clothes at all. They were floaty bits of material that seemed held on by nothing more than a light breeze.

'No. You look very . . . not like a boy.'

She held his look for a long and predictably disconcerting moment. A smile twitched at the edge of her mouth. Somehow, somewhere – actually in the pit of his stomach – he found that hint of the smile the most disconcerting thing of all.

'I *am* very not like a boy, boy. No boy could do this.'

And then she reached out and took his hand again, and leapt into the air. His stomach flipped and his arm was half wrenched out of his socket, and then she hoisted him higher and put an arm under his armpit and held him, his back tightly clenched to her as she soared up, spiralling around the curved skyscraper.

He saw the office floors, layer after layer, as they rose and circled towards the swelling middle of the building. He saw empty desks and winking computer screens. He saw a conference room with men and women sitting round a long table. He saw a man in a suit standing on his head against a wall as a couple of business-suited women laughed and applauded. And he saw entire empty floors with a lone cleaner pushing her cart through the anonymous maze of booths and dividers. And then the building ceased to belly outwards and started to taper, and Ariel twisted in mid-flight, laughing as she gave them a widening panorama of the whole city below.

He saw the sparkle of the river and the closer high-rises, and then the distant skyscrapers at Canary Wharf to the east, and he began feeling as giddy as her laughter, as the circuits around the building got narrower and narrower as they neared the apex.

And then the whirling panorama really did start to blur with the velocity at which she was circling and then they reached the rounded point at the top of the building and the circling became a pirouette that got faster and faster until George felt like one of those ice-skaters spinning on one skate, so fast that they ceased to be a recognizable person and just became a high velocity whirling smear.

'Please,' he choked, half laughing, half panicking. 'Please. Ariel. I'm going to hurl . . .'

And her spinning slowed and eased and then ceased and once she had stopped, it took a while for his brain to settle back on its gimbals and stop its own sympathetic whirligig.

Ariel stepped gently down to the rim of the building's cap and lowered him on to it. He grabbed a bar set into a recessed hole and clung on tight.

'No, don't—' he began, but she did.

She let go of him, and there he was, sitting on top of the world, a shiny glass and metal world, that curved away from him so radically that there was nothing to see but drop-off whichever way he looked.

Ariel stepped in front of him, spun on one toe and curtsied, as if she had just completed a virtuoso performance. She looked expectantly at him, a prima ballerina waiting for applause.

'There's no way I'm letting go of this bar in order to clap. It's just not going to happen,' he explained, deciding that given his precarious position, anything other than complete frankness would be suicidal. 'But you're right. No boy could fly like that. That was amazing.'

'Amazing?'

A single golden eyebrow curved higher than its mate.

Obviously amazing wasn't doing it.

'Brilliant. Crazy. Superb.'

Her eyebrows regained their symmetry.

'Yes,' she said. 'It was superb.'

'Yes,' he nodded, really hoping that she would take the compliment and put him back on the ground. He had a sudden horror-struck premonition about being left there, perched on the sharp end of this fantastically elongated egg shape as the night drew in and darkness covered the city. He knew if that happened he would eventually fall asleep and slide off the curving edge and into death.

He saw with huge relief that she was smiling triumphantly. She looked off into the west and pointed.

'There is a boy who lives over there, a babyish boy in a babyish park who thinks he too can fly. Should you ever see him I would be eternally in your debt if you could repeat what you have just so kindly said. Especially the "superb" bit. He is an odious crowing coxcomb of a boy. And he flies with all the grace of a thrown turnip.'

'Thrown turnip. Gotcha,' he said, clenching on his hand-hold like a very determined limpet. 'Could we please go down now?'

'You want to go down so soon?' She stretched languidly, her hands back to back, fingers intertwining, reaching for the sky: her toes straining on point. 'But you can see everything from here.'

'I know,' he said. 'Except I can't see Edie, and I can't see the Gunner, and frankly . . .'

And here all the frustration of being snatched up and put down and snatched up again and flown all over the city boiled over and choked him.

'. . . frankly, I'm fed up with all this. I've got friends in trouble, and they need help and I need help to help them, because they're my responsibility, yeah? And all that happens is I seem to be being carried further and further away from any place I might find them. So please. Ariel. I have to do what has to be done. So the flying is tip-top, OK? But what I *really* need to know is: can you help me or not?'

He ran out of words and stared at her. She watched her fingers make a butterfly as they descended to her sides, and then she smiled at him.

'Of course,' she said. 'To help do what has to be done. That's why I came for you.'

He didn't know what she meant.

'I'm sorry?'

'I'm not. I told you what I was.' She flashed a grin.

'A spirit of the air?' he guessed.

'A minister of Fate,' she said, with a gasp of exasperation. And then she tugged his ankle again and he lost his grip, and the whole falling thing happened again, only this time he was ready for her to catch him, which, thankfully, she did.

'There's an easier way to do this,' he choked as they angled groundwards in a shallow dive.

'Ah, but you don't get the easy way, do you, boy?' she laughed as they flew down and cut north up the street known as St Mary Axe. 'You get the Hard Way.'

And the way she said it, the way she knew it suddenly, made his stomach drop faster than any of the flying had done, and then he heard a sound that made everything much worse.

Ahead of them, somewhere in the darkness he heard a single bell tolling as if for a funeral, deep and low and solemn. And he knew with absolute certainty that it was a warning bell, and that the warning was for him.

18

THE ICARUS ALONE

The Icarus flapped its rigid wings and gave a series of short muted shrieks of agony as it flew over the office buildings that made up the Broadgate development.

It was screaming because it hated people, and the more of them that it saw in one place the worse it felt. It preferred the safety of its plinth, where it could stay hunched inside the contraption that attached it to its wings and close its ears to the noise they made as they walked past.

The reason it was shrieking was partly because it had accustomed itself to the habit and partly because the flying harness was so ungainly and heavy that being attached to it was like being permanently jammed in its own personalized torture chamber.

It found it hard to fly effectively because the wings it had been given were more like ragged and sawn-off windmill sails than anything designed for graceful passage through the air. This meant it could only fly short distances without exhaustion, and never got higher than about six metres off the ground. Whenever it had to overfly anything taller than that, it had to do it in a series of hops, using sinewy man's feet that had become accustomed to a new life as talons.

It was shrieking particularly intensely because the length it had tried to fly was too ambitious, and it was going to have to land in the middle of the crowd of people dressed up and heading for a night out. Its hatred of human beings was so intense that it had convinced itself, somewhere in the back of its mad mind, that the closer they came to him, the more it hurt.

It landed in front of the only group of unmoving people amid the flow – six black figures, frozen in time, tired and work-weary men and women who would never make it home because they were cast from bronze.

The taint stood in front of them, protected from the real people flowing past by their tight, immobile grouping.

Six unmoving pairs of bronze eyes watched the taint panting and sobbing as it flinched from any contact with the people passing it.

The real reason the Icarus was mad was because it didn't know who or what it was – man, machine, animal or bird. That's why it couldn't fly very well. That's why it walked like a bull on its hind legs. That's why it lived its life in a scream.

The only other creature who had ever been able to understand it or soothe it was the Minotaur, because the Minotaur had been made by the same Maker, and had the same mad split at its core.

And the boy and the glint had killed the Minotaur. And the Icarus would hunt them down, no matter how much the hunting hurt.

It took a great ragged breath and launched itself into the sky.

It would find them.

19

DIGGING IN

The Gunner's wrongness seemed to be getting worse. He felt tired beyond normal exhaustion, and his hands and limbs were beginning to not do what he wanted them to, as if the instructions coming down from his brain were subject to a game of Chinese whispers and losing a lot of the detail in translation.

His hands had begun to feel as if their normally strong, agile fingers were wrapped in stiff new boxing gloves. His back ached, and he was fighting the overwhelming desire to find the piece of gravel and just sit down for a bit. He knew this last was a fatal impulse, because once he sat he was pretty sure he wouldn't want to get up again. So he wiped his now clumsy hands across the rough stone of the wall and confirmed to his satisfaction that there were no more heart stones left on it.

He grinned to himself and hefted the oilskin bag that his groundsheet cape had become. It clinked satisfactorily.

He had two choices, he thought: he could drop the bag under water, which would leave the Walker floundering around in the dark, trying to find the heart stones. The only trouble with that was that the tank floor was barely two metres below water at its deepest points, and a lot shallower over most of its area. Floundering around would eventually lead the Walker to trip over the package, and then when he opened it he would have all the light he could want.

'Bury it,' he grunted. 'Smart-arse didn't say I couldn't dig *downwards*, did he?'

He stumbled up on to the gravel, moving by touch alone. He found the back wall, and dropped to his knees. He put the bag of heart stones on the ground next to him, and allowed himself the luxury of a cigarette.

The match scraped and he ignited the end and sucked in the smoke. He pulled the pewter plate out of his jacket and looked at it in the light of the match as it burned down to his fingers.

'Dream of four castles my Aunt Fanny – know what you are, my beauty?' he asked it as the match died and darkness swept back in from the edges of the tank. 'You are a bloody short-handled shovel.'

And he rolled the cigarette to one side of his mouth and chunked the plate into the pea-gravel at his knees. He hoisted a plateful of stone to one side and dug in again, pleased to see that the injunction forbidding him to dig upwards was not preventing him digging in the opposite direction.

And as is often the way of it, once he was working, he felt less tired. It was as if the physical labour took some of the stress out of him and the rhythmic shovelling left less space for him to worry about the wrongness of things at his core.

He knew he had plenty to worry about, not least of which was the fact that he was running out of time. Turn o'day must be approaching up on the surface. And if his plinth was empty at midnight, he knew he was a goner. He didn't know how being a goner would work with the fact he seemed to be under a curse. Perhaps it meant he'd be a walking dead statue, a pair of dead hands, the same way taints were, only ever moving from the plinth to do the Walker or the Stone's bidding. The thought of becoming a taint in spit's clothing turned his gut, and he took it out on the gravel by digging faster and harder. Whatever happened, even if he kicked the bucket at midnight, he was going to bury the Walker's profane booty as deep as he could. He dug so hard that the pewter plate buckled and he threw it aside and started digging with his hands alone.

And for the longest time in the darkness the only sounds were the chunk and hiss of gravel being scooped out of a hole and tossed aside on to more gravel and the quiet pop of a man working with both hands and a cigarette parked in the side of his face.

He wondered what George was doing right now.

20

FRIAR'S DEAL

'Where's the boy?'

The Black Friar glowered down at Edie.

'Gone.'

'Gone? Gone how? Gone where?'

Something in the accusing way he asked gave the strong impression that whatever had happened was going to turn out to be Edie's fault.

'Just gone. Don't know how, don't know where.'

Her chin jutted forward as she refused to look away from his eyes.

'You don't know how, you don't know where. And now . . . you're here.'

'Yep.'

He exhaled, a long and noisy out-breath whistling out

of his nose like a safety valve taking the pressure off a steaming boiler.

'Well. That's fine and dandy, no doubt. Capital, even. And I suppose you—'

'I thought you might know why.'

He didn't look like someone who was used to people interrupting him so bluntly. He cleared his throat.

'You thought I might know why you're here?'

'Why George has gone.'

The safety valve blew as the Friar detonated in a spluttering explosion.

'Why he's gone? You think I know why the boy has gone? Sunder me from my bones, girl! I assure you it's nothing to do with me! Why, the very thought of—'

'I thought you might know if it's to do with the Hard Way.'

The explosion stopped. The Friar ran his hand over his bald head and down to his chin. It was as if he was wiping off the look of shocked indignation and replacing it with one of genuine puzzlement.

'The Hard Way?'

'You said if he didn't put the dragon's head on the Stone, he'd be guaranteed the Hard Way. I wanted to know if suddenly disappearing was part of that.'

The Friar stepped back. Looked less ominous. Scratched his head.

'You're saying he *didn't* put the head on the stone?'

'Yeah.'

'Because he ran out of time? You surprise me, indeed you do. I saw the mark he bore, I sensed the power within, I felt he would succeed.'

The monk looked genuinely puzzled. 'Well, devil me kidneys . . . I'd have wagered on him finding the Stone Heart, indeed I would. I thought more of the boy.'

Edie had a sudden flashback to George, his face set and determined as he held the pistol steady, aimed right into the Minotaur's eye. She remembered how he hadn't flinched, not even at the thunderous detonation when he'd pulled the trigger.

'He didn't run out of time. He found the Stone Heart. It was the London Stone. He worked it out. He followed the map of words you gave him. He did other stuff too. He was a bit amazing. He just chose not to put the dragon's head on it. He chose the Hard Way. And I want to know if that's why he disappeared.'

'He chose the Hard Way? You're telling me he actually CHOSE the Hard Way? Trophies and trumpetings, why would he do that . . .? Unless . . .'

The Friar looked at Little Tragedy. Then at Edie. And then slowly took three steps back to the bar. He reached over it and grabbed a Coke bottle. He popped the metal cap thoughtfully between his teeth, and held the bottle out to her.

'Have a drink, in as much as this hellish soda water can be called a drink, then tell me everything – leave nothing out. And then we'll see what we can see and mayhap do what can be done.'

Edie took the bottle and sat down on a stool and, suddenly very conscious that the broken dragon's head was in the pocket of George's coat only centimetres from the Friar's elbow, started to talk.

She told him of everything that had happened since they left this room the night before, and ended on the Gunner being spirited into the mirrors by the Walker.

'And that's why I want to know about the mirrors. And that's why I want to know about the Hard Way. I have to find George and we have to help the Gunner.'

'And why is that?'

'Because it's the right thing to do,' she answered, without thinking. And when she heard herself say it she realized that that was exactly why, for her, it had to be done. Take a life, save a life.

And then, and only then, did she drink from the untouched bottle of Coke. The bubbles rose inside her and she burped thunderously and looked defiantly at the mountainous spit.

'And you have told me everything that happened?'

'Yes,' she said, crossing fingers in her mind. 'I've told you everything I saw.'

Which was strictly true. They had left here last time pretending that they had to go and fetch the broken dragon's head, not telling the Friar that it was with them at the time, in George's coat pocket. And that brought her eye back to the same coat and the same heavy pocket lying on the bar-top by the Friar's elbow. She looked away and hoped he hadn't noticed the weight inside it as he'd pushed it aside to reach over for her Coke.

'I didn't ask you if that was all you saw. I asked you if that was all that happened.'

For a being made of bronze his eye was disconcertingly steely.

'That was what happened.'

'Still not quite what I was asking, but close enough for a glint, perhaps.'

She heard Little Tragedy try and stifle a small snort of derision. He didn't do a very good job, and the sound irritated her more than she would have expected. Her head came up, eyes bright and defiant.

'I've got nothing to hide.'

The Friar peered at her for a moment, and then his shoulders started to twitch, and the twitch turned into a quake, and the quake rumbled into a laugh, and soon the whole room was reverberating to the deep rolling mirth of the mountainous figure at the bar. He reached for a towelling beer mat and dabbed at the tears streaming out of his eyes as he chuckled and chortled and generally did a very poor job of trying to control himself.

Being laughed at unexpectedly is never a very pleasant experience. Being laughed at by a ton and a half of bronze in a cassock is even more annoying.

'Hoi,' she said, trying to stem the tide. 'What's so funny?'

'Sorry,' gasped the Friar. 'Intolerable rudeness, eternal shame, gross lapse of hospi—hospitality. But a glint. Having nothing to hide? Why, the thought of it! A glint is nothing but a veritable pantechnicon, stuffed to the gunwales with hidden things. The hidden and the hiding are two sides of the same coin, as you know in the core of your young being, whether you acknowledge it or no. A glint absorbs the hidden in the world and needs must hide to survive in that world. Why, if it were not so nearly a symmetry it might be a paradox!'

And he erupted into a fresh spasm of laughter, shoulders heaving and chins wobbling at the sheer hilarity of it all.

She had no idea what the avalanche of words meant. It felt as if he was using his booming voice to bludgeon her. She did understand what a paradox was, and it *was* a paradox that this laughing figure who seemed all hospitality and good cheer was, in fact, particularly frightening. It was as if he'd found a way to use all that cheeriness as a weapon. He was a million miles away from the smiler with the knife who'd pursued her on a distant beach in what seemed a different life; but still, there was something about all the mirth that seemed to suggest if not a hidden knife, then a hidden agenda that might be just as fatal to her as a blade.

All the laughter and the good-cheer had the effect of making it hard to think, and thinking was how Edie stayed ahead of things.

'Hey,' she said. He kept on laughing.

Without thinking why she was doing it she picked the bottle cap off the table in front of her, held it between thumb and forefinger and flicked it at the Friar. Metal hit metal as the cap hit him square on the forehead with a distinct 'tink' noise that chopped off the laughter like an axe. The bottle cap bounced up and off the sloping head, glinting in the headlights of a car passing outside the window, and the Friar's left hand snapped out and opened and closed in one astonishingly fast reaction from a man who seemed so mountainous and fat. It caught the cap and crushed it in one movement. Then the hand opened and gently dropped the mangled disk on the table in front of her.

'Oh, oh,' said Little Tragedy behind her.

'Silence, you imp!' boomed the Friar. And then he lunged forward, hoisted the knees of his cassock, and sat on the stool in front of her. The crushed bottle cap was still rocking on the small circular table-top between them. Edie decided to be intimidated later. Right now she needed answers.

'The mirrors,' she said. 'I told you all that happened. Now you tell me about the mirrors, and then tell me about the Hard Way.'

The Friar rubbed his chin with one hand while the other drubbed out an irritated tattoo on the table. Then he stopped the finger-tapping and looked off to one side at the mirrors.

'I'll make you a deal,' he said shortly.

'A deal?'

'A deal. Something for you, something for me.'

'What kind of something?' she asked, trying hard not to look at the coat on the bar-top with its suspiciously bulging pocket.

'I want your word. I want your word that if the boy lives and you find him that you will bring him to me.'

'You want George?'

'I want to talk to him. I want him to talk to me.'

'And that's all.'

'And that's all.'

She didn't need to think.

'Deal.'

The Friar peered at her, peered so intently that she felt he was in fact peering into her, and then spat in his hand and held it out. She was unsure what to do. Little Tragedy cleared his throat from the shadows at her back.

'Spit in your 'and and shake 'is.'

Her mouth, now she thought about it, was too dry to muster any extra spit. She worked it, trying to generate some moisture.

'It's more for the look of it than the actual spittle, my dear,' said the monk.

So she dry-spat into her hand and let the big bronze fist close round it. She was surprised by how soft and warm the smooth metal was.

The Friar sat back with a smile.

And for an instant she wondered if she had just unwittingly betrayed George in some way.

21

THE LAST KNIGHT

George heard the bell tolling ahead of them — deep, regular and doom-laden. They flew straight, as if locked on to the source of the noise like a homing beacon, missiling through the sheets of rain that were now gusting down with a vengeance.

Ahead of them black metal railings and a spiked gate loomed between two worn stone gatehouses, barely larger than sentry boxes. Ariel flew over them and between two old colonnaded brick buildings that led into an inner courtyard complex beyond. At the back end of the courtyard were modern glass-fronted office buildings, and as they flew in George saw one or two umbrellas hurrying through the rain as people headed home through the downpour. There was so much water on the ground that he could see the rain-pocked reflection of Ariel, gold and bright against the louring night sky beyond.

And then she swerved and landed so delicately that it wasn't clear where flying ended and walking resumed, but it *was* clear that they'd arrived. The tolling of the bell was very loud against the white noise of rain that was coming down like stair-rods. She pointed to the side of one of the renovated warehouse buildings.

There was something red and boxy high on the wall above them, but because the rain was falling directly into his upturned eyes, it took George a couple of seconds to realize that it was the bell and its mounting. It must have been a fire-bell at one time. Now it rang its relentless funeral note and sat there in the rain, red and slick as new blood.

He knew he wasn't going to like the answer to his next question, but he asked it anyway.

'What's that about? Why are we here?'

Ariel smiled brightly at him, spun on a toe in a single pirouette and came back round without a hint of the smile or laughter in her eyes.

'Never send to know for whom the bell tolls, boy. It tolls for thee.'

'OK,' he said, very deliberately. He wasn't surprised, because he'd known the bell was for him from the first clang he'd heard, but he wasn't any clearer either. 'Why is it for me?'

She stretched a long arm out with a theatrical flourish and pointed over his shoulder.

'It is a summoning bell. It is summoning you to meet the Last Knight.'

He turned slowly. Ten metres away, on a raised patch of grass surrounded by a low box hedge, was a full-sized knight in armour sitting on a fierce looking mount, carrying a long lance at the ready. The knight's helmet covered his face except for a narrow slit in his visor, and the horse wore a surcoat made of interlinked plates of metal set with round disks of blue glass in a Celtic wave pattern. They made a majestic pair, though there was something almost skeletal about the horse's head. He could see through the nostril. He could see through several bits of the horse, in fact, because it wasn't solid at all. It was hollow. And then George looked more closely and saw that the sculptor had made both the man and the horse out of plates of armour. The Knight was a hollow man. Which raised the question – a pointed question, given the sharpness of the lance in the Knight's right hand – of whether he was a spit or a taint.

'Ariel,' said George quietly. 'Why is the bell summoning me, exactly?'

A fine shower fanned out in a flattened halo around

her as she shook the water out of her hair before speaking. George noticed that there was something theatrical about everything she did.

'I told you, boy. You chose your own fate. You picked the Hard Way. That starts here.'

George had been pretty sure the Hard Way had begun when he was knocked into the sky by Spout, if not even earlier when the Gunner had been taken from them. He didn't like the idea that that had just been a warm-up for something much worse.

'And who is the Last Knight?'

'He is the Last Knight of the Cnihtengild.'

She pronounced the strange word 'ke-nik-ten-gild'.

'The what?'

'They are a Guild of Knights. Spelt the old-fashioned way. That writing explains it,' she said, pointing behind him.

There was a plaque on the shallow wall beneath the hedge that surrounded the Knight.

He walked slowly forward, keeping an eye on the Knight and his charger as he went down on one knee in the rain-splashed puddle in front of the plaque and read:

King Edgar (959–975) granted this derelict land to thirteen knights, on condition that they each perform three duels, one on land, one below land and

one on water. These feats having been achieved, the
King gave the knights, or Cnihtengild, certain
rights . . .

He got no further, because the horse blew an irritated harrumph and stamped its hooves, and he looked up to see the Knight was leaning forward, the dark shadow of his eye-slit pointed at him. And as George stared back, the shadows lightened and he could see a pair of dim blue lights beginning to kindle where the eyes would have been hidden. Before George could decide whether to straighten up and run away or stay where he was, the Last Knight spoke. His voice was deep and sonorous, and shared the brassy harmonics of the bell tolling in the background, as if his voice was the bell put into words.

'Will you stand?'

It was a simple question. George could see no harm in it. He straightened up and wiped the rain from his face.

'Yes. Hello.'

'And will you stand?' repeated the Knight.

George looked down at himself then back at the blue eye-lights, staring out from within the blank helmet. The horse pulled against its reins and pawed the ground with a great metal hoof.

'Here I am. Standing,' he answered, a little puzzled.

The Knight pulled at the horse's bridle, which made it snort and stop the pawing.

'And then will you stand?'

The repetition was getting strange. Or maybe just annoying. Or perhaps the knight couldn't see very well out of the narrow slit in his armour.

'Yes. I'll stand. I am standing. I do stand. As you see.' He spoke slowly, with exaggerated politeness, so as not to cause offence. 'You've asked me that three times already.'

The horseman's neck straightened and his mount snickered through its curling nose holes.

'And you have accepted three times, good knight.'

George decided the statue was obviously a bit mad. As far as he knew there was no reason why statues shouldn't be as mad as anyone else. He hadn't accepted *anything* once, let alone three times. He decided it was time to try much harder to get back to Edie.

'Yes. Well. Good night to you too,' he said, and turned away.

'HA!' The next toll of the bell was augmented by a simultaneous roar and clash of arms.

The sound hit him like a physical blow. It was so loud he saw rainwater bounce up out of the puddles around him. It was a shout of approval, and it came from many more throats than just the Last Knight. It was the sound of a great host shouting and hitting their shields with swords or lances. And in a flash of something like lightning or a sheet of flame George saw the Guild gathered round him in a living frame, like ghostly projections on the rain. But these were no brightly coloured fairy-tale knights from a child's book. These were grim combat-worn figures, clinging to their saddle-horns with the last of their strength. Their armour and chain-mail weren't shiny but hacked up and skeined with blood. Their sword edges were nicked and dinged, and their shields bore so many gouges that it was hard to make out the heraldic designs that had once been painted on them. Those that carried their helmets had faces grizzled with stubble, and dark shadowed eyes stained with battle-weariness. Several of the faces were bruised and bloodied, and many of them sat awkwardly on their mounts, shoulders dropped or curled over the pain of wounds he couldn't see. To complete the sense that they had all just paused in a battle, breath panted out of their mouths and the nostrils of their horses, pluming in the cold. And they all held drawn weapons in their hands.

George saw all of this in a flash, and when it was gone the modern buildings reasserted themselves and he was staring at Ariel, still with his back to the Knight. One thing that had changed, however, was that there seemed to be hundreds of bright blue lights radiating out from behind him, making a starburst on the surrounding walls of the courtyard, like an intense disco ball.

'He meant good knight with a K,' said Ariel.

There was another flash, timed with the tolling of the bell, and he saw the other knights once again, the Guild, moving slowly in.

'Okey-dokey,' said George slowly, really not wanting to turn round and see where all those blue lights were coming from. 'And what does that mean exactly?'

'It means he's honouring you as a fellow knight for accepting the three challenges. It's chivalry.'

'Er, no. It's rubbish,' he hissed desperately. 'I didn't accept any bloody challenges, let alone three!'

'Yes you did, boy. You agreed to stand. You agreed three times.'

'But I didn't know what he was saying! I thought he couldn't hear me or something. I thought that was why he was repeating himself . . .' he lowered his voice. 'I thought he might be a bit deaf. Or mad . . .'

'HA!' The bell tolled and there was another intense flash and the sound of a host shouting, and George saw the Guild again. They were moving in, making a long alley on either side of him.

'Good luck, boy,' Ariel said, and walked backwards away from him.

'What am I meant to do?' he hissed.

'Stand and fight. Three duels, three trials of strength, none to be fought on the same ground as any other. You must fight on the earth, under the earth, and on the water. You read the plaque. That is the way of the Guild.'

'But why must I fight?'

'Because in choosing the Hard Way you chose to remain. Now you must prove you are worthy to.'

'And if I don't?'

Another toll of the bell, and this time a flash with no shout, just the vision of the Knights. This carried on happening every time it rang. It was like seeing them in a very slow strobe, a tempo dialled down to the funereal tolling of the bell.

'Then you will not remain. Here or in any unLondon. This world will have seen the last of you.'

She pushed up his sleeve and tapped the metal flaw twining out from the Maker's Mark.

'Each of these flaws will start to move towards your heart when you begin a duel. They do this to make you finish each contest, for if you run away, the flaw will continue up your arm and pierce your heart. So do not run from any of the duels. You must stand and prove yourself. Only in that way will you show what you are made of.'

Desperation was making his breath come faster. He clenched his fists and clasped at a last straw as he heard the horse behind him nicker and shake its bridle chain.

'But I can't fight. I don't have a weapon!'

She smiled, a sad smile of farewell, and pointed behind him.

'Then pray that your wits are sharper than his lance, boy, because here it comes.'

He turned, and in the next flash saw that the Guild had now hemmed him into a narrow jousting space that bristled with weapons and fierce looking faces. And more than that, at the other end of the gauntlet he saw the source of all those lights. It was the Knight and his charger.

The blue glass disks that were interlinked in the horse's surcoat had each lit up, lancing blue light in all directions as the knight spurred the charger slowly forward off the dais. The lights bounced and waved hypnotically on the surrounding walls and windows, mirroring the sinuous rippling of the surcoat as the great horse stepped daintily over the low hedge, one hoof after the other clopping on to the wet stone floor of the courtyard.

The Knight was shrugging his shoulders and rolling his head on his neck, like a boxer loosening up before a fight. He seemed every bit as murderous and businesslike as the rest of the Guild looked in the flashes that George kept seeing every time the bell tolled.

He kept moving back, roughly along the alley made

by the now visible/now invisible knights. He wondered if they were actually there all the time, or only when the flashes happened. He stepped sideways, planning to run into the low brick colonnades where the Knight would be too tall to follow him easily and he could at least grab one of the metal chairs to use as a weapon.

Something hard, like the flat of a sword, smacked his head and made it ring, but not before he had heard the jingle of harness close by his ear and the word 'COWARD' hissed at him.

He held his ear and stumbled back across the now obviously more-than-imaginary jousting ground. He must have staggered too far, because something big and flat and hard like a shield batted into his face and sent him sprawling back into the centre of the narrow space.

And being hit in the nose was perhaps the thing that saved him. Being hit in the nose hurts a lot, but it also spikes adrenaline and makes you very angry, instantly. And George got very angry very quickly, and the treacly black feeling surged up into his throat and nose, and he wiped his hand across his face and wasn't surprised to see a thin streak of blood on it. He remembered the Gunner; just after he'd first saved George way back at the beginning of their nightmare journey, when he'd looked down at him and said:

'You're angry. Sometimes angry gets things done.

This isn't one of those times . . .'

But he also remembered the way the Gunner had channelled his fury when fighting the Minotaur. That had been one of the *other* times, when angry did get things done. This, he knew, was the same kind of time.

'OK,' he said to himself. 'Fine.'

And even though he was soaking wet and there was no point to it other than show, he turned, rolled up his sleeves and set his legs a shoulder's width apart. And the Gunner may have been physically absent, perhaps lost for ever, but there was definitely something of him in the way George planted his feet and held his ground.

And he spat into the puddle and faced the Knight at the other end of the courtyard.

'FINE,' he shouted. 'Do your worst.'

There was a flash, and in it he saw the Guild again, looking as if they were somehow both projected on to and made out of the pelting rain itself; and they were all looking at him.

They didn't look like a happy band of knights in armour who were devoted to courtly poetry and rescuing damsels in distress, or slaying picturesque dragons.

They looked like a nasty hard-nosed bunch of mediaeval muggers.

'Anyone going to lend me a shield or something?' he asked.

In another flash he saw no one moving. It just made him angrier.

'Good. Nice chivalry. To hell with you all anyway.'

He felt the scar on his hand twinge badly, and he knew without looking that what Ariel had described had started. The metal flaw had jagged up his arm and was heading for his heart. He looked at his hand and held the Maker's Mark out for them to see. Then he showed it to the Knight.

'I don't know what this means, but I am a maker. You might not want me to get my hands on you.'

He was of course bluffing, but bluff was all he had going for him. The Knight stopped and cocked his helmet.

'Show me the hand.'

George's spirits rose. Maybe the bluff was going to work, though he had no idea why it would. He held his hand up.

'A dragon did this . . .' he began, hoping the extra detail might impress someone.

'You carry the mark,' boomed the Knight.

'Yes I do,' said George quickly. 'I do carry it . . .'

'The mark of the Ironhand,' continued the Knight.

The bell tolled on the next flash of light, and in it George saw the Cnihtengild craning forward in their saddles for a closer look. He felt he was getting somewhere.

'Yes,' he said, trying to sound like he had a clue what he was saying. 'Yes. That's right. Um . . . I am the Ironhand.'

Here was a pause. Nothing moved but the rain.

'No,' said the Knight. '*An* Ironhand. There have been many. You have the mark that says you may be one. Only time, your ordeals, and how you face them will tell.'

'But an Ironhand's a good thing, right?' said George, trying to catch up.

'It is.'

'So . . .' said George, slowing up suddenly, realizing he should negotiate the next bit very carefully because he might be at a very important junction where the right reply would send him down a road where he wouldn't need to fight the big statue with the even bigger pointy lance: whereas the other road would end with his being neatly – or probably not so neatly – kebabed.

'. . . so,' he continued, 'so you're good. And I'm good. So me being an Ironhand – sorry, a *maybe* Ironhand – means what? That we don't have to fight, yes? I mean, it makes a difference, right?'

He injected an eager note of 'hey presto' into the last question, as if he was stating the obvious.

And then his heart suddenly bucked and soared as he saw the Knight slowly nod his great helmet. He made a doubly imposing figure sitting on a horse at the centre of a moon-burst of blue lights radiating out from the horse's mailed caparison. George forgot to breathe, waiting for the Knight to add words to his silent affirmation.

'Yes. It makes a difference.'

'Great!' George exploded in noisy relief. 'That's great. Just great. Brilliant—'

The Knight lowered his lance and aimed it right at George's chest.

'It means you are a worthy adversary. Now.'

George froze in horror. That 'now' definitively pricked the bubble of his newly inflated hope.

'Now?'

'Now – *à outrance!* Have at you!'

And he jagged his spurs into the horse's side, and the horse bunched muscle and leapt forward, and there was another shout and clash of arms and a flame freeze-framed the ranks of the Cnihtengild hemming George in and all he could see was nowhere to run and the sharpened lance point barrelling in towards him like an express train through the rain.

21A

BLACK NEWS

The Walker paced back and forth on the corner of Bury Street and St James's Court. His hands were clasped behind his back, and as he walked his head was cricked to one side, watching himself.

He was looking at his reflection in the highly polished black granite stone adorning the corner of the building.

The edge of the building had been sculpted so that a stylised steamship appeared to be ploughing its way out of the corner and into the street. The Walker let his hand trail over the frozen bow wave the boat was making, a 'V' of tight stone curls peeling off the façade like black wood-shavings.

The Raven sat patiently watching him from its perch on the bowsprit of the boat, the only thing blacker than the granite around it, apart from its eyes. The eyes flickered, and then the Raven hopped on to the Walker's shoulders.

'The eyes of Tallyman have seen something?' hissed the Walker.

The bird clacked its beak in his ear, the Walker listened and then nodded.

'Puddle Dock, they say?'

He turned on his heel and walked back in the other direction.

'A glint walking down Puddle Dock, seeking succour or knowledge would likely be on her way to see a friar. A Black Friar.'

He ran his hands over the black mirrored surface, as if testing it. Then he turned away with a snap.

'Black is a lucky colour. Tell the Tallyman where she is bound. Now she is found, it would pain me to have her lost again.'

22

A WILDERNESS
OF MIRRORS

Edie thought for a moment about the fact that she might have just betrayed George. It was a short thought, but a sharp one.

And then the Friar was talking and she was listening, and what he told her quickly pushed the uncomfortable thought to the back of her mind into a place from where she could unpack it later.

'The mirrors are gateways. Not all mirrors, just mirrors that are set up parallel with each other. They work in two ways: firstly, by stepping into a mirror a being may move himself from where he is to another place within the city, so long as there are parallel mirrors set up there too.'

'That's wild,' said Edie, despite herself.

'Oh it's much more than wild, I assure you. It's much more than a mere 'transporter'. It's very powerful, and it's very, very dangerous . . .'

'Why?'

He stood up, the swiftness of his movements making her flinch. But he was only gesturing to her to take a position in the archway.

'Stand there. Between the mirrors. Do not touch them, because now you know what they can do they may be open to you. But look.'

She saw the images of herself and the dimly lit bar concertinaing away into the distance.

'You think you are seeing reflections of yourself, again and again. But you are not. You are seeing moments in time. Even a single reflection in a mirror is never yourself in the present, because it takes a thin slice of a microsecond for the light carrying the image to bounce off the mirror and back to your eye. A face in the mirror is always a face in the past, by that tiny fraction. And because of that we never see ourselves as we are, only as we were . . .'

He smiled at her.

'Look at the images of your face, repeating off to infinity. Each one seems the same, but that's only because the images you can see clearly are the ones where the differences are so minimal as to be beyond detection.

Travel further through the layers and you travel deeper into the past.'

She looked into the mirrors, trying to see where the differences began. She couldn't. But she felt uncomfortable.

As if the mirrors were gazing back at her somehow.

'How does it work?' she said, looking away.

'The "why" of it doesn't matter. It's just something that "is", the same way the sky or a sparrow just is. It's like that and it's always been like that. London is a place of power and it was a place of power before people erected the first shelter here. It was a place of power before people built stockades or roundhouses or temples or huts on it. Why, it was a place of power before the thought of temples had even occurred to man. It was a place of power when the wide arch of the sky was temple enough for all men. Look along the river; look at the Tower of London. Ancient? It's a Johnny-come-lately. It was a Christian church, and before that a Roman temple and before that a shrine to a Celtic crow-god and before that a shrine to a god with horns on his head and before that only the Raven himself remembers. All pasts are all still there, layered under the skin.'

His eyes were shining. He ducked through the arch next to her and she turned, uncomfortable in the thought he might be trying to get behind her in the dark.

'So the mirrors not only transport you through space. They can also move you through time, into past Londons,' she said.

'You're quick, little girl.'

'I'm not a little girl. I'm a glint. I know all about the past.'

'And of course it holds no terrors for you.'

Edie rolled her eyes and blew her cheeks out at him in impatience.

'It holds plenty of terrors for me. Don't be stupid. The past's not a nice place, is it? I'm just saying I understand about being able to go to the past because it's sort of what I do. I can get my head round that.'

His face broke into an anticipatory grin, eyes flashing theatrically at her. She shrugged.

'You don't seem impressed, child.'

'Not really. I got enough trouble coping with this particular present. I don't need more.'

'You don't "need" more?'

The more outrage he showed at her lack of response, the less she wanted to appear impressed by the vista of possibilities he was opening up.

'Nah. Sorry. I just can't really do the past layers of London thing. I mean I hear what you're saying and all, but it's just a bit . . . crap.'

She hadn't meant to say crap. She'd meant to say

weird. Or maybe scary. But her mouth had taken control before her brain could hit the anchors, and she'd said it. The Friar looked shocked.

'A bit . . . "crap"?'

'Yes,' she replied. She supposed she'd meant it, having said it and all.

'You think different realities, layered pasts, are a bit . . . "crap"?'

'Yeah.' She just wasn't going to be bullied. 'Yeah. No offence, but it's the sort of thing saddoes talk about when they've bonged a bit much or got all boozed up and out of it, you know what I mean? All that magic mushroom mumbo-jumbo they think makes sense of what's going on in their messed up heads, stuff like all the molecules in their fingernails being galaxies with little worlds spinning round them and all . . .'

As someone who had spent most of her life trying *not* to see strange and frightening things every time she accidentally touched something, Edie had strong views on people who voluntarily monkeyed with their heads in order to attempt to experience strange things. And as someone who'd slept rough in the city and been in and out of more hostels than a young girl should have, she had also come across people who went to extreme lengths to get out of their heads, usually for the understandable reason that they couldn't get into the warm.

The Friar rose to a height that seemed at least half a foot higher than normal.

'Saddoes? You think this is something for "saddoes"?'

He spat the word, hissing the S's on each end in disgust. Once again she decided not to show she was intimidated by him.

'Well. It does all sound a bit crap, doesn't it?'

'What it sounds like to your young ears is something I have no control over, glint. What it *is* . . .'

And here he raised his hands over his head and did something to the chequered circular mosaic in the ceiling. It looked as though he was moving two of the rings in different directions.

'. . . what it is, I can show you.'

There was a crump and crunch, and somehow the world jerked a bit and felt suddenly a lot darker and more serious. And the Friar looked less like a monk and more like a demon as the shadows danced across his face, lit from below. And the main reason he looked like a demon is because the light that was casting these sinister shadows across his face was red and shimmered like flames, and there had – a moment ago – been no flames in the room. And Edie turned to see where the fire was coming from and only got halfway to looking behind her, because firstly she felt a great heat-blast sear the side of her face and then her eyes stopped as they swung past the mirror to her right, the mirror that had contained the endlessly repeating reflections of herself, and now contained a blast furnace vision of hell and falling walls and screaming people.

The shock of it made her leap back – and for an instant she felt the cool glass of the other mirror behind her. And she heard the Friar yell, 'NO! STAY AWAY FROM THE MIRROR!'

And then the cool hard glass at her back gave way as gently as a soap bubble popping and the world lurched as she started to fall through into a howling firestorm and blasts lashed her face and something grabbed her foot . . . and that's when things *really* started to go wrong.

23

THE STROKE DOLOROUS

The Last Knight barrelled in through the rain, his lance aimed unwaveringly at George's heart. George backed up until he felt a wall behind him, and then he ducked and rolled sideways.

He knew the invisible knights had him hemmed in, and had the throbbing nose to prove how hard it would be to try and barge through their cordon. It was a thick impenetrable wall of horses' bodies and shields and men with weapons. But he also noticed, when the knights became visible at the next flash and toll of the bell, that lower down, under the horses' bellies, there was plenty of space to escape at ground level.

So that's what he aimed for as he ducked and rolled for safety, hoping he wouldn't find a hoof in the way. As it happened a hoof found him, and gave him a glancing blow on his shoulder, but apart from that his plan worked pretty well. As he rolled, the bell tolled and in another flash and he saw the belly of the horse above him and then he hauled himself up on to his feet and sprinted across the courtyard to the relative shelter of the low brick colonnade.

He heard a roar of disapproval from the Cnihtengild, heard someone clearly shout 'CRAVEN!' and turned in time to see the Knight hurriedly raise his lance to the sky and try to apply the brakes by leaning back and hauling on the reins. The charger's head came back and its hooves locked into a slide. He could see why the Knight had raised the lance, because if he hadn't he would have definitely speared himself a nice big office building.

George ducked sideways, flattened himself against the inside of a pillar and held his breath. In front of him was the plate-glass wall of a coffee bar. The bar was closed, but a girl was stacking the chairs and wiping the table-tops. She looked up and George was sure she saw him, so sure that he was about to shout for help when he heard a horse's hoof slowly clopping closer, and saw in the reflection in the window the lights on the war-horse's surcoat step slowly into the arch behind him.

He saw the Knight try to bend his head low enough to get into the colonnade, but there wasn't enough headroom. He looked down and saw the lance jabbing in beside him, tapping his leg.

And that's when he remembered that if he could see the Knight in the reflection of the coffee-shop window, then the Knight could see him right back.

'You must fight,' said the Knight. 'You must come out and fight, or you must forfeit as a craven varlet.'

His voice echoed ominously in the low-roofed space.

'I *am* fighting,' said George. 'I just don't have a weapon!'

A twinge of pain in the scar made him look down at his hand. He remembered how it had cut through the tentacled arm of the earth creature that had grabbed him in the underpass the day before. He remembered how the Temple Bar dragon had looked at his hand in a kind of wonder. He remembered making the bullet that had killed the Minotaur. He remembered the Gunner's look of awe as he had told him he was a Maker.

And then he looked at the lance that was tapping him on the leg. Somehow the tapping was too ignominious to bear. The Knight was cajoling him to fight as if he was a toddler having to be coaxed out of a hiding place in a Wendy house.

He thought of the power in his hands. He thought of how he had just been called Ironhand.

And then he moved. His hand flashed down and

grabbed the lance about a third of a metre from the tip. He knew what he would do, and he tried to focus his mind in order to do it. He was going to snap the lance and then he would have a pointed weapon of his own, and the lance would be blunted. This would be a good thing on many levels, not least because he was pretty sure the sculptor who had made the Knight had decided not to equip him with a sword.

It was an act of desperation, but somehow George knew from the pulsing pain in the scar in his hand that it would work.

His hand closed round the lance shaft and he tried to put every ounce of strength and will into it. At the very least he would bend the thing and render it useless.

It was a good plan and he did put everything into it. He put so much willpower into squeezing and tugging at the lance that when it neither snapped nor bent he remained clenched on to it for too long, and when the Knight kicked his horse so that it sprang backwards, he was dragged out into the open, like a terrier refusing to loosen its grip on a particularly enjoyable stick.

As he was dragged out, he suddenly had a horrible vision of what his hand would look like if he slid down the lance and the blade at the end sliced it open.

And without thinking, he flinched.

He flinched because he let the fear in.

And as he flinched the Knight flicked the lance sideways and sent him skimming across the rain-slick courtyard floor as effortlessly as a man twitching a fishing rod.

George spun to his feet and looked for the next place to run.

The bell tolled and he saw the Guild advancing behind him in a solid and ominous wall of armour and general purpose grimness.

'You must stand. You cannot run. You must fight. Refuse to fight and you forfeit,' bellowed the Knight.

'I am fighting,' shouted George. 'You've got a bloody horse and a weapon. All I've *got* is running!'

However, he was in a dead end. So he stood his ground, because when there's nowhere to run and all the talking hasn't worked, that's almost all you can do.

And when the Knight pricked his horse forward and lowered his lance, George did the one other thing he hoped the Knight wasn't expecting: he ran towards him.

He didn't plan it, but it came to him as he was already kicking into a sprint. His dad in the park, a rugby ball, cold winter afternoons. And the words:

'The trick is, zig when they expect you to zag.'

The stutter-step. The key to wrong-footing the tackler on the other team. His dad had spent hours trying to help him get the hang of it. Do it right, and a hefty opponent closing in on you at speed didn't have enough room or mobility to change his direction in time to catch you. It was the perfect tactic.

The only problem was, he remembered five steps into the run, was that he'd never really been that good at rugger and was particularly crap at selling the stutter-step. Often he just tripped up and tackled himself.

He erased the thought and focused on the tiny circle of the end of the lance as it sped towards him. And when it was two paces away he jinked left – but went right, and the lance tip tried to follow him, and whiffled past his ear as he ducked and dug in, his left shoulder grazing along the side of the horse's mail as they passed.

He reached the safety of another colonnade and looked back to see the big horse outlined by the office building beyond, trying to 180 at speed, sparks flying from its hooves as its skid sent up a huge backlit wall of spray.

He didn't wait to see them get their balance again. The bell tolled and he saw in the accompanying flash that the Guild were arranging themselves in another long line, cutting off his most obvious route to escape. But he also saw, at the end of their gauntlet, not a blank wall but the sentry-box style gatehouses he'd flown in over with the golden girl. And beyond the gatehouses the traffic and lights of the city beckoned.

He didn't think twice, just clenched his fists, ducked

his head and ran his heart out, tearing past the sporadically visible walls of knights. He had to get there before one of them positioned himself at the end of the line and cut off what he was pretty sure was his last chance of escape.

He ran so fast that his heart bounced alarmingly hard against the inside of his ribcage, but he saw that he'd made it.

None of the Guild was going to be able to block his exit. He didn't let up on his speed. He wasn't going to slow down until he'd put a lot of ground between the Knight and him. Or until he threw up or had a heart attack or something. He felt the jag of elation as he closed on the open gate. Two paces out he allowed himself to look back.

This meant he was facing the wrong way when the gate slammed shut.

He hit it in a pile-driving shoulder charge. He hit it so fast and so unexpectedly that the impact was somehow dulled with shock. He saw stars, bright tiny stars that whirled round in front of his eyes. It didn't really hurt so much as take all the breath and hope out of him in one bone-crunching impact. Except no bones crunched. The only thing that broke was his spirit.

He opened his mouth to say 'What?' but didn't have the breath to voice the word. He turned and saw a flash of gold beyond the tightly arranged black bars of the gate.

He couldn't believe it.

'*Ariel?*'

Her slender arm serpentined through the bars and her hand found his upper arm. She squeezed it gently.

'You cannot run. You cannot refuse the duel.'

He shook his head in disbelief, trying to shake some of the stars out of it.

'You closed the gate? *You . . .?*'

She squeezed his arm again. Given the fact that he saw in the next flash of flame that the Knight was now aiming at him from the other end of the two long ranks of the Guild, her gesture didn't give him the comfort he imagined she intended it to impart.

'Open the gate!'

She shook her beautiful golden head sadly. And he was sure he heard real regret in the catch in her voice. Which made what happened next almost worse.

'I cannot, boy.'

The Knight lowered his lance for the third time and kicked the horse forward. Its hooves danced through the puddles, sending up great sheets of spray as it bore down on him.

'OK, fine,' he said desperately. 'Let go of my arm and I'll climb over.'

'I cannot do that either.'

And her hand clenched round his upper arm like a manacle and pinned him to the gate.

'But why?' he shouted, heart freezing at the sight of the inbound knight.

'Because I am a minister of Fate . . .'

And the new note in her voice was as hard as diamond and cold as ice.

'. . . and no one, absolutely no one, cheats Fate, boy.'

She spat that last 'boy' as if she was getting something really disgusting out of her mouth. And no matter how hard he struggled he couldn't break her iron-hard grip as it pinned him to the metal gate like an unmissable target.

'HO!' The bell tolled its final note and in the flash he saw the Guild rise in their stirrups and shake their weapons at the sky in celebration of his death, and the fatal lance-tip sped in towards his heart – three metres, two metres, one metre – Game Over . . .

And he reflexively jerked his head away, and actually sensed the wings of Death flying in to gather him as he closed his eyes and felt a tremendous impact and something went horribly wrong and he heard his scream of pain as if it was already coming from outside him, and he felt himself leave the earth on one brutally savage jerk and his head seemed to explode, and then his spirit soared into the sky and he opened his eyes knowing he would see himself being drawn into the light—

. . . and instead he saw Spout looking down at him with its implacable stone eyes as it flapped into the night sky.

'Gack?' the gargoyle enquired dryly, tightening the grip on George's chest and then swaying into another lopsided wing-beat, circling north.

George looked down, still half expecting this to be an out-of-body experience, still imagining he was going to be looking down on his impaled body.

And what he saw instead was the Knight and the horse and the lance thrust through the gate, up to the hilt, and he also saw that the figure writhing on the end of the weapon was the source of the screaming, not him, and her golden shape was the last thing George saw before his eyes fluttered shut and unconsciousness swept in and anaesthetized him.

24

TYBURN'S LAST VICTIM

In the darkness, in the cold, in the absence of hope, the Gunner dug on.

The scoop and scatter noise had been added to by a new sound, which was a hollow splash as he dug in. The reason for this was that he had dug so deep into the gravel so that he was now below the level of the surrounding water in the tank. He was so far down that he had one leg inside the hole, and was bending and stretching as he dug, waist deep in a gravel ringed pool of his own excavating.

The tiredness that he was now feeling was a real tiredness, the tiredness of hard work, not the wrong feeling that had been churning inside him in the absence of any distractions. It occurred to him that if he'd put all this effort into trying to dig upwards he might have reached a surface by now. Then again he might not have been able to if the roof had fallen in – shifting a stone to start digging might have ended everything before he'd even begun.

'Could have brought the house down,' he said aloud. The sudden sound of his own voice in the echoing chamber made him pause. And then he became even stiller, as he felt something moving around his ankles. It was the water in the pond.

There was a definite movement, the ghost of a current, barely there, but definitely present.

The Gunner didn't know it, but the current he was feeling was the pull of the Tyburn, one of the lost rivers of London, the one that gave its name to the place where London's criminals used to be hanged. And now it was exerting its dark pull at the Gunner's ankles. He didn't know that, any more than that he was standing in a lost mediaeval water tank below Marylebone. All he knew was that moving water meant a stream, a stream meant a channel for it to flow down, and a channel might, just might mean a way out of this rat-hole.

If he'd been of a reflective bent he would have said, like most soldiers, that the ideal way to die was at home in bed, surrounded by the great grandchildren. But since that wasn't an option, he thought he might as well die trying not to.

He doubled his efforts, and as he bent and shovelled the urgency of his movements tipped his tin hat into the water in a great splash. It took him a moment to realize what had happened and retrieve the helmet. And when he did, the obvious hit him.

'Must be getting stupid,' he muttered and started digging with the hat. Now he really was making progress. The hole deepened, and he was even able to feel the top of a low arch in the wall beginning to appear. As he dug he wondered why the hole had blocked up. It's the nature of an underground stream, if blocked, to silt up with the debris it washes down, and this was how the bank of gravel in the tank had been created.

Something had blocked the exit pipe from the tank, and as the Gunner's hat suddenly skidded sideways instead of digging in, he found the reason. He put his hat aside, and reached down. His first thought was that it was a tree root. Then it came away in his hand, and he felt it. He had a sudden horrible feeling he knew what it was. He reached into the water and found more pieces. And then his hand tangled in hair.

He carefully disentangled it and shook his hands dry before lighting one of his precious matches.

Although the flame reflected off the surface of the

pool he could see enough to be sure: staring back at him were the two wide eyed sockets in the skull of a woman. He could tell it was a woman because there was a long hank of hair, dark as aubergines, hanging off one side of the skull, and there was a gold ring glinting on a finger-bone next to a small bundle. He reached in and moved the bundle and then he realized it wasn't a woman's skeleton at all, because another face smiled back at him. It was a crude face, carved out of some kind of wood, but it was unmistakably a doll's face.

The dead woman was no woman, but a little girl.

And he knew without needing to be told that the girl was a glint, and that she was one of the Walker's victims, possibly even his first.

The little bone hand that clasped round the smiling doll's face did something to the Gunner. It filled him with a murderous blackness.

'Right, you bastard. Fate or no fate, I ain't bloody dying tonight. I'm coming for you.'

And then he lit another match and looked into the small skeleton's eyes. He didn't see anything gruesome in the bones and fragments of flesh and clothing that remained. He saw a little girl who had died clutching her doll for comfort that didn't come. He imagined the sobs that had filled this stone chamber before she went quiet. His jaw clenched tight.

A statue can't cry of course. Everyone knows that. It must have just been water from the splashing and digging that rolled off the upper curve of his cheek and plopped into the Tyburn below as he reached gently into the water and began to move the bones, laying them softly on the gravel bank in as close to the right order as he could manage. Despite the growing clumsiness in his tired hands, the Gunner managed most of the time to be as delicate as a father putting his child to bed.

'Sorry, love. I got to move you. But it's only so as I can have him. And I WILL have him, straight up. I'll swing for him, wherever he is.'

25

BLACK MIRROR

The King's Library sits off the west side of the great, circular, glass-domed courtyard of the British Museum. It's a long elegant room, and the mixed collection of curios on display come from all the ages and regions of the world.

There are delicate fossils and brutal Maori war clubs, exquisite alabaster vases as high as a man and slender Native American spears tipped with meteorite blades. There are Greek sculptures and busts of the great men who assembled the collections. There are ancient manuscripts and fine gold jewellery, savage flint axes, rude Roman wind chimes, and all manner of obscure religious relics and paraphernalia.

To most people this looks like a charming hodgepodge of collectable objects from the Age of Enlightenment; only a very few people know that there are things in this compendium of seemingly mismatched objects that are there because they keep each other in check – things of power, dark things and light things, cancelling each other out by the careful way they are arranged round one another.

The lights were off and the rest of the Museum was silent.

And then there was a very distinct popping noise, and the Walker stepped out of one of his small mirrors. He reassembled them, snapping them together, face to face, and slipped the disc into the pocket of his coat. He stood in front of a tall free-standing display case and feasted his eyes on its contents. He pushed back the hood of the green sweatshirt he wore beneath his flapping overcoat, releasing the Raven that had been travelling with him, and leant forward, both hands on the glass of the cabinet as he stared at the contents.

The Raven stretched its wings and flapped across the width of the room, finding a perch on the railing of the walkway that ran round the bookcase at first floor level. It fixed its unreadable black eye on the Walker and the glass case whose contents he was engrossed in.

The contents were as follows: three wax discs of different sizes, two small one big, all thick as cheeses, decorated with magical symbols like pentacles and forgotten names of great significance; a 'shew-stone' or small crystal ball, not much bigger than a golf ball; a thin gold disc, engraved with the same concentric circles and simple turrets that had been scratched into the surface of the pewter plate in the underground water tank: and perhaps strangest of all, a mirror stone. The other objects looked just the kind of occult paraphernalia anyone would expect to see in a magician's lair: the mirror stone was a different thing altogether. Its lines were so simple and unadorned that it looked timeless, simultaneously both completely modern, and irretrievably ancient. Carved and polished from flawless black obsidian, the label described it as being of Aztec origin.

'Aztec,' he snorted, spat derisively. Spittle dribbled down the sheer wall of glass between him and the offending label. 'Collectors with the brains of pigmy shrews.'

The truth is that he knew this black stone mirror was old long before the Aztecs in Central America developed their strong taste for human sacrifice; and it was into the highly polished face of this stone, which looked in shape just like a hand mirror, with a handle and a hole in it for a long-perished thong, that the Walker stared so intently.

'Birds and butterflies. Imagine that . . .'

He looked at the Raven as he pushed up the right hand sleeve of his coat.

'The Aztecs sacrificed them in their hundreds of thousands to their god Quetzalcoatl. Hummingbirds rather than ravens mainly, so you, my friend, would have been fine. But I should have liked to see that. It takes a particularly exquisite sensibility to think of sacrificing a butterfly . . .'

The Raven, for whom the insect world was essentially an all-day buffet, didn't think killing butterflies was especially unusual, but he kept his beak shut. The truth was the Walker liked to talk and he was doomed to listen.

He reached out and splayed his hands against the glass opposite the circular crystal ball. He closed his eyes and spread a hand as if measuring it and committing the size to his memory. Then he peered into the dark glassy surface of the mirror again.

'The mirror is no use alone. Without its twin it's little more than polished rock.'

He smiled darkly up at the Raven.

'An ordinary pair of glass mirrors will open a portal to wherever in this world you wish to go – anywhere in space or time – if you have the knack. But compared to what a stone mirror can do, that is a mere parlour trick for pewling infants. A pair of stone mirrors can open a portal into another world entirely. And from that dark world a cunning man may bring and harness powers the like of which this world has never seen.'

If the Raven was impressed it chose a strange way to show it, as it squittered a prodigious bird's mess on to the bald marble head of the eighteenth century worthy below it. The Walker didn't notice.

'And they thought they could clip my wings by separating them and hiding the other stone mirror where I have never found it. And yet it never occurred to them that with eternity spread ahead of me I would have time in time to find a glint and a master maker to choose a stone and carve me a new one. Fools . . .'

The crystal ball was beginning to spin inside the case, answering a hidden force emanating from the Walker's spread fingers – and the faster it spun the more it seemed to wobble on its axis.

A bead of sweat trickled down the Walker's nose and splashed to the parquet floor as he struggled to contain a powerful answering judder in his hand, and then with a gasp his open hand snapped closed and he lashed it back and forth, flailing his clenched fist across the air in front of the cabinet. And as he did so the ball whipped and ricocheted around the interior of the glass cube, matching the movements of the fist, bouncing off the sides faster and faster until the noise of the sharp percussive impacts sounded like the rip of a machine-gun, and then all the glass in the cabinet shattered at the same time and fell to the floor like a dropped crystal curtain.

An alarm bell began to ring prosaically in the distance, and the dim lights came on. Ignoring all that, the Walker stepped over the shards of glass and deftly snatched the ball from its now stationary position in midair in the centre of the case, and pocketed it.

His hands re-emerged carrying two crumpled and mismatched gloves. He speedily put them on, and then equally quickly he spread a scarf out and placed two of the protective wax discs on it. Then he picked up the obsidian mirror and put it on top of the discs, letting go of it as soon as he could, as if not wanting to touch it any longer than he had to, even though he was wearing gloves. Then he sandwiched it with another protective wax disc and tied the corners of the scarf tightly together, making a bundle. He pocketed the gold circle with the Dream of Four Castles on it, and then stepped back.

'Come,' he said.

The Raven flew on to his shoulder. He held the ends of the scarf wrapping the bundle containing the stone mirror in his teeth as he exchanged gloves for mirrors in his pocket, and then, just as the first Museum guard was running through the door, he stepped into one of his small glass mirrors and disappeared.

26

HUNTER'S MOON

Edie fell into the mirror behind her. She felt the surface bend and pop as delicately as a soap bubble, and then she was falling into the fire. As she fell someone grabbed at her ankle, but they weren't able to hold it, and she hit the ground with a thunderous crash like the gates of Hell blowing open.

She fell on her back and rolled, so that the first thing she saw were her legs in the air above her, and beyond them the dark sky and the bright disc of a full moon staring back down at her, the pale night-sun of a hunter's moon, framed for an instant between two familiar scuffed boots.

And then she felt the sharp dig of a broken brick in her back, and she lost contact with anything familiar as she flinched and squirmed to her feet, just in time to see long bright-white fingers of light sweep across the sky, cutting it into jagged segments, and then she was conscious of the hungry crack and pop of a fire very close to her.

Whcih was when she realized that the crash she had heard was not her landing on the ground; it was the sudden introduction to the continual hellstorm of noise that shook the world around her, the world she had fallen into: the sound of a world blowing itself apart. There were deep explosions, and crashes and screams. And behind the screams was the low moaning sound of a siren rising and falling, and behind that there was a rhythmic throbbing engine-rumble from the sky itself. And there was the sharper counterpoint of anti-aircraft fire from a hidden battery nearby, and mixed in all this were urgent shouts and jangling ambulance bells and more screams and huge earth-shaking thuds she could feel through the soles of her boots.

Unwilling to look round at the source of all this horrifying sound until she had to, she looked at her feet, and saw they were on the step of a shop. There were fragments of brick and glass all around her. She looked to her side, and saw a mirror on the doorpost. She saw her face staring back at her, a white smear of shock, side-lit by flames. And then before she could see if there was a matching mirror on the other side of the door, there was a huge thump that knocked her to her knees as the ground kicked and buckled beneath her. And when she looked up, stunned by the violence of the invisible blow, halfway back on to her feet, she saw something that stopped her moving at all. She remained there, one knee on the ground, eyes wide, mouth open, staring at the infernal vision towering over the other end of the street.

It was a firestorm. And out of it, out of the very centre of the flames rose the familiar dome of St Paul's Cathedral, wreathed in conflagration and black smoke – but untouched. It was a vision of the end of the world – except, from the heat on her face and the twingeing pain in her shoulder where she'd rolled on to the half-brick, Edie knew this was no vision. She wasn't glinting this.

This was real.

When she glinted the past it was real enough, but the vision of the past came in jagged slices, and it always came to an end eventually. And she never ended up with brick-dust in her mouth. This wasn't glinting, this was being.

'Hey! You, girly, get off the bloody street, get down the shelter!'

A man's voice shrieked at her from the other side of the road. She turned to see a middle-aged man in a suit with a canvas bag over one shoulder and a tin hat like the

Gunner's, except the Gunner's didn't have a white 'W' painted on the front. He was waving at her angrily, thin moustache bristling like a furious hairy caterpillar.

'It's that way, down the end. You trying to get yourself killed or—'

The side of the ancient brick building behind him jerked as if it had been kicked from the other side by an unseen giant. The man never got to what came after the 'or' because the front of the building dropped on him in a brutally short avalanche of brick and stone.

Edie put her hand over her mouth instinctively as the dust cloud rolled out, and then it thinned and she saw the white 'W' of the hat slowly rolling towards her. It hit the kerb at her feet and turned over. She got a glimpse of something wet inside it, and looked away.

In the inferno surrounding the unscathed dome of the Cathedral there were plumes of water arcing futilely into the roiling mountains of fire. At their base were the dark outlines of small groups of men wrestling fire hoses. In the sky above, the fingers of searchlights quested back and forth, as intermittent lines of tracer fire squirted into the dark heavens like fiery echoes of the water jets playing on the devastation below.

Edie realized she had her hands jammed over her ears, trying to keep the jarring assault out of her head.

And then something grabbed her arm.

She spun to see the Friar. His normally jolly face was tight and worried.

'Come,' he shouted over the sound of another building crashing to the ground in the next street. 'Back in the mirrors. You don't want to die here.'

For once in her life she didn't even think of arguing. She let him drag her back towards the shop entrance where she saw, with relief, two mirrors facing each other either side of a bookshop window. That was their way out of this nightmare.

And then the Friar stopped dead.

'What?' she began.

And then she heard it, an instant before it hit: a whistling sound from out of the chaotic sky overhead – shockingly, intimately close.

Then there was another sharp jerk on her arm and the Friar pulled her to him and turned away from the bookshop and the safety beckoning in its mirrors only a pavement's width away. He curved round her, enveloping her in his wide bulk.

And then the bomb hit and her feet were blown out from under her. Only the unbreakable grasp with which he held her to his chest stopped her falling. The very air seemed to punch them viciously, and there was a sudden jagged horizontal silver hailstorm as the windows of the shop blew out. If she hadn't been completely shielded by the arched metal back of the Friar, she'd have been just a red mist and so much stewing steak, blown across the cobbled street. The shop window was followed by the shop's contents. Whole books spilled across the pavement, and a snowstorm of pages from volumes shredded by the explosion swirled around them.

After a second the Friar straightened and they turned to see that they were in the middle of a slow moving blizzard of paper, some pages on fire, some not, but all whirling up into the night sky on the updrafts created by the heat around them.

The Friar crossed the pavement in four fast paces, batting the airborne page-storm out of his way as he went. Edie stumbled after him, and she stopped when he stopped.

The mirrors were gone, shattered off the pilasters by the same blast that had destroyed the shop window. Even through the maelstrom of the blitz around them Edie could hear the single sharp tutting noise the Friar made. It was more ominous than a building falling.

'Those were the mirrors,' she said.

He tutted again.

'Those were our way out,' she went on, voice rising.

He peered up at the sky. She tugged at his robe. Glass shards fell out of the folds and tinkled to the ground round his feet.

'What do we do now?'

He looked up and down the street. Seeing him behaving so unsure made her more frightened than she already was. Finally he looked down.

'Can you run?'

She looked up at his great-bellied bulk standing over her.

'Can *you*?'

The ghost of a smile flickered across the flame-lit face above her.

'Lady. When my survival depends on it, I can practically *fly* . . .'

And he hoicked up his cassock above the knee with one hand, grasped her hand with the other − and ran. And even though she would never have admitted it later, the fact that he held her hand pulled her out of her stunned state and she ran alongside him, matching his every long pace with two of her own.

And the details of that headlong dash through the firestorm and the falling bombs blurred together and happened so fast that later she could not remember exactly what happened when: but single moments seemed to happen, disconnected to each other, one minute there, next minute gone: an old fashioned taxi with spoked wheels was blown across the road in front of them, burying itself upside down in a second-floor bay window. They ran on. At some stage a stream of fire suddenly flashed out of an alleyway, blocking their way. The Friar just grabbed her and hurdled it. There was one point where she remembered running past a London bus, on its side, and she registered the curling staircase that ran up the back to a top floor that had no roof. She turned her head away before her brain could make sense of the twisted coat and hand sticking out from under the side of the bus, between it and the pavement.

They ducked down narrow lanes between vertiginously high walls, and at one point dodged through an old churchyard that appeared out of nowhere in the warren of streets. She remembered the whump of a bomb hitting the churchyard behind them as they left it, turning to see a long box toppling back down out of the sky and dashing itself to pieces on the church wall, and looking away before she had to see what was in the coffin. And she remembered the Friar saying:

'They'll be burying those poor souls again in the morning.'

And then they were running on and on, through strangely empty and quiet streets one minute, then through flaming ruins the next. And it was only when she saw a street-sign hanging off the corner of a building reading 'Puddle Dock' that she realized where they were running to.

And though tired, she redoubled her effort, and they skidded round the final corner to see the Black Friar standing on the prow of his building above them. He didn't look down to see himself running past – or if he did, Edie was sprinting too quickly to notice it.

The Friar pushed open the door and they tumbled in. She had time to notice that the windows were crisscrossed with tape, before he yanked her forward in between the two mirrored arches.

'Right,' he panted. 'Home, James, I think.'

'James who?' enquired a familiar voice from the alcove within.

She peered in but couldn't see him. What she could see was a poster, a finely drawn cartoon of two men leaning on a bar, talking – and the bottles and even the beer-pump handles behind them all had the familiar face of a man with an angular sweep of hair and a – in fact *the* – Hitler moustache, listening carefully. And below it the message 'Careless Talk Costs Lives'. It was a colourful and funny looking poster.

'You're right,' she said into the darkness, aiming her voice towards where she knew Little Tragedy would be listening. 'I do like the poster.'

And then the Friar snorted and pulled her arm and they were falling back into the mirror, and then she staggered and found she had different carpet under her feet and the world outside wasn't blowing itself to hell, only grinding itself quietly down with the traffic beyond the windows – windows now no longer crisscrossed with anti-blast tape.

'I think,' said the Friar, 'that that explains the mirrors.'

'Yep,' said Edie, trying to stop her legs and voice from trembling. 'Got the mirror thing. Definitely not for saddoes. Definitely real.'

And then she sat down suddenly, right there on the floor, because something had to give, and her shaking legs just got there first.

27

EIGENGANG

It was the football that woke George up, that and a man's voice shouting energetically somewhere far away.

'Over here, my son – on the 'ead!'

And then there was the unmistakable dull thump of a boot kicking a wet leather football, and he opened his eyes and came out of the dark and saw a white and red ball spinning up into the air below him, and then slowly drop away and meet a group of players rammed in round a crowded goalmouth. There was a tussle and some muddy hacking and then the ball billowed the back netting and one of the players pulled his shirt over his head and ran off in a victory circuit, hand held high, and there was the sound of good natured laughing and catcalls from the others, and the only abnormal thing about it was that George was seeing it from a teetering bird's-eye view.

And then he felt the stone talon wrapped round his chest, and remembered Spout and the fact that he was meant to be dead and the screaming golden girl on the end of the lance, and the past dropped back in and hit him like a bag of wet cement.

The floodlit green space below was Coram's Fields, an oasis of grass and trees just south of the Euston Road. Spout was flying faster now, as if he was nearly home and didn't have to conserve its energy. The rain had eased, but was still coming down – a light drizzle instead of the stair-rods that had soaked him earlier.

George was wet to the skin, shivering badly and trying to figure out exactly why he wasn't dead.

Ariel had pinned him and held him to the gate, so hard that he couldn't move. And the Knight had thundered in behind the lance. And George had looked away at the last minute and closed his eyes. And then he'd felt the colossal impact. And so he really *should* be dead.

Except now he was conscious again, he replayed the final moment more slowly and realized that the thing that had felt terribly wrong was not the impact as much as the direction it had come from. The lance had been about to punch heart-high through his chest, impaling him like a butterfly on a pin. But the impact hadn't been from the front. It had been from the side. And now he thought about it, he remembered hearing Death's wings flying in to gather him, and he understood that it hadn't been Death but Spout, diving out of the night sky at the very last minute and snatching him out of the way, so that the Knight's lance had punched through the empty space where George now *wasn't*, and through the gap in the gate railings into the space where Ariel still *was*.

And then there had been a feeling like his head exploding, and that must have been Spout clattering him into something like the roof of the sentry box as he snatched him into the sky, because George could now feel a definite bump throbbing behind his ear.

So that was how come he was now being flown over the Euston Road towards the lavishly ornamented roofscape of St Pancras Station: Spout had snatched him back. Spout had rescued him, just as earlier Ariel had saved him from the gargoyle. Out of the frying pan, into the fire. The only thing was, he wasn't sure who was frying pan and who was fire any more. He was pretty certain Spout hadn't suddenly changed from an enemy into a friend, so it had to be that the rescue was accidental, and Spout had taken him back for his own reasons. It was all too complicated and he was hurting and cold and confused.

The memory of Ariel – her smile, her joy in flying round the gherkin, pirouetting on the top of the world – all that hurt him somehow too, especially when overlaid with the ice in her voice as she had gripped him and held him for the Knight. The hurt was because she'd betrayed him.

Spout was slowing as they flew up and round the tall illuminated clock-tower on the eastern end of the building. George registered the green slate roof thrusting sharply into the sky above the clock-faces on each of its sides, and the accompanying pinnacles decorating each corner as they circled the massive, exuberant confection of orange brickwork and clean white stone.

The long engine-shed of King's Cross passed on his right shoulder, and then Spout was flapping down the roof of St Pancras, over a sharp ridge with a narrow flat runway on the very top, leading west between tall chimneys that swept up from the vertiginously sheer roof-slopes on either side. Before the building curved abruptly and ended in a squatter but equally pointily tower on the far end, there was another tower, and it was to this one that Spout was flying. As it loomed ahead of them Spout stopped flapping and spread his wings wide, making them act as air-brakes, slowing their speed to stalling point. Just when it was clear to George that flight was no longer viable and they were going to start falling, Spout reached out a talon and stuck to the corner of the wall.

'Geer!' he coughed. And put George down on the narrow space behind him. There was no question of George running away from this position. Spout's eyrie was a small area where three angles of roof met, and then fell away sheer. There was a lead gutter box, a sort of inset tray with a hole and a piece of broken masonry wedged in one corner of it that provided a place for George to squat and watch the gargoyle as he settled into position. Except – unlike all the other gargoyles that George could now uncomfortably see dotted all over the building, who were all facing *out* at the city – Spout turned and looked *in* at George.

George had no clue as to what was going to happen next. The gargoyle stared at him and then slowly stretched its wings, shook himself like a dog, and then folded them neatly back down around his back. It was the first time George had really had a chance to look at Spout properly, at rest. Every time he'd seen him before he'd been moving, running, flying or chasing. And George had been so busy trying to stay as far from the creature as he could that he'd never had a chance to really take him in, in all his glory.

Not that it was very glorious. He definitely had, as George's dad used to say, been hit with the ugly stick. He was a stringy feral cat with wings where his front legs should be. There was something strained and tortured in the way the sculptor had made him, and life on the roof had clearly not been kind to him either. He was streaked with dirt, his mouth leaking green from where George had pulled out the old copper pipe. The weather had not only beaten him, but shattered off the knuckle-tip of one wing, which gave him a lopsided quality. In fact George wondered if it was this missing bit of wing that made Spout fly so lopsidedly too.

Spout bared his fangs and George saw how deep the green staining went, curling out round the lower teeth like blood.

'Gack,' rasped the creature.

'Yes,' said George. 'Nice place you've got here.'

He had his arms wrapped round himself and was hunched down into a ball, trying to get some warmth trapped in the middle of himself.

'Shame you haven't got central heating,' he said. He must be getting light-headed.

'Gowk,' said Spout, leaning in and tapping his own mouth then prodding George back against the tiles.

'Gowk!'

He was trying to say something, George realized. He

was definitely trying to communicate. And he looked irritated at George's inability to understand what it was he was trying to say.

'GOWK!'

'Yes, gowk,' said George. Spout didn't look impressed. His fangs ground against each other in silent irritation and the creature's throat worked like he was trying to cough out a fur-ball or a fishbone.

'Sorry. I don't speak gargoyle,' George apologized.

Spout shook his head and batted at his mouth again, wingtips clattering against the bared fangs. And George suddenly realized what he must be saying.

'Gowk – spout. You want the spout! The gowk – I mean spout – I pulled out of your mouth. Yes, of course. I'm sorry . . .'

Now it all made complete sense. It explained why the creature was so tenacious in its pursuit of him. He'd wrenched an important part out of its mouth. In fact before he'd done that he couldn't remember the thing making any noise at all. And these attempts to speak sounded so painful that he wasn't surprised that the gargoyle wanted it back.

His hands scrabbled in his trouser pocket and eventually managed to disentangle the corroded metal pipe. He held it out like a peace offering.

And then he got clever, just in time, and snatched it

back, out of Spout's grasp.

'Although . . .' he said slowly, thinking as he spoke. 'Although, perhaps we can make a deal. You put me down on the ground, and then I give you your spout back. You understand?'

And he mimed flying down and then handing over. Spout cocked his head. And then his talon flashed out and back with surprising speed, and George's hand was suddenly empty. The gargoyle looked at the metal pipe it now held in its own grasp.

'Yes,' said George. 'Or you could take it now, and *then* put me back on the ground. If that works better for you. I'm, um, easy . . .'

He knew he was clinging on to the frayed coat-tails of a very forlorn hope, and so he folded his arms back around himself and tried to look on the bright side.

'Still. As long as you got your spout back, I'm happy. I'm happy, you're happy, and . . .'

Spout stopped looking at the copper pipe and stared at George again with a stony intensity that stopped him talking. Spout twirled the pipe once in his talon, and then tossed it over his shoulder without the least interest. George stared at him as they listened to the pipe ping and clatter its way down the roof and on to the engine shed below. George swallowed.

'Gowk!'

Spout clattered his wingtip against his chest and then poked George insistently.

'Gowk – eigengang. Eigengang – gowk.'

Somewhere all this made sense, but not on any planet George was presently inhabiting.

'Sorry. I don't know what "eigengang" means, either.'

Spout lunged forward, and for a moment George thought he was attacking, but then the gargoyle grabbed the broken lump of stone in the gutter-box under his feet and tugged it out. George tipped backwards and his hands flailed against the tiles to stop himself falling into the void below. When he looked up, Spout was thrusting the stone at him like a club.

He raised his hands to shield himself, but Spout hissed in frustration and sat back on his haunches. He waved the broken piece of stonework at George. Then he lunged forward again, put the stone fragment down and grabbed George's hand. The scar with the Maker's Mark twinged badly as he pulled George forward so he was standing on tiptoes, and then it rubbed George's hand with the edge of his wing, in the place where the weather had shattered a large lump out of it.

'Ow!' cried George, whose hand was being sandpapered by the abrasive surface. Spout hissed angrily and stepped back. George was suddenly alone and unsupported; worse than that, he was on tiptoe, and very aware that hundreds of feet were sucking at him from below. He tottered and fell back into the gutter-box. The broken piece of stone jagged into his side as he landed and he arched his back and pulled it out of the way. And as the stone pressed itself into the soft flesh of his hands and fingers he knew.

He knew without having to look at the shape lopped out of the gargoyle's wing that he was holding the broken piece. His hands felt the identical rough texture, his fingers knew that he was feeling the negative shape of the one he'd felt on Spout's wing. He knew it was the same rock and he knew it would fill the space exactly. And he knew the two pieces of rock not only belonged but, in some way he couldn't explain, *wanted* to be together again.

'Oh,' he said. And sat down. He looked at the piece of wing in his hand, and then at Spout.

'Oh.'

Spout squatted back in front of him and angled the broken wing-knuckle towards George. And although he was more frightened of this stone monster than anything he could imagine, he couldn't help putting his hand out and feeling the stone wound again.

'You want me to mend you.'

He felt the stone surface. He put the broken piece into the wing. It fitted perfectly.

'Eigengang,' said Spout, nodding.

'If eigengang means mend, I can't. I'm sorry. I mean, it's not just a matter of putting it back. It's got to be fixed.'

His mind flashed back to the ordered mess of his father's studio. He heard his dad breathing in the sucking-air-in-the-side-of-his-mouth way he did when he was smoking but couldn't spare a hand to remove the cigarette. He saw his dad using two hands to hold a broken piece of sculpture together. It was a ballerina that had belonged to his mother and George had broken it and they were trying to mend it before she noticed. It had been a conspiratorial moment between the two of them – boys together, working against the clock. And he remembered his dad saying it wasn't just a matter of glue. That you couldn't just rely on glue. That for a repair to work you had to make a mechanical join too, as well as the glue. Especially if you were going to put pressure on the break. George thought of the immense pressure that Spout put on his wings every time he flapped, trying to keep his great mass airborne.

'It's complicated. It's got to be glued or mortared or something. And then it's probably got to be screwed or pinned. I'm sorry.'

His hand squeezed the wing apologetically. And as it did so he felt the stone becoming hot.

Spout looked at him sharply.

'Eigengang.'

George squeezed again. The heat became fiercer. As he moved his hand along the seam between the two pieces of stone, it became hard to work out where the heat was coming from. And then he realized he wasn't feeling heat coming from the stone.

He was feeling heat coming from his hand.

He didn't know, afterwards, why his eyes closed, but he found he had blanked out the world and just focused on what he could feel. And his hearing seemed to dull too as he felt the rough surface of the stone, and the tiny crackle and popping that was occurring within the crack, as split granules of stone found their sundered neighbours and knitted back together under the heat coming from his hand.

And then he slumped back, strangely exhausted and panting for breath, a dull empty feeling beneath his breastbone. Whatever he had done, it had cost him. He was drenched in sweat, and steamed slightly in the cold air.

Spout shook his wing, as if testing it. The broken piece was solidly a part of him again. He nodded his head with enthusiasm.

'Eigengang!'

And then he sat back on his haunches.

George did the same.

'Wow. That was . . . something,' he said. And he looked up at the night sky, trying to concentrate on the tingling aftermath in his hand and not the emptiness in his chest.

'And it's stopped raining.'

Spout's head came up fast, his eyes wide, his ears back, all the hackled spines on his back raised.

Something was coming.

28

QUEEN TAKES KNIGHT

After dark the narrow streets in the City of London become quiet. The workers have all gone home, and the twisting canyons formed by the high-rises jammed into the ancient street pattern are not thoroughfares to anywhere else, so traffic passing through the City blasts past on the wider roadways as side-streets that are busy by day become a ghost-town.

The Red Queen drove her horses slowly along the road, the ancient design of the war-chariot beneath her feet strikingly at odds with the shiny modern buildings towering over her on either side.

Her daughters rode with her, scouring each side street and alley as they passed, looking for Edie or anything that might give a clue as to where she was.

They had the intense look of their mother. They were fierce, mostly silent girls. But when they needed to move, they did so firmly and decisively. They had her fearlessness running in their veins, but whereas their mother allowed her fire to blaze freely whenever she chose, the girls had chosen to keep that fire banked up quietly.

The one on the left heard it before the others.

She touched her mother's arm, and the Queen instantly reined in the horses.

And then they all heard it.

The noise of other hooves, coming closer.

The Queen gripped her spear, and then the source of the sound came slowly round the corner, and the three of them stood stock-still.

It was the Last Knight. He rode at a slow, funereal walk, his lance lowered in mourning, his head bent forward in sadness. And across the saddle in front of him was draped the limp golden body of Ariel.

The Queen and her daughters watched the Knight walk towards them, keeping so still they seemed frozen in a pocket in time. And then, when it became apparent that he was going to pass without acknowledging them, the Queen spoke tightly.

'Sir Knight. A word, if you please.'

He just carried on past.

The Queen nodded at her daughters. Without

comment they leapt nimbly from the chariot and ran towards the Knight, soundless on their bare feet. She threw her spear to one of them who caught it almost without looking and ran ahead of the Knight. As the Queen snapped the reins on her chariot and turned it, the daughter with the spear stood foursquare in front of the warhorse and the armoured man towering above her jabbing the spear at his throat in warning. He stopped the horse. The other daughter grabbed the bridle reins and held them as the Queen trotted up.

She looked at the golden girl lying across the horse's neck. Then up at the Knight.

'What is this?'

There was a pause as the Knight slowly looked round at her.

'An accident.'

'And what are you doing with her?'

He nodded ahead.

'I had thought to scale the building and put her on her plinth before turn o' day. I would not have her die on my account.'

The Queen looked at her girls.

'And was it on your account that the accident happened?'

'It was.'

The Queen nodded at her daughters. The one holding

the reins came round the side of the Knight and pulled Ariel off the horse and on to her shoulders.

'It is my obligation—' began the Knight in protest.

'You have done enough,' said the Queen, seeing the large hole in Ariel's side. 'If you had done but a fraction more I could have ridden my chariot through the wound you have put in this poor girl.'

'It was not meant,' he protested.

'It never is,' she snorted. 'Go back to your Guild, Knight. And play your sword games with each other. That is all you are good for. We will take care of her from here and make sure she is on her plinth by turn o'day.'

The Knight looked at her, then bowed his head and backed his horse into a turn and rode slowly away.

The Queen watched him as her daughters carefully laid Ariel on the back of the chariot.

'See, girls? It's as I always tell you: it never does to send a man to do a woman's job.'

29

DEATHSLIDE

High on the roof of St Pancras, George could hear them coming for him. And hearing them, he looked over the edge of his precarious perch and saw that a great many stone things were crawling over the green tiles and chimneys below.

In the middle of everything George had forgotten what the Gunner had told him about gargoyles: that they might be taints and bent on his destruction, but they always had to answer their first purpose – which was to be highly decorated waterspouts.

This meant that when it rained they had to go back to their places on whatever roof they came from, and funnel water. Decoratively. It also raised the question of why Spout alone had suddenly been able to fly freely through the rainstorm. George had a strong feeling it had something to do with the fact he'd somehow changed the gargoyle by giving it a name and ripping out the metal spout that had been gagging it when they'd had their first confrontation. It was, however, not a thing that George was going to have time to concern himself with right now.

The question crawling, slithering and hopping towards him was what he was going to do now that the rain had stopped. All the gargoyles in the St Pancras rookery had come alive and were converging on him from all sides. That was the sound he'd heard — stone limbs and talons scraping relentlessly closer over wet roof-tiles and dripping chimney-stacks.

They moved slowly, but there was something much worse about that than if they had come in a rush. If they'd come in a rush he wouldn't have had time to see them in all their brutal detail. They came in different shapes and sizes, but all had jaws stretched wide in gaping snarls, panting through their mouths as if they somehow smelt with the backs of their throats. Some were worn and weather-beaten to a point where their features had begun to erode into almost abstract masks of hostility and threat. Some had obviously been carved more crudely than others, and several of them must have been recently restored, because they looked newer and their lines were more finely incised.

The larger ones dragged their wings after them like great capes, while the smaller ones hopped from perch to perch, leapfrogging each other from gable-end to dormer-window to chimneystack as they came.

George wondered if this was what Spout had intended, if this was his end; to be torn apart by this pack of blank-eyed taints, high above the uncaring city. Spout, however, turned to him and held out a talon.

'Gung,' he said urgently.

He was shaking like a dog does when its blood is up and it smells trouble. George didn't understand why the arrival of his friends was upsetting the creature so much.

'Gung ear!' hissed Spout, motioning with his talon whilst keeping an eye on the approaching gargoyles. And George had just enough time to wonder if he was trying to say 'Come here' with a cat-like mouth that wasn't designed for normal conversation, when something tumbled out of the sky above them and buried its teeth in Spout's shoulder, and the momentum knocked him off his perch, and George's eye met his for one appalled moment, and then Spout and the smaller gargoyle who had dived on him from the spire above fell over the edge and out of sight.

George scrambled to the lip and looked over just in time to see Spout and his attacker crash down on to the flat roof below, landing on another gargoyle who instantly joined the fight. The gargoyles on the roof stepped back, and for a few moments the three creatures ripped and tore at each other in a snarling hissing ball that rolled back and forth across the narrow space. At one point it looked as if they were about to plunge into the forecourt below, but Spout hooked a great talon on a protruding gutter and heaved himself and the two monsters who were attached to him back into the middle of the roof.

Spout slammed himself back into a chimneystack, stunning the small gargoyle on his shoulders. It fell to the ground and Spout savagely back-heeled it over the edge. The gargoyle locked on to Spout's front tried to get his fangs into Spout's throat, but the lopsided gargoyle struck faster and closed its fangs on the other gargoyle's head.

The surrounding creatures hissed in fury as Spout shook the smaller gargoyle back and forth in his jaws. And then the circle of gargoyles closed in on Spout, and he spat the lifeless creature on to the tiles and grabbed the first new attacker that rushed in on him, stepping nimbly aside and using its momentum to throw the creature straight past into the solid brick chimney behind him. Spout then grabbed the stunned assailant by a wingtip and whirled him round like a club, cutting a swathe in the surrounding horde as they backed off to avoid being hit by the flailing gargoyle. George realized Spout was fighting his way back to the foot of his tower.

And then the wing of the creature Spout was swinging like a battle-axe snapped off with a crack like a rifle shot, and the body and other wing spun away into the night.

The surrounding gargoyles froze. Spout looked at the wing fragment in his talon and sort of shrugged. He hefted the improvized club as if to say 'Who's next?'

And then three big gargoyles, two Spout's size and one bigger, rushed him from different points of the compass. He kicked the first one out of his way, but the other two tackled him and their impact knocked the wing fragment from his grasp and took them all out into the darker air over the engine shed . . . and they were gone.

Half of the gargoyles below rushed to the edge, but the other half turned to look at something more interesting.

George.

He was staring back down at them and wondering what to do when a gargoyle blindsided him by crawling round the roof and grabbing him from the side.

He found himself airborne again, but only for a short flight, as the gargoyle that had grabbed him was one of the medium-sized ones with quite stubby, not particularly aerodynamic wings, and it clearly didn't have the lift necessary to keep himself and his human prey in the air at the same time.

They crash-landed on the narrow ridge below. It happened slowly enough not to hurt too much, and it happened awkwardly enough for George to end up lying on the creature's arm.

The gargoyle tugged its arm, trying to get out from under.

In the struggle, George banged his head on another piece of stone – the broken wing fragment that Spout had used as a club.

Before he thought too much about what he was going to do, he grabbed the broken wing and scythed it into the gargoyle's face in a crunching haymaker. He could tell it was crunching because crunch is what he heard. The gargoyle looked at him, groggy and puzzled, then it shook its head to clear it and snarled.

So George just hit it again, carbon copy blow, and then once more, even harder. And the gargoyle's head was smashed sideways in a ninety-degree arc with the first blow, but it came back round snarling in fury – just in time for the second blow to send it 180 degrees the wrong way on its neck. The crunch this time was followed by a 'thunk' as the head dropped off the body on to the floor.

It wasn't just George who was shocked at the result of his despairing blow. The gargoyles around on the roof were suddenly very still. He took advantage of this to roll to his feet and get the solid brick of a chimneystack at his back. He figured if they were coming for him, he'd do better if they could only come from in front. He'd seen how far trying to fight a 360-degree battle had got Spout.

The gargoyles began to hiss, starting quietly and then getting louder.

'Right,' he lied, waving the broken wing in front of him. 'I can do this all night. Who's next?'

His bravado didn't slow them one bit as they slowly began to close in.

George didn't have a plan. He was outnumbered and out of options. The only chink of hope he might have, he realized, was the ray of light beaming straight up from the roof about twenty metres away. It was a skylight, and though jumping through a window is not usually the most sensible thing to do, in this situation he thought it might be the safest option. Out here he was surrounded. If he could get inside the building there would be corridors and rooms and places to hide. If he could sprint through the advancing tide of stone killers and hit the glass with both feet, and then roll like a parachutist when he landed, he might have a chance. Of course the chance depended on a) not getting too sliced up by the falling glass he'd have gone through, and b) the skylight dropping him into a room on the floor below, and not something else – like, for example, an unending light-well that ran down the whole height of the building.

'I can do this,' he said, trying to ignore the other voice in the back of his head that told him he was still lying.

If he was going to do it, if he was to have any chance of getting off this roof, he would have to do it now, before the gargoyle horde closed in any further and got too dense for him to run through. So he gripped the fragment of wing, and ran.

As he exploded into motion the thought flashed that this was the second time he'd tried to get out of a tight spot by running forward instead of away. The thought gave him strength as he remembered how well it had worked on the Knight.

The first gargoyle he came to reared up and snatched at him, but he ducked under his wings and powered on. Coming out from under the wing he found another gargoyle in front of him, and before it could move he jumped at it. His front foot hit the creature in the chest and it went over backwards. George went with it, using it like a springboard as he jumped over the gargoyle's body and raced for the skylight in the roof ahead. A small monster leapt at his face, but he managed to club it back with the fragment of stone.

And then there was nothing between him and the rectangular skylight, except four paces of clear roof. A big gargoyle had launched into the air on the other side of the glass, but he wasn't going to intercept him in time to stop his desperate para-jump through the glass.

George hit the edge of the skylight and leapt high. He registered with relief that all there was on the other side of the glass below was a drop the height of one room, on to a pile of old boxes.

He brought his feet together in midair, said a brief prayer for the foot whose only covering was a sock, and slammed his heels down on the glass in one mighty smash.

One thing about London is that the people in charge of how things are built have very strict ideas and rules about materials that have to be used. One of the rules about skylights is that they have to be made from safety glass. And if the skylight is to be in a roof just below a tall tower that has stone decorations that may shatter in frost or fall off in high winds, then that safety glass has to be as safe as safety glass can get. It has to be tough — the kind of tough that doesn't just go to pieces at the first sign of danger.

His heels smashed down on the glass and didn't break anything except his fall.

The water lying on the rain-slick surface did,

however, combine with his considerable forward momentum and turned the rectangle from a skylight into a skating rink.

George's feet flew out from under him, and he hit the slippery glass with his tailbone, only just managing to get his chin down into his chest in time to stop him dashing his brains as he fell backwards. But that was where his good luck ended and the very bad luck began.

True, he did slide beneath the airborne gargoyle that had been leaping at him from the other side of the skylight, but only because he was now tobogganing at high speed towards the edge of a very steep roof and a long drop on to the engine shed below. He scrabbled and shimmied, desperately trying to get some friction going, some kind of stick that would slow him down or help him stop.

Hope flickered as a new gargoyle appeared over the fast-approaching roof edge. He stuck his feet out, hoping to slow himself against it, but the gargoyle was heartbreakingly quick-witted for a lump of stone. As he was about to impact – it simply flattened its ears and ducked.

And so George flew onwards, over its head, off the roof – and into the void.

30

THREE CHALLENGES
AND A BETRAYAL

Edie had got her legs back under control, but she was still sitting on the pub floor, absorbing what had happened to her. Finding herself actually in the midst of World War Two London at the height of the Blitz had been quite different to the sharp pain of merely seeing slices of the past when she glinted normally.

Being *in* the past rather than just seeing it wasn't painful as such. It just left an overwhelming feeling of nausea and a kind of empty horror inside her. Maybe it was being there and coming back so suddenly that did it, she thought, concentrating on this rather than on the hand she'd seen sticking out from under the tipped omnibus. Perhaps this time lag was like jet lag, only worse.

The Friar watched her from where he leant against the bar, getting his breath back. He pushed George's coat to one side and heaved his great bulk up on the bar top, bare legs and sandals dangling out of the bottom of his cassock, somehow startling in their powerful nakedness. He looked as if he was sitting on the side of a river, about to paddle. He only lacked a fishing rod to complete the illusion. Instead, he looked at her and flicked his words over her head like a fly.

'And the second question?' he said in a voice so honeyed and solicitous that, despite the shock still flushing through her body in a pounding torrent of bad adrenaline, she felt her hackles begin to rise again.

'Second question?'

'Apart from the mirrors and how they work. You said you had a second question.'

Though it had been only minutes ago, it felt like she'd asked that question in a different life. She shook her head to clear it.

'Yeah. Right. The Hard Way. You said if George didn't make his sacrifice by putting the broken head on the Stone then he would have to do things the Hard Way.'

'Indeed,' he purred with the kind of smugness on his face that in Edie's book would normally have been asking – in fact begging – for a slap. Somehow, in her present state she didn't have anything approaching a proper slap in her, real or verbal. She took a deep breath instead.

'What exactly is the Hard Way? Is it why he just vanished off the face of the earth?'

He twirled George's coat round on the bar-top. Then hung it neatly on one of the beer pulls.

'Maybe.'

Somehow having been dragged back from what very possibly was and certainly had felt like, the end of the world hadn't put Edie in a mood for 'maybes'.

'I need you to tell me a little bit more. Please.'

The 'Please' stuck in her throat, but she got it out with a good attempt at a smile as a sugar-coating. And to her surprise he told her. He told her that he must stand and fight the three duels, and that they all had to be fought above or below ground, in the air or in or on water. And he explained this was so because the challenge of three contests was one of London's forgotten rituals, but that just because it was forgotten it didn't mean that it didn't underpin the city in an important way.

'After all, my dear, who remembers the keystone that was laid beneath the cathedral or the church? But they are there, and though forgotten it should be remembered that the whole edifice would tumble without them.'

'You mean it's like tradition,' she said.

'It's nothing like tradition. Tradition is like giving votes to the most obscure class of people, namely your ancestors. My word, no. Tradition is merely the democracy of the dead. No, this is part of the living warp and weft of the city itself. Nothing dead about it at all. He has to fight three duels to earn his place in the fabric.'

'What if he doesn't fight?'

His eyebrows rose and fell one after another in a small ripple of outrage at the very thought.

'He has to. To refuse a contest is failure. To fail is to become a Stone-Servant and walk in thrall to the power in the Stone for eternity.'

She absorbed this carefully.

'So that's bad.'

'So that, as you so perspicaciously put it, is bad.'

'But if he doesn't know this, if he doesn't know the Hard Way is the way of three duels, he might refuse a challenge. He might. I would. I'd run away unless I couldn't avoid it!'

'Then you'd better find him and tell him that, had you not?'

'But how can I find him?'

'Look for him.'

She spluttered with frustration at the enormity of the task he was outlining for her.

'In this city? It's like searching for a needle in a haystack!'

'Then don't waste time . . .'

He hooked his thumb and jerked it towards the door behind him.

'. . . be on your way. The first step in finding a needle in a haystack is to start.'

She sat tight.

'Will you help me?'

'I thought I just did.'

'Help me find George,' she added.

'Why would I help?'

'Because you're a spit.'

His expression didn't change by a flicker.

'OK then,' she continued. "Because you're not a taint.'

Maybe something ticked under his eye, but even if it did, she was pretty sure it was irritation. He sighed shortly.

'Absence of hostility does not mean presence of benevolence, my child. It can also mean indifference, and I, uncharitable and uncharacteristic as it may be to admit it, find that I am sublimely and ineffably indifferent.'

'But why?'

He looked over her shoulder.

'Why, she says, why?'

There was a small, needling 'Tchah' of disbelief from behind her as Little Tragedy tried to express how extraordinarily dense she must be not to know why the

Friar was suddenly, inexplicably, changing tack.

'I mean it,' she said, hating the plaintive note that had crept unbidden into her voice. 'I don't know why you've gone all like this, why you won't help.'

The Friar deliberately scooped George's coat off the beer pump handles, and then let it fall to the counter-top with a distinct and giveaway thunk.

Little Tragedy scuttled out of the shadows and nimble-fingered his way into the pocket. In an instant, he pulled out the broken dragon's head like a conjuror producing a rabbit, eyes wide as soup plates.

'Ooooh,' he said 'Look at that. It's little George's little dragon. Blimey.'

'Blind you indeed I should, you scamp, if you don't stay where you ought,' barked the Friar, snatching the carving from his hands. 'Blind you indeed I should, were my heart not so damnably soft and sentimental.'

'Sentimental' and 'soft' were the last two words Edie would have used to describe the look on the statue's face as his eyes locked on hers across the dragon's head.

'Why? Because it appears that the boy did not trust me, and neither did you. And trust, milady, is a two-way street. And that street is now closed. I cannot abide a liar.'

He glared at her with an intensity she found hard not to blink at. She wanted him to turn back into the Friar who had shielded her from certain death and then run her to safety through the Blitz. But that Friar was gone. Too late, she realized she hadn't thanked him for following her into the mirror and saving her life.

'Look, I'm sorry, and I should have thanked you—'

There was a tap at the window that stopped all conversation. She followed his gaze. Three figures were outlined against the night beyond. Two of them had noses pressed to the frosted glass, so close that it was clear their eyes were black Raven eyes. The figure behind them was less distinct, but he was tall and seemed to be wearing a hood.

'The Tallyman—!' piped Little Tragedy. The Friar cut him off with a look and slid off the bar, landing on the floor with an ominous thud. He paused to put the dragon's head back in the pocket of George's coat, and then walked to the door.

'Keep her out of sight until I tell you,' he hissed over his shoulder.

Edie felt Tragedy tugging at her urgently.

'Come on, Glinty. Time to be somewhere else.'

She let him pull her back into the shadows behind the arch. They could see the bulk of the Friar blocking the door as he opened it, and then he stood in it like a roadblock, whispering earnestly with whoever was on the outside.

Edie's blood ran cold, in a way she'd heard talked

about but never felt. If the figure on the outside was who she thought it was – the man who'd sent the Minotaur after her – the man who'd calmly threatened to slit her belly and casually spill her guts on the floor like a bag of peas – worst of all, if it was he who she'd seen drowning the girl with her face in the ice-hole at the Frost Fair – then her blood had every reason to turn cold in her veins.

Because if it was the Walker, then Death had come to call.

31

SIEGE IN THE SKY

When George slid pell-mell across the wet skylight and was launched into the void above the glass-roofed engine shed far below there was an instant of actual and momentary weightlessness that battled a sickening sense of disbelief as his world went quiet –

– and then gravity did its thing and 'off the roof' turned into 'down towards the ground'.

George had heard that people who fall off high buildings lose consciousness before they hit the pavement. It was one of those playground facts that kids told each other, like the one about drowning – how gentle it was in the end. George had always wondered how anyone knew this stuff. It wasn't as if you could ask dead people how it had felt. He fell through the air like a flailing starfish, watching the humped glass roof of the train shed coming up to meet him with appalling finality.

He didn't lose consciousness. In the few seconds of free-fall his mind remained as sharp as the glass panels he was about to hit. His life didn't flash past his eyes. He didn't experience a moment of relief, of oneness with the universe. He just felt alone. Brutally, sadly and irrevocably alone. And he just had time to think what a terrible waste this was, how terrible it was to have wasted such a precious and extraordinary miracle as life. He felt ashamed at how little he had made of what he had been given – more ashamed of anything he'd ever done or not done in his life.

And he wondered if this terrible pain had gone through his father's mind in the instant of the car crash that had killed him – and then as he accelerated towards impact his last thoughts tumbled after one another, and they were these: he knew his father had definitely felt all this, and he knew that his last thought had absolutely been of George, and he knew that the pain of that last thought had been an unspeakable one. He knew it just as surely as he knew he had gone to sleep every night since wishing for just one last word with his dad. And then he thought of his mother and remembered the good times and the laughter and realized, just as he ran out of air and hit solid, that she would now spend her life unable to say those last words to him. And the sudden pain of that realization was worse than the impact.

The impact wasn't too bad.

What took the edge off it was the tonne or so of flying sandstone that swooped in at a shallow angle and caught him, flattening off his downbound trajectory and slowing his velocity into a survivable deceleration. George had the air knocked out of him as the gargoyle almost fumbled the catch, and things went black for a microsecond, but then he saw the wing that was flapping above him, and he saw the mended seam, and twisted his head to see the gargoyle's face, and the face spared him a quick look and said:

'Gack!'

'Hello, Spout,' said George, fighting a ridiculously inappropriate bubble of hysterical laughter that was rising in his throat. 'We've got to stop meeting like this . . .'

Spout swerved suddenly. A large gargoyle swiped a talon at them, and then a second one flew at them from above. Spout only managed to avoid a collision by flying into the side of the building and bracing himself against the scaffolding. George reflexively grabbed on to the plastic safety webbing shrouding the scaffolding. Spout punched away another assailant with a snarl and then turned and slashed at George. For a moment he thought the creature had perversely snatched him from death only to have the satisfaction of decapitating him. And then the talon whistled past him and slashed a hole in the webbing. And before he could quite realize what was happening, Spout had grabbed him and pushed him into the relative safety of the decking within. He sprawled on the splintery boards and then turned in time to see Spout poking his head inside.

The great stone mouth opened and produced the first clear word George had heard from it, probably because it actually did begin with a 'g', because that was the only sound Spout's vocal set-up was really good at.

'Go.'

George was shocked by the clarity.

'You're saying "go"?'

Spout nodded fiercely. One eye scanning the sky above him.

'Go, Eigengang, go!'

And George got it.

'Eigengang? You're trying to say Ironhand! Only you only do "g"s. You're calling me Ironhand!'

Spout exhaled heavily and rolled his eyes as if George was actually denser than the rock they'd been carved from – and then was savagely yanked back into the blackness as a gargoyle dropped on him and tackled him round the neck.

George didn't waste any time wondering why he had

started to talk. He just decided anywhere was going to be better than where he was right now. And as he saw gargoyles buffeting the protective mesh round the scaffolding, he decided to try for an anywhere with solid brick walls around it. He ran along the clanking aerial walkway, trying each window as he passed. Four windows along, he got lucky. The glass was in the process of being replaced, so there was just a dark hole in the brickwork.

He vaulted in and rushed blindly through a dark room full of timber and workbenches, and saw a door at the far end which he ran for.

As he burst through the doorway something grabbed him in an all-enveloping tackle. For a jolting moment he knew it was some fresh, hellish monster, and then he got himself disentangled and realized he'd just run into sheets of plastic that had been hung to keep the workmen's dust in one room. He pushed through into a long dark corridor and stumbled abruptly, his foot – the one without a shoe on it – finding a step where the floor should be and crunching down on to a rough surface below. He looked down, and in the mirk realized he'd gone through the floor and on to the lath and plaster of the ceiling below because half the floorboards had been removed and were stacked on the side wall of the corridor.

He got up and made his way forward, picking his path

as fast as he could past the long holes in the floor – hoping he was going to find a staircase soon. He thought he could hear stone wings and talons keeping pace with him on the scaffolding that ran parallel with the corridor, one short room away. He was sure he heard great stone knuckles rapping on the windows behind him, testing them. He bumped against a bench and something heavy thudded on to the floor.

It was a club hammer, the big heavy kind used for hitting cold chisels.

He picked it up. Having three pounds of drop-forged steel on the end of a stout hickory handle was just the confidence booster he needed. There was a piece of rope like a thong looped through a hole drilled in the bottom of the handle, and he put it round his wrist.

He remembered a comic book his dad had in his workroom, a memory of his own childhood – *The Mighty Thor*. He'd been a superhero with a hammer like this. George didn't feel much like a superhero right now as he teetered his way carefully along the skeletonized floor joists. The sound of gargoyles tracking him seemed to be coming closer and closer.

Then he pushed through another curtain of plastic sheeting and found himself in a great long room that was so full of builders' equipment that in the dark it seemed like an obstacle course: scaffolding towers and ladders hugged walls which were in the process of being scraped down to the brickwork beneath, big sacks of plaster and stacks of paint-cans were piled next to blocks of sheetrock panels, and there was even a cement mixer in the middle of the floor. George closed the door behind him and, since there was a bolt on his side of it, locked it for good measure. He stood there shivering and wet and now that he was still for a moment, realized how very cold he was.

The room had windows on both sides; he was pleased to see the ones on the side with the scaffolding were all boarded up. So were most of the ones on the other side, facing the Euston Road. He moved slowly around the edge of the room and wondered if he was safe. He couldn't hear any more noise from the gargoyles outside, though maybe that was because they too were keeping silent and trying to listen for any sounds he might make from within, trying and figure out exactly where he was.

If that was so he gave them a big clue by immediately knocking something off a table, something that clashed like a cymbal as it hit the floor. He bent down and stopped it rolling before it made any more noise. It came apart as he lifted it back up and nearly spilled its contents. He caught the lid awkwardly because his free hand still had the club hammer in it. It was a biscuit tin and he was holding it upside down. He put the hammer on a table-top, turned the tin of biscuits the right way up, grabbed a handful and ate them greedily, as he moved away from the table, scanning the room for anything else useful. He wondered if there was a heater in amongst the jumble, and if there was, whether he would get the chance to warm up in front of it. He squeezed between a stack of cylinders that looked solid but gave and wobbled as soon as he touched them. They were rolls of roof soft-insulation. He reached a hand out to stop them toppling –

– and then he went very still, as out of the edge of his vision he saw an ominous group of men standing behind him, faces distinct in the relative darkness of the corner of the room.

He didn't look directly at them but carried on as if he hadn't seen them. They were so still that there was definitely something not right about them. He didn't know why a line of men would wait in the dark, just watching him, but he knew it couldn't be for any good reason. He drifted slowly back to the table where he'd left the hammer. He wanted the reassuring heft of it in his hand before he confronted them, and he figured the way to do that was to act nonchalant. His mouth was suddenly dry as he reached for another biscuit. He crunched into it and then put the lid back on the tin.

He reached for the table-top, hoping they would

think he was just going to put the tin down. He placed it on the table, and then grabbed the hammer and whirled, holding it ready to lash out if they tried to rush him.

'OK,' he hissed. 'What do you want?'

As he pulled the hammer from the table he caught a coffee mug that went spinning off the edge. The only answer he got was the sound of it smashing noisily somewhere in the darkness.

The men didn't move. He was now facing them directly so he could see this clearly. They just stared at him, great white moon faces impassive in the gloom.

He tried to swallow, but the biscuit had gone to sawdust in his dry mouth, and he choked. Choking made him angry and he stepped towards the line of men, determined that it was better to face them than turn his back on them and run away. There was something very unnatural in their stillness.

He dry-swallowed the biscuit fragments.

'Seriously, who are you . . .?'

One step closer and then he stopped dead.

They weren't anyone. They were just a line of white hard-hats and overalls hanging on the wall. It was only his fear and the darkness turning them into people.

He lowered the hammer in relief. Even better than not being people, they were dry clothes. He quickly rummaged through and found two donkey jackets and a padded shirt-jacket. The shirt-jacket had the flat, slightly sour smell of plaster, but he was in no position to be choosy. He stripped off his wet shirt and shrugged into the dry shirt. The quilted interior was cold against his skin, but he buttoned it up and tied the arms of his wet shirt round its waist to keep his body warmth in. Then he put the smaller of the two donkey jackets on top of it. It was rough dark wool with some kind of plastic covering on the shoulders, but it was warm. Almost immediately he could feel the heat returning to his outer body. He stumbled over something at foot level, and was pleased to see it was a pair of paint covered workman's boots, the kind that were like leather Wellingtons, without laces. He jammed his bare foot inside. The boot was big, but not unwearably so. He toyed with the idea of carrying on with odd shoes on, and decided he'd take off his one shoe and wear both of the boots. He stuck his shoe down the back of his belt, cinched it tight, rolled up the sleeves of the shirt so it fit and went back to the table where he filled the jacket pockets with the rest of the biscuits and looked for something to drink.

There was nothing except a paint splattered plastic kettle, so he drank the water from that, all the time keeping his ears open for any sign of gargoyles trying to get in: the only sounds he could hear were normal, night-time city sounds – traffic, the occasional thump of a passing car stereo on the street below, the high pitched whine of a scooter, and in the distance the wah-wah and shrill electronic chirrup of a police siren. He crossed to the street side of the room and looked out of the windows. No sign of trouble.

A gust of wind blew in cold from the window space next to the one he was looking out of, and a rattle of chains alerted him to the fact that it was somehow accessible to the night air. He hurried over and found that it was open, but blocked by the huge circular mouth of a rubbish chute. It was one of those long segmented tubes that you see attached to the side of buildings under renovation, the kind that are essentially made from many bottomless dustbins chained together to form a long slide that drops all the builders' debris into a skip below. This one was slightly curved so that he couldn't see what was at the bottom.

He stuck his head out of the small triangular gap at the side of the chute to see if the angle was shallow enough for him to even think of using it as an escape slide. The bad news was that it wasn't really. The *worse* news was that something hissed on the wall to his right and he looked up to see three gargoyles flattened on the exterior of the building like geckos, all staring at him.

He ducked away fast, but not fast enough to miss seeing that the outside of the building swarmed with stone creatures, all listening at windows or scanning the brickwork. He ran back to the door, knowing he had to get out of there. He bumped off obstacles as he went – sending the teetering pile of roofing-felt rolls scattering ahead of him. He hurdled one and then caught his shins against the sharp hard edge of a paint-can and made the door in an ungainly stumble, dropping his hammer as he reached out to steady himself. It clattered loudly on the floor. He figured that the gargoyles must know where he was by now, so he definitely had to get somewhere else fast.

He tugged at the deadbolt on the door. It was stuck. He'd rammed it too tight when he'd locked the door. He gritted his teeth and pulled harder. It wouldn't budge no matter how he pulled – then something hit the other side of the door and that freed the bolt and the door flew open, sending him flying backwards.

Two stone talons appeared on either side of the door-jamb, and then as he scrambled up on his feet, a gargoyle head that had once had two horns but now only had one snarled into the space between them. The gargoyle was too big to get into the room without ducking and edging in sideways – and that was what saved George.

He knew he was too far from his hammer to get it, but his hand closed on the wire handle of one of the paint-cans he'd tripped over, and as the gargoyle was ducking sideways and starting to unfold one wing into the room, George lunged forward, swinging the paint-can in a desperate haymaker.

The weight of the can developed a powerful centrifugal force as he swung it up and back over his shoulder, so that by the time it was coming round on the upswing it was going at quite a speed. The gargoyle snarled and launched a wild bite at him – and thereby stepped into the blow. The can caught it right under the chin. The force of the blow jarred George's hand, but he managed to keep hold of the can as the gargoyle went cartwheeling backwards out into the corridor and ended up flat on its back. It lay there stunned, then shook its head, trying to right itself.

George felt adrenaline spiking in his nostrils, and heard his teeth grind against each other as he clenched his jaw and went after the creature. He swung the can left and hit it hard on the side of the head, and then he caught it on the backswing. The can burst as the gargoyle bounced back on to the floor, and sprayed red paint all over its face and wing.

George saw its neck go slack and backed up fast, re-bolting the door behind him. Something else was rattling the boards that obscured the windows on the opposite side to the street. As the bolt slammed shut the thought occurred to him that unless he came up with a plan for getting out of the room, he might just be caught like a rat that had locked itself into its own trap.

He wondered if he could survive the five-floor drop sliding down the rubbish chute. Then he thought of the skip that it must empty into, and all the lethal hard and sharp rubbish it could be filled with. Bad idea. His legs were starting to shake with frustration, wanting to run but having nowhere to go. And now something started rattling the boarded-up windows on the chute side of the room. It really was time to go. He kicked out in frustration, to stop his leg-shake as much as anything else, and connected with the soft roll of roof insulation. It thudded across the room, and as it did so he knew what he was going to do. He picked up the nearest roll. Although it was unwieldy he managed to stagger across the room with it and threw it down the chute. It just fitted, with about ten centimetres on either side. He turned and grabbed another, threw it after the first, and then went for another one, working fast and methodically so he wouldn't have time to listen to the second thoughts banging insistently on the back door of his consciousness.

There was an alarming splintering noise from the blocked window behind him, and he saw that the creature on the other side had managed to get one corner of the boarding free. It was definitely time to leave.

He took a deep breath and swung one leg into the chute. And then one of those second thoughts got through. If he reached the ground in enough of one piece to walk away, exactly how was he going to do that? The gargoyles on the outside wall would recognize him and swoop down on him.

He swung his leg back out and ran across to the hooks where he had found his jacket. He quickly jammed a second donkey jacket over the one he was already wearing. It was a tight fit, but now he felt bigger and fatly padded. Then he pulled a hard hat on to his head, snatched up a pair of heavy-duty gloves from the table and jammed his hands into them as he ran back to the chute, trying not to look back at the new banging noise rocking the door on its flimsy hinges.

He didn't let himself think twice this time, though he did grab the hammer and another roll of insulating felt as he passed. He tossed the roll down the chute and swung straight after it into the yawning plastic gullet.

As his hands released the rim of the chute he heard a loud crack from the door behind him — but then he was gone, plunging groundwards at speed.

His stomach leapt skywards as he fell in the opposite direction. Everything happened at once as he tried to remember to keep his mouth closed so he wouldn't bite his tongue on impact, as he'd once done on a high flume at a water-world. His hard hat bobbled off and fell after him as he attempted to slow his descent by braking himself with his boots and elbows and gloves, bracing his back against the curved interior surface of the pipe.

The outward friction didn't seem to slow him much but he hoped it was enough to do more than turn a clean but fatal free-fall into a juddering death-slide. His attempt to slow himself kicked dirt off the sides of the tube, so he was falling into a blinding cloud of choking dust as he went. He tried to stop breathing in and was about to wonder how he'd know when to stop his feet pushing outward and bring them together so he could attempt a parachute landing, when it all became academic: he hit bottom with a slamming jolt that knocked out all the air in him as his knees pistoned up towards his chin – and then he stopped dead. But alive, he realized, with a wave of elation that didn't diminish when his hard hat caught up with him and bounced off his head a moment later.

He stayed very still, surrounded by the soft pink plug of roofing felt that had cushioned his fall, trying not to cough and splutter in the dust-cloud he'd kicked up. And then, when he'd really believed the evidence of his senses and ascertained that nothing was broken, he grabbed his hat and gripped the hammer tightly as he squeezed himself down through the roofing felt and into the half empty skip beyond.

It was covered with a tarpaulin and tied down against the wind, but he found a gap and managed to serpentine head-first out of it. He risked a glance upwards, and saw that all the gargoyles were massed around the windows of the room he'd just left, five storeys above. He darted into the protection given by the overhanging scaffolding, and walked as quickly and quietly towards the corner of the building as he could manage.

If the gargoyles hadn't heard him falling down the chute, he was sure they must be able to hear his heart hammering. He remembered to put the white hard hat on his head as he came to the end of the scaffolding, and walked out into the street with only the slightest hesitation. Not looking back was almost the hardest thing he did, but he knew he mustn't. Because any gargoyle who looked down could see his face and realize that the bulky man walking away beneath the hat was in fact a boy.

His shoulders itched and his ears strained for the sound of anything whistling in out of the sky behind him, but by the time he had walked halfway past the next building he thought he might have got away with it. As he passed the cascading fonts announcing the entrance to the British Library he gave himself the luxury of twirling nonchalantly on his feet as he walked, and saw the coast was clear.

His knees almost buckled with relief and he hurried on down the Euston Road.

He didn't notice a huge statue turn its head and look at him from a vantage point set back in the piazza outside the British Library. The huge male figure was bent over a large pair of dividers, as if measuring the world. He looked as though he had been made, then cut up into chunks, and then badly re-assembled, with gaps where the joins didn't quite meet.

The giant looked at him, then up at the rookery on St Pancras. And he put his fingers in his mouth and whistled.

32

ESCAPE TO SILENCE

'Come on, Glinty, time to be somewhere else,' said Little Tragedy, tugging Edie back through the mirrored arches, back into the dark alcove beyond.

At the front door of the pub she could see the Friar talking earnestly to whoever was on the other side. Being somewhere else seemed like exactly the right idea. The only thing was that once she looked around she realized that there was no door out of this cloistered space. It didn't feel like a place of escape. It felt like a dead end. And she suddenly felt badly trapped.

As if reading her thoughts Little Tragedy put his finger up to his lips, and then monkey-swung up on one of the wall lamps and did something to the mosaic roundel in the ceiling. Then he dropped to the ground, nimble as a cat.

'Trust me. I know somewhere the Tallyman won't find yer.'

He beckoned her to the parallel mirrors. Her feet braked on the carpet. She had no intention of going back to the Blitz. He shook his head impatiently.

'S'all right. I changed the wossit in the ceiling. We ain't going to the past, just somewhere else in the city, somewhere they can't find yer. It's an 'ouse, a safe one, don't worry. Look: it's nuffink bad.'

And he pointed into the mirror. She let her feet take her close enough for a look. There was no conflagration on the other side of the mirror. There was just an empty grey room, bare grey walls meeting dusty grey floorboards. The only relief from the plainness silvering everything was the crisscross shadow thrown across the floor by the window in the moonlight. There was nothing else in the room, and no shadows where danger might lurk.

She heard the Friar raise his voice in the doorway. She heard the word 'Walker' and 'Stone', and that alone evaporated any misgivings she was having about re-entering the mirrors.

She nodded at Little Tragedy, and her eyes slipped over his shoulder and were caught by the sight of

George's jacket, hanging on the beer-pump handles. He saw what she was looking at, and nodded.

'You're right. Don't want to forget the dainty, do we?'

And he nipped out into the bar-room proper, and quick as thought had snatched the coat and was back at her side.

'Ladies first,' he whispered. And just before she stepped into the mirror she had a second thought, and hesitated. What if—?

And before the thought could go further Little Tragedy had clucked with impatience and pushed past her and into the mirror, tugging her arm as he went. And she stepped in after him, feeling the surface tension on the mirror stretch and pop as before, and then she was in the room beyond.

And this time, instead of her ears being assaulted by a hellish barrage of noise, she experienced the opposite – complete quiet. It was the sound of a city at peace with itself. It was so silent that she could hear her heart begin to slow down from the panicked tempo it had risen to when she had been in the pub only an instant before.

It wasn't just the lack of explosions and fire that was different from the last trip she'd made into the mirror. It also wasn't hot. In fact it was the opposite. The air was still, so there was no draught, but it was not even warm.

'It's cold,' she said, watching her breath plume as she turned to look at Little Tragedy.

'Sometimes it's cold, sometimes it isn't. It's a funny old room,' said the boy. He was looking at her over the top of the jacket he had taken from the pump handles.

There was something in his eyes that she hadn't seen before. He still had the cocky urchin's grin, but his eyes didn't match. His eyes weren't grinning. They were saying something completely different, something not cheery, or chirpy, or cheeky.

They were saying sorry.

' 'E's not a bad man. 'E's always looking after glints. 'E told me. 'E said no one looks after them better.'

Her heart froze and her hand was already in her pocket, closing round the well-worn disc of her sea-glass. And even as she pulled it out into the grey room she knew what she would see, because it was already hot to the touch, already blazing with warning light. And as the light shone out and cast her finger-shadows on the grey walls, she completed – too late – the thought she'd begun in the pub just before Little Tragedy had pulled her into the mirror.

The thought was this: if the Friar had shielded her from a bomb blast and saved her from the Blitz, why wouldn't he save her from the Walker? And of course the answer was that he probably would save her from the

Walker. Which raised the question of why the boy-imp had pulled her into the mirror behind the monk's back, and why he was looking so *wrong* . . .

'You're not talking about the Friar, are you?'

His eyes swivelled this way and that, anywhere but at her face, at the shock and rising horror in her eyes. He held out the jacket, as if making a peace offering.

' 'Ere, take yer coat. It's parky in 'ere.'

She looked at the mirror behind him, calculating how she could get to it without him stopping her.

'Thanks,' she said slowly, taking the jacket. She knew how to do it. She'd take the coat and then throw it over his head and jump past him in the confusion. And then she remembered the broken dragon's head in the pocket and thought that she'd better take that with her, and then she realized the heavy weight wasn't in the pocket at all, and she hesitated, confused for an instant and then she looked up and saw it.

Little Tragedy had the broken carving in his hand, and he took advantage of this shock to back up to the mirror in two fast steps.

'You can't take that,' she said, voice hoarsening. 'Don't do this.'

His smile was really just hanging on by a thread, and his eyes looked so sad peering out from his mismatched face that he might have been a Tragic boy wearing the mask of Comedy, rather than the other way round.

'Don't leave me here,' rasped Edie, looking round at the bare grey walls and something moving slowly beyond the windows, a new terror gripping her.

' 'E's not a bad man. 'E told me,' the urchin insisted. And then he put one leg into the mirror. He paused, as if he wanted to be gone but his conscience wouldn't let him make a quick exit. As if what he really wanted was for her to tell him that what he was doing was all right.

'Tragedy, no, please . . .!'

He shook his head. Something glinted in his eye.

' 'E'll be along in a while. You'll be hunky-dory, no bother.'

And as she leapt for him, trying to get in the mirror, he jumped back and out of the room, and she hit nothing but hard cold glass.

Her first impulse was to smash her fists into it, but sense took over and halted them in mid-punch. For some reason she couldn't get back in the mirror, but if she calmed down, maybe she could find a way.

She stepped back, trying to clear her head, pushing the panic and outrage at Little Tragedy's betrayal down far enough that there was room for her to think.

She spun round. There was a door, four walls, and a window. The door was the obvious choice, but for a reason whose tapping was becoming more and more insistent at the back of her mind, she didn't want to open it, or even touch it.

She crossed to the window and looked out. It was, of course, barred. The thing that she had seen moving beyond the window was still moving, and the warning bell it had triggered jangled louder and louder in her head.

It was snow.

And the rooftops it was falling on all around her were not the rooftops of the London she had just left. There were no sodium street lights, no TV aerials, no satellite dishes – no neons or any flickering bloom from TV screens in the windows beneath them. There was no hard-edged electric light out there at all.

It was quiet way beyond the fact that the snow was deadening every sound as it blanketed the city. There was simply no traffic noise. No cars, no buses, no whining motor-scooters. There was a distant sound of a barrel organ, and the jingle of harness.

She looked down through the bars, and in the narrow slice of street that she could just make out, she saw a horse pulling an old fashioned hackney cab, its wheels slowly cutting a twin furrow through the deep snow on the street. The driver sat on his high seat, cracking his whip at the horse's hind-quarters, a short top hat tied on to his head with a muffler, his legs swathed in a horse blanket. And then he was gone, leaving nothing but the twin wheel marks in the snow.

She knew then that the imp had lied about more than one thing: she knew she was not in her present London. She was in an older London, a London deadened with snow, an icy London where horses pulled wooden wheel-furrows through white streets, a London where it was cold enough for rivers to freeze over and for girls to be drowned in ice-holes.

And she knew too that he had lied about this being a safe house. This was not a safe house, because she could always tell if stones held sadness or anguish or horror, and this was why she didn't want to touch the grey walls or even the door handle a couple of metres away across the floorboards.

She knew all this even without hearing the distant sound of sobbing that came from a lower floor, beyond the door.

This was no safe house. This was the House of the Lost.

33

THE EUSTON MOB

George hurried west on the Euston Road, leaving the British library behind him. He had just heard an urgent, ear-splitting whistle and though he hadn't seen the whistler, he had a feeling that whatever it was he'd do no harm quickly getting as far from it as he could.

Now he wasn't actually fighting for his life he was able to focus on his urgent worry about Edie and the Gunner. As far as Edie was concerned, he was pretty sure that she would continue on to the Black Friar as they'd planned. One of the things about her was that she didn't go to pieces when things got hard. The Black Friar would surely be able to help her. He hoped she would find the broken dragon's head in the coat pocket and use it to bargain with the Friar if it was necessary. He couldn't believe how much time had been wasted since they'd sat together in the shelter of the skip, working out the first step in their probably futile plan to save the Gunner. Now he was safe the whole business of being picked up and flown all over London seemed like a desperate inconvenience. He still had no idea how to find or save the Gunner. The frustration of it hit him with the intensity of a blow and he stopped, trying to think straight now the adrenaline was flushing out of his system.

He realized he was walking with no sense of where he should be going. He should be heading for the Black Friar's pub. Edie would still be there – if she had gone there in the first place – and even if she had left, the Friar would tell him where she'd gone. Of course, going to the Black Friar's pub meant crossing back into the City, and that meant finding a way past the City Dragons that stood watch on each thoroughfare leading across the old boundary, but he'd have to deal with that problem when he came to it.

He was level with the entrance to Euston Station. If his sense of direction was working, then he needed to turn south and east. His London geography was a bit sketchy about how exactly to get there from where he was, but he thought if he turned in that direction he would eventually hit the river, and then all he reckoned he'd have to do was to head east.

So he turned, and the scrape of his oversized plasterers' boots on the gritty paving-stone was echoed by another stony scrape in front of him, and then there was a hiss, and he looked up, and there were two massive stone bat-wings blocking his way as the gargoyle he had hit with the red paint-can dropped softly on to the pavement in front of him. The red was splashed across it like blood, and its head was cocked, the one paint-spattered eye screwed shut while the other seemed to bore into George, despite its stony blankness.

He looked round for somewhere he could hide. To his left was a big blocky gatehouse, one of the pair leading into the station. Unfortunately it was too far for him to be able to get to it before the gargoyle got to him, and even if it hadn't been, there was no door that he could see in the façade, which was carved with the names of battles fought long ago in far away places.

With nowhere to run, George knew that his battle was about to be here and now.

He knew it from the look on the gargoyle's face as it scraped one talon forward on the paving stone, and then dragged the other one after it. And he knew it from the twinge in his arm – from the dragon's scar and the three flaws entwining his forearm.

He gripped the hammer, ready to go down fighting. And then his hand twinged again.

The pain gave him an idea. It had bought him a moment with the Knight. If it bought him a moment with the gargoyle, maybe he could think of something that would stop it tearing him to shreds.

'Hey,' he said, holding his hand out. 'Back off.'

The big taint cocked its head in the opposite direction and then, amazingly, stopped.

George saw his wrist extending out from the donkey jacket sleeve, and caught a glint of metal reflecting the streetlights on a part of him where he should just have seen his skin. He realized with a sickening jolt that the stone and brass grooves braiding round his arm had definitely moved further towards his elbow. He decided he didn't have the time to worry about that now. He had to keep his advantage over the gargoyle going.

'Yes,' he said, submerging the shake in his voice. 'A Maker's Mark. An Ironhand. You back off, or I'll . . .'

He couldn't think what to say. So he took one step forward, brandishing his hand in front of him as if it was a magical talisman.

'Back off or I'll . . . I'll . . .'

'Most likely bleed all over him, like.'

The voice from behind George was not one he'd heard before. It was a Geordie voice with the flat, hard, matter-of-fact vowels of North East England.

'I was you, bonny lad, I'd lower the hammer and step back.'

George wanted to look behind him, but he didn't want to take his eyes off the gargoyle.

'Big Red there's not fussed about your 'and, Sonny Jim. He's fussed about four Lee-Enfields pointing right at his ugly mug,' rasped another voice that sounded like it came from South London and had smoked way too many cigarettes on the way.

George realized that the gargoyle wasn't looking at him at all. It had stopped because of something that was behind him.

'Now, why don't 'ee step back to us, lad. Be safer, all things considered,' said a third voice, humming with a west-country twang in which all the s's sounded like z's.

George turned.

Four bronze World War One soldiers were behind him, tall men in long flapping army great-coats. Three stood and one knelt, resting his elbow on one knee. They wore soft peaked hats instead of tin helmets, and they all held rifles levelled unwaveringly at the gargoyle. One of the standing riflemen's jaws were in constant motion, as if he was chewing tobacco or gum.

The kneeling soldier took his trigger hand off the weapon and beckoned George towards him, nodding slowly as if to say it was all going to be all right.

George backed up fast. The standing soldiers made a space for him without taking their guns off the taint as George walked through them and turned to see what would happen next. The rifleman who was chewing stepped forward into the space that he had just vacated and spat a large gob of something dark on to the paving-stone at the gargoyle's feet, splashing his talons as he did so. George decided it must be chewing tobacco. The chewer gestured to the sky with his gun.

'Haddaway, ya greet sackless cuddy!'

And when the gargoyle didn't move, he took another step forward and prodded it in the chest with his gun. The gargoyle flinched, hissed, and then threw itself backwards into the air, its great wings beating downwards, causing the soldier's greatcoat to billow behind him like a cloak as it pulled itself higher and higher into the sky, until it disappeared behind the rooftops behind it. There was a general easing of tension and uncocking of guns, and then the soldier next to George turned and nodded at the chewer.

'It's all right; we never know what 'e's sayin' neither, do we, Westie?'

George looked at the soldiers as they all crowded round him, looking down with interest.

'You'll be the boy we heard about, most like,' said the

one called Westie. 'Us got a pigeon, tellin' us to keep a sharp eye out, friend of the Gunner's, it said?'

George nodded. The chewer looked round.

'Said tha was wi' a lass too, kiddar?'

'Edie,' said George. 'We got split up.'

The soldiers tutted and sucked their teeth.

'Who are you?' said George.

The soldier nearest him paused in the action of lighting his cigarette.

'Rifleman South,' he said, his accent turning 'South' into 'Sarf'. He thumbed introductions over his shoulder without looking. 'These are my oppos. Corporal North's Geordie bastard as you can tell, so we don't understand 'ardly nothing what 'e says. Westie here's a bit of a wurzel, but once you get used to 'im 'e's all right. And Private East there don't say much anyway, but 'e's a nugget, lets 'is fighting do the talking, so don't you worry about 'im. We're all good men in a scrap, none better. They call us the Euston Mob.'

He jerked his thumb at an obelisk with four empty plinths at its base.

'That's where we stay. We was railwaymen, see, before the war, so they put us in front of the station. That's our billet. Plinths on points of the compass, 'ence the names. Come on, out of the street.'

He led George back towards the obelisk.

George looked up at the night sky into which the red gargoyle had disappeared.

'You think he's really gone?'

South hunkered down against the stone, rifle across his knees, enjoying the smoke.

' 'E won't 'ang about. Westie here may seem slow but 'e can shoot the eye out of a running squirrel without breaking a sweat, leastways that's what 'e's always tellin' us, eh, Westie?'

The other soldiers joined them sitting against the monument's base, except for East who seemed edgier than the others and stood apart, keeping watch on the sky towards St Pancras.

' 'E won't be back, not if 'e knows what's good for him,' agreed Westie, taking a light from the end of South's cigarette.

'The Gunner's in trouble,' said George. 'I need help.'

'Everyone needs 'elp' said South. 'All right Sonny Jim, why don't you start by tellin' us what's going on then.'

And, conscious of the three interested faces turned towards him, George did. In as few words as he could manage he sketched everything that had happened to him since his nightmare began. They didn't interrupt him, but he was aware of them looking at each other at certain points in the story. And when he told the bit about how the Gunner had broken his word and then been taken by the Walker, even East turned away from his watch on the night sky and looked at George intently. And then he finished, and was conscious of nothing so much as that he just seemed to have wasted more time he didn't have.

'So anyway,' he concluded. 'I started out to help the Gunner, and now I've got these three duels or contests to fight as well!'

'Oh yeah, you gotta fight 'em. You can't duck 'em. Duck 'em an' you're done,' said South. 'Them stripes on your arm, they're the marks of your task. Each stripe is different, see, like the contests are. And they're on the move, right?'

George stared at the flaws corkscrewing towards his elbow. Two were slowly moving up his arm, but the metal one had just started to circle it in a tight coil. As if it couldn't go further. He nodded.

'Ar well, it'd be worse than the black dam if you let one o' they buggers get to your heart,' said Westie.

'What do you mean?' George asked, knowing he was going to hate the answer.

'Why, you'll likely croak . . . or worse, lad,' he went on flatly, looking at him through a skein of cigarette smoke.

'What's worse than croaking?' asked George in horror.

There was a pause. South and Westie glanced at each other for a moment. Then:

'You met the Walker, yeah?' puffed South, and widened his eyes, as if no further explanation was necessary.

' 'Ee just must face up to the three contests and, one by one, happen the lines will disappear,' Westie explained. 'That's why you must stand. Because if you don't, you'll lose anyway, because you won't stop the line reaching your 'eart, see?'

Now George was panicking, despite all his intentions to keep a clear head.

'Wait, but with the Knight. I didn't finish the fight – I mean – am I already doomed?' He stared at the soldiers' faces. 'Am I going to croak?'

North reached over and took his arm. He pushed the sleeve back and looked at the scars. He looked at South.

'Well,' exhaled South, 'that's a matter of opinion: it seems to me you didn't duck a fight as such. Seems to me you was on the point – a very sharp point – of losin' one. And then this gargoyle, the one you called Spout, he flies in and snatches you, yeah?'

North and West nodded.

'Reet. Wasn't tha running away, like. Was a *deus ex* wotsit . . .'

North snapped his fingers, trying to conjure the word that was on the tip of his tongue.

'*Machina*.' South cleared his throat and looked at a watch that he pulled out of his pocket. 'You didn't run, is what I'm sayin'. Worst you could say is rain stopped play.'

'I don't follow.'

'Maybe you don't follow, chum, but I reckon the Last Knight will. I think 'e'll follow you till the fight's all done. It's your fate, mate. Your first duel ain't over, it just got cut short. Postponed, as it were. I'd say you're half a scrap down and two more to go. Look at 'ow that metal vein must have started to move, but then stopped. If you'd chosen to run away it would have continued on and split your 'eart and we wouldn't be wastin' valuable time talkin'. It's just coiling round and round, markin' time until you meet the Knight again and finish the duel you started. But that ain't the problem right now.'

He tapped his watch.

'This is.'

George stared at the timepiece. If he'd felt sick before, he felt sicker now.

'You're saying I'm out of time. The Gunner's out of time. It's nearly turn o'day . . .'

'Aye, lad – exactly,' said North.

'Ar, and if 'e isn't there, if 'is plinth is empty by midnight . . .'

'The Gunner's a goner . . .' finished South.

George felt the night closing in on him, as the rising

266

claustrophobia of hopelessness began to take over.

'But I'm out of time, I'll never—'

'You want to talk less and listen more, chum,' said an unfamiliar voice. It was East. He pointed at Westie. 'What did he say?'

George reran the conversation in his head. He heard the soft west-country burr saying 'If 'e isn't there, if 'is plinth is empty by midnight . . .' But it didn't make sense, and they were all looking at him . . . and then he got it.

'If his plinth is empty, you mean . . .?'

North nodded. 'Canny lad.'

George was on his feet. Urgency took the place of the rising hopelessness and squashed it back down into place.

'. . . you mean, if someone takes his place on the plinth, he won't die?'

Four bronze faces nodded solemnly at him.

'Well, why didn't . . .? That's easy . . . I'll do it!'

South shook his head.

'Standing to ain't easy, Sonny Jim. It's not just standing there – there's other things to be dealt with, see, and—'

'Fine, whatever, I'll do it!' George was almost giddy with relief.

'Nobody 'ere doubts that. It's just, when you get there . . . I need to warn you about something.' He broke off suddenly and looked at his watch. 'Oh, gorblimey. Never mind that – that ain't the question.'

'What is the question?'

Rifleman South held out the watch. George looked at it and started doing a horrible calculation in his head.

'Question is, how fast can you run?'

George didn't waste any time answering, because he had no time. He just nodded and sprinted westwards. He did remember to stop when he got to the edge of the traffic – and he took advantage of the enforced second's pause to turn and hurl a hurried 'Thank you' back over his shoulder as he did. And then a hole opened in the cars and he dashed across the road, vaulted the central divider, and jinked west, running at full tilt.

He was running so fast he didn't see the homeless man in the doorway track him with Raven black eyes. And he was too intent on finding his way to Hyde Park Corner to hear the tramp saying:

'Boy maker running west on Euston Road.'

34

THE HOUSE
OF THE LOST

Edie stood very still for a long time. After the distant fit of sobbing the house was quiet, but not quite silent. Outside the window the snow-deadened city continued to leak the sound of a distant barrel organ, but apart from that the only noises she could hear came from within the house, and they were the noises of the house itself: a door whose hinges needed oiling opened and closed somewhere below; a short sliding noise and then a sudden thud as an unseen hand opened, or perhaps shut a heavy bolted lock; floorboards creaking as something moved across them.

And then there was silence, a silence that Edie added to by not moving at all.

One reason that she didn't move was because she

knew that when she did the dusty floorboards beneath her feet would creak, and she had the distinct feeling that the silence that she was listening to was *exactly* the kind of silence that was listening right back.

It was a silence that was patiently waiting for her to make the first sound.

The other reason she stayed still was that she was in the middle of the room, as far from the walls as she could get. A normal person wouldn't have noticed it, but Edie was a glint, and being a glint, the walls growled at her with a kind of low frequency hum, a horrid magnetic attraction enticing her to touch them and release the stored trauma in the brick and plaster. It was the same intensity of sadness she felt as she passed cemeteries and churchyards and old hospitals, somehow willing her to reach out and draw it from the stones.

She steadied her breathing and tried to keep her mind off the tug of the distress stored in the walls by calmly checking the room for anything that might help her. The insistent pull made her bunch her hands deep into her pockets, in case they wandered off on their own and touched something without the permission of her conscious mind.

There really was not much to see. There was the barred window, there were the two mirrors and there was a thick layer of dust over everything. And that was it.

Having exhausted the contents of the room, and keeping her ears on alert for the slightest noise beyond the door, Edie turned her attention to the floor.

Now she focused on it she realized that the sick tug of pent-up anguish that came at her from the walls also dragged at her from below, like a dark undertow. She was glad she was wearing shoes. She had never been in a place that held so much potential malice and sadness stored in it, so much that there was a foretaste of it in the air; she could tell it was bad in the same way that you can tell what food will be like before eating it just by the cooking smell. It crackled invisibly all around her like static electricity.

She had never been in this house, but it felt like home.

It didn't feel like home in a warm way, not like the few tattered happy fragments of home she remembered from the good parts of her childhood, nor did it feel like some idealized vision of 'home' – a place of security where everything would always be all right, everything understood, everything forgiven.

It felt like the other one, the home she'd never been to, the one where secretly – ever since she'd killed her step-father – she knew she belonged: the dark home where yesterday's secrets are exposed so that today's pain can be justified and tomorrow's punishments planned.

A single tear makes little sound as it falls to the floor,

but the sight of it splashing in the dust jerked her out of the paralysis she'd fallen into and she remembered to breathe, sucking in a deep and desperately needed lungful of air. She wiped the back of her hand angrily across her eyes, determined that the one treacherous tear would have no company.

Then she focused on the floor again: it was thick with dust, but there were distinct footmarks which she could see were hers and the bare feet of Little Tragedy. There were also paw marks that had nothing to do with either of them. They were like dog paws, but bigger than any Edie had seen, and then there was a swirling drag mark serpentining into the room from the door. It came about a third of the way inside, and then stopped, as if someone had perhaps started sweeping and then given up the idea when the thickness and the pervasiveness of the dust had dispirited them.

Edie was standing there, trying to piece together the evidence in front of her eyes, when she became aware of a tickle in her nose.

The tickle was the result of the dust she had already stirred up by her arrival and argument with Little Tragedy. It wasn't a bad thing in itself; but in her nose it was going to lead to a sneeze. A sneeze is also not a bad thing in itself. Edie had once spent a summer's afternoon looking up into the sun because it made her sneeze and sneezing, on that day, had made her feel good. On this night, sneezing was not going to make Edie feel good. It was going to make her feel very bad, because on this night she knew she would be sneezing into a listening silence that was just waiting for her to break it.

On this night Edie knew one sneeze could well be fatal.

Before she could think how to stifle it it exploded. She grabbed her nose and clamped it shut, and jammed George's balled-up jacket over her face to muffle the sound – but the noise of the air convulsing its way out of her just redirected out of the side of her mouth in a sharp detonation.

She stayed where she was, bent over her hands, ears straining for a reaction to the noise she'd made. For a moment she thought she'd got away with it – but then she heard floorboards creak. The sound changed in tone and tempo and became the unmistakable noise of someone coming up stairs. She could hear a dragging sound too, a sort of rustling and the counterpoint of smaller clicking footsteps alongside the noise made by the bigger thing.

There was an especially sharp crack from a floorboard that seemed to be the sound of the larger thing or person reaching the landing, and then the sounds moved closer to the door. Edie had time to see a golden strip of wavering light appear in the crack beneath it, as if the figure approaching was carrying some kind of lantern – and then the footsteps and the scuffling stopped suddenly.

Edie grimaced and very quietly slipped her arms into George's coat again. Whatever was going to happen she thought another layer couldn't do any harm, either offering protection or warmth.

Then she heard the sniffing.

Two dark shadows broke the golden strip under the door, and from them came hungry intakes of breath, as if whatever was outside was trying to inhale the inside of the room in big hungry nasal gulps of air.

Edie looked down and saw the warning stone blazing a shaft of light out of her pocket. She closed her hands round it, extracting some faint support from the familiar sea-rounded edges and accompanying heat.

The door opened.

A woman stood in the opening, a tall woman in an old fashioned grey dress that covered her from high on her neck down to the floor and beyond, where her full skirts bellied out and trailed on the ground around her. She wore a wide belt tight around her middle, and her hands were covered by thick protective gloves, made from rough suede, that reached up to her elbows like welders' gauntlets.

Edie couldn't see her face, because she held a candle

high in front of it, and all she could make out was the impression of a high forehead and dark hair scraped back from it into a severe bun on the back of her head.

'What is your name?' the woman said in a disturbingly quiet voice.

'What's yours?' said Edie, reflexively defiant.

There was a pause as Edie saw the woman cock her head as if adjusting to what she'd just heard. When she spoke again it was almost a whisper, as light and dark as a Raven's feather, but not so quiet that Edie couldn't hear the rising note of surprise in her voice.

'You are a young girl?'

Edie looked down at herself.

'Er, yeah . . . What are you? Blind?'

The candle lowered as the woman answered.

'No. I'm not blind, child. I just choose not to see.'

It was the word 'choose' that made what Edie saw so much more disturbing than it already was.

The woman's face was gaunt and almost ageless in its severity, but the most striking thing was the eyes above her high cheekbones.

They were sewn shut.

Four workmanlike stitches closed each pair of eyelids with thick black cobbler's thread. The only thing that made the sight worse was the hint that the woman had done this to herself.

'Why would you do that?' said Edie, despite herself. 'Why would you let someone do that?'

The woman sighed as if the answer to the question was so obvious that any answer was a waste of preciously hoarded energy.

'Eight short stitches? It's nothing, child, not if you wish to stop seeing . . .'

'But why?' Edie couldn't stop herself asking in outrage.

'Come. You know why. You know what happens when we do what we do. You know willpower is not enough to keep our eyes closed. You know however hard we try that the eyes always open and then they see what is stored in the stones. And you know that the shards of the past stored in the stones are seldom happy and almost always terrible.'

The meaning of what the woman was saying hooked into Edie's gut like a suckerpunch.

'You said "we" . . . you mean, you're a glint?'

'I was. And it is my lot to live in this house. Can you feel what is in this house?'

Edie nodded, her mouth too dry to answer. Then she realized that the woman couldn't see her, but before she could say anything the woman was speaking again.

'Of course you can. You'd do the same to yourself, girl – close your eyes, wear thick gloves and sturdy boots to avoid any contact with the fabric of a building whose every touch invites an agony a hundred times worse than a mere needleprick . . .'

And then her foot kicked out from beneath her skirt and stamped sharply on the floor, making the dust jump. Her voice remained unnervingly quiet in comparison.

'Now. Enough talk. You must come with me.'

Edie had a very strong sense that she was being taken somewhere worse than this. And even though they hadn't worked, she wanted to stay close to the mirrors and the door they might open back into her normal world and time.

'Forget it,' she said. 'No way.'

'You must do as I say, girl. You must not say no.'

'Watch me.'

There was a low growl. For a moment Edie thought it came from the blind woman. Then she realized it came from behind her. It was the kind of low growl that you feel through the soles of your feet. It was the kind of growl you ignore at your peril.

'I cannot. And I am not used to being disobeyed . . .' said the Blind Woman in a voice as dark and delicate as beetles scuttling across a black silk shroud.

Edie knew that if she gave in to being scared she'd go to pieces, and she knew that if she went to pieces she was done for. So she set her chin and dug her heels in.

'Well, get used to it. I'm—'

Edie didn't even get as far as 'not' before the growl started again, and then the Blind Woman's skirts billowed out on each side and two brindled mastiff dogs the size of small ponies came into the room, heads low to the ground, ears flattened, teeth bared, double spiked collars gleaming sharply in the moonlight, hunched and ready to spring.

'You can come now, or you can beg to come later.'

The Blind Woman's voice was pale with disinterest as the dogs prowled forward, their great heads a hand's span above the dusty floorboards, eyes rolled up and fixed on Edie as they came closer. The spittle leaking out from their snarls left a trail in the dust as they moved across it.

Edie stood still until they were close enough on either side for her to feel hot breath on her hands. She clenched them and pulled them higher in an unconscious but futile effort to keep them out of harm's way.

'Look—' she said.

The dogs leapt at her, teeth clashing, loud angry barks hitting her with the force of actual blows. Dog-spittle ribboned across her eyes as her hands reflexively snapped up to protect her face from the sharp fangs clashing millimetres away from it.

And then, despite herself, her survival mechanism kicked in and she was pushed back by the enraged barking and snapping teeth as the dogs herded her across the room and her hand touched the wall and there was a jolt as the waiting past flashed into her.

She went rigid with shock and the dust billowed out around her in a mini blast-wave from an unseen detonation, and what she glinted in harsh jagged slices was:

The room in summer.

Sunlight shafting in through the window, making diagonal beams of light through the dust suspended in the air.

A short-haired woman in a light blue sundress with a sprigged daisy pattern across it crouched in the centre of the room. She was staring round her in bewilderment, Her feet looked defenseless in a pair of white flip-flops.

Time sliced and the woman was suddenly shouting 'No!' at the door with such intensity that the tendons on her neck stood out like whipcords.

Another slice and Edie saw her hands scrabbling something hanging on a chain round her neck to protect it from whoever was standing in the door. Clutching it tight, almost hiding the tell-tale light blazing out from its sea-rounded edges.

It was a brown piece of sea-glass – a heart stone.

Edie saw the short-haired woman go very still. She saw her clench her jaw – saw it in a way that she felt in her own clenched jaw.

And then she saw two huge brindled shapes leap into the living frame barking furiously, and she heard a scream —

— and then time sliced and on the floor where the woman had been was nothing except the sea-glass and a white flip-flop, upside down in the dust.

Edie jerked her hand away from the wall and the glinting stopped abruptly.

She saw the Blind Woman working her mouth as if choking down a rising wave of nausea. The dogs had taken half a step back, but only half a step.

'Whatever you saw, child,' whispered the Blind Woman. 'Whatever you saw, it will be worse when it happens to you.'

The dogs snarled.

Edie thought of George. She thought of the Gunner. She saw the Gunner smile, and she saw George smile at her too. She knew that giving in was betraying them as well as herself.

She felt the dogs' breath on her hands. Hot and wet and meaty.

And then she decided she wasn't giving in. She was living to fight another day.

'Fine,' she said. 'Fine.'

And she reached into her pocket and folded her hand round her heart stone before stepping carefully past the dogs towards the Blind Woman. The dogs moved with her, growling more quietly now.

'If you try and run, if you do anything other than what I tell you, they will bite,' the Blind Woman murmured as gently as a midnight breeze caressing its way through a cemetery hedge. 'Now come to me.'

Edie came and stood in front of her, shadowed by the dogs. She stared into the whip-stitched eyelids.

'Happy now?' she gritted.

The Blind Woman didn't move. It was as if the unseeing eyes were somehow seeing Edie. She slowly pulled off a glove, and an unexpectedly soft hand traced the contours of Edie's face. She found the wet tracks of her tears and traced them.

'Spirited,' she said, and put the gloves back on. 'I was spirited once.'

'Tell me what you want,' said Edie, swallowing something bitter at the back of her throat.

'I want nothing that you can give me. I want my warning stone,' said the Blind Woman simply. 'He stole it.'

'The Walker?' said Edie.

'Who else takes our heart stones?' sighed the Blind Woman. 'Follow me.'

'No – wait,' said Edie, desperately trying to make sense of what she was hearing. 'Why does he take our heart stones?'

'He wants the power in them, the power that makes them blaze, the power that gives us just enough strength to cope with glinting the past.' She let a bitter half laugh escape. 'It's such a small piece of power, but it means everything to one of us. Whereas the only way he can use the stones to get enough strength for his needs is to collect ALL of our stones and add their little powers together to make one big one.'

She turned and walked to the door.

'Why does he need this power?' asked Edie, dry-mouthed, measuring the distance to the door to see if she could get past and put the woman between her and the dogs.

The Blind Woman turned and looked at her, pausing in the doorway for an instant. And without eyes, it was hard to see if her smile was pitying or just sad as she replied:

'Ask him. He's coming . . .'

35

ROAD RUNNER

For the first time in a long time George felt he was running towards something. It made a difference. Fear was pretty good at getting him running, but that was running fuelled by the flight part of the fight-or-flight reflex. This running was taking its fuel from the fight part. Maybe that was why he was able to dredge up the reserves of strength he needed.

He stopped worrying about taints swooping down on him, not because he wasn't scared of them, but because worrying about things he couldn't possibly stop was an obvious waste of energy, and he had none to spare. Every ounce was going into keeping his legs and arms pistoning forward. He would just have to deal with any attack if it happened, as it happened. He had one shot at getting to the Gunner's plinth, and he wasn't going to let anything distract him from it.

He ran in a kind of trance state: somewhere he knew all this was hurting and that he had run through several stitches, and that his breath was tearing out in great ragged gasps that would have sounded like sobs if anyone had been noticing, but he didn't care. He just ran, clutching the hammer.

And as he ran he realized that his mind was clearing of all the things he didn't understand and leaving only the things that mattered, only the things he could deal with. Firstly he was going to be able to buy another day for the Gunner, if he just made the run in time. And then he would find Edie and she would tell him what the Black Friar had said, and they would find a way to get the Gunner back. There was no doubt in his mind, because there was no room for anything that would slow him down.

Unfortunately he turned into a narrow alley and suddenly found there was no room in it for him and the low sports car that was heading straight for him.

It honked its horn and flashed its lights, but George kept on running. Luckily the alley was so narrow that the driver was going slowly so as not to scrape his expensive wing mirrors on either side, so when George didn't stop he had enough time to slam on the brakes without skidding or running him down. The car came to a stop, entirely blocking the alley.

George didn't miss a step. He just jumped up on the bonnet of the low-slung muscle-car, over the roof, down on to the boot and off into the empty alley beyond before the driver knew what was happening.

Of course the moment the driver realized that a boy had run over his car he went berserk. George could hear a torrent of shouting coming from behind him, then a series of angry blasts on the horn, and finally the sound of someone trying to slam an expensive gear-box into reverse, managing to engage the gear at the third shrieking try, and then the boom of exhausts as the driver angrily tried to back up and catch George.

He took the time to glance backwards for an instant, saw reversing lights approaching at speed as the driver wobbled to keep straight in the narrow alley, had just time to see him catch one wing mirror and explode it into expensive shards against a drainpipe, and then he turned away and ran on, pausing only to pull a rubbish bin into the alley behind him to discourage further pursuit from the driver now leaning out of his window and screaming at him.

He ran out of the alley, and adjusted his bearings as he crossed the road and carried on. He could see the trees of the park beckoning at the end of the road.

Seeing the park again reminded him of Edie, of the first time they'd met in the underground garage beneath the grass. She'd been sparky and aggressive and had hit him when he tried to be nice to her. But then she'd turned out to be a brave and resourceful ally in all the adversity they'd had to face together. He wondered suddenly if she might already be there at the Gunner's plinth. Of course, the Friar probably told her the same thing he'd been told by the Euston Mob. The thought of seeing her again put more energy in his legs, and he hit Park Lane with a renewed burst of energy. He chicaned through the late-night traffic and slipped into the park.

Running on grass, beneath the sodium-lit tracery of the trees, was a lot easier.

He saw a clock-face on the side of one of the buildings on Park Lane as he passed, and as he ran under the tall modern hotel his heart was pumping like a trip-hammer, but now it was because he knew he was going to make it to the plinth before midnight.

Hang on, Edie, he thought. *I'm almost there!*

36

THE MAKERS
AND THE STONE

The Blind Woman led Edie down two flights of stairs as calmly and precisely as if she could see.

The rest of the house had no carpets, no pictures no furniture – no decoration of any kind. Dust greyed it all into nothing more than a background. Edie heard the big dogs following behind her and clenched the heart stone tightly in her pocket. The woman stopped in front of a door and felt at her waist for a large key-ring that was hanging from her belt. Once more she took off her glove and felt the various keys, searching by touch alone for the one she needed. She found it, and Edie noted that she put the glove back on before she put the key in the door and turned the lock.

'There is a chair,' she said softly. 'You will walk forward and sit on it. You will wait. If you move? The dogs will bite.'

Edie saw that the Blind Woman stood to one side as if afraid to enter the room. Edie heard a low growl behind her, and walked through the door.

There was a chair in the middle of the room. It was solidly built and rested on small iron wheels attached to each leg.

The room was lit by a single candlestick on a desk in the centre of the floor. It looked as if it had once been designed as a library, but was now a library without books. There was no furniture except for the high desk or workbench, and shelves covering every inch of wall. It wasn't, however, empty. Instead of the regular ranks of leather-bound volumes that may once have peopled its shelves, there were irregular lumps and bundles filling their space, from the bare wood of the floor to the dangerously sagging lath and plaster of the ceiling. Piles of paper covered the desk and the floor around it.

Edie walked to the chair and sat in it with a shiver.

She noted that the windows were a lattice of diamond-shaped glass pieces joined with lead. There was no obvious way to open them, so there was no question of throwing herself out of them in a desperate bid for freedom. The two dogs padded in after her and lay at her feet, eyes locked on her.

The Blind Woman stepped back from the door into the hall and sat on a high-backed chair against the wall, facing the doorway.

And for a long time the only sound was the dogs breathing and Edie's heart beating. She shifted in the hard chair, and the tiny creak immediately made both of the dogs growl sharply to their feet and raise their hackles at her.

Edie looked through the door at the stiff-backed figure staring sightlessly back at her.

'What were you?' she asked.

'What was I when?' replied the Blind Woman, in a voice scarcely above a whisper.

'Before this happened,' said Edie. 'What were you?'

More silence answered her. And then, just when Edie had decided the woman wasn't going to answer, she did.

'I was a teacher.'

'That figures.'

'What do you mean?'

'Never liked teachers much,' said Edie. 'Never seemed to tell you the stuff you really needed to know.'

'And what do you need to know, child?' murmured the Blind Woman. 'What could someone so young and unaware possibly want to know, when any knowledge will blight and not enlighten?'

'That's rubbish!' snorted Edie. 'Knowing stuff, the right kind of stuff is good. In fact, it's all good, isn't it, even the bad stuff, because how can you make a plan or keep yourself safe without all the info?'

'You can't keep yourself safe with it either child.'

'Yeah well, excuse me for living, but I haven't given up yet.'

The Blind Woman allowed the pale moth of a smile to flutter across her face, and then it was gone.

'You will. Everybody does.'

There was something pulsing at Edie from the shelves, exerting a stronger force than the background pull of the wall. She looked at the strange assortment of indeterminate shapes lumped together all round the room.

'What's on these shelves?'

'Stones.'

'Why?'

She wanted the Blind Woman to keep talking. The silence left her mind too empty, a blank canvas for the malign hum of the house and its contents to bleed their terror on to.

'Because he collects them. Like he collects our heart stones. Looking for the power hidden in a very different

290

kind of stone. A much stronger and darker stone.'

'What . . .?' began Edie. Then she stopped and re-formed her question. 'Why is everything about stones?'

'Because it is,' said the Blind Woman shortly. And then said no more.

Edie waited, and when it was clear that that was all that was going to come, she grunted in disgust.

'Typical teacher.'

The Blind Woman's head came up, bridling at Edie's tone.

'What?'

'It's like I said. Never tell you anything useful. Ask them a difficult question and you get "You don't need to know that", or "That won't be in the exam", or "Just because". You must have been a really rotten teacher.'

The Blind Woman sat so stiffly upright that you could almost hear her spine crack.

'I was a good teacher,' she whispered, soft as dust. 'I was a very good teacher.'

Edie stared at her. Unless she was mistaken there was a single tear cutting a pink trail through the dusty skin at the edge of the Blind Woman's sewn lid.

'Then why don't you tell me why this is all about stones?' said Edie, just as quietly.

'It can't help you,' she replied.

'Maybe it can help you,' said Edie carefully.

'Nothing can help me, child.' She laughed almost inaudibly. 'I am lost, so mired in darkness that I cannot turn back.'

'Then don't turn back' said Edie. 'Stay where you are. But why don't you be a good teacher again? Why don't you tell me why everything is about the stones?'

In the silence one of the dogs turned and looked at the Blind Woman. She worked her mouth as she thought.

Her hand rose and smoothed non-existent stray hairs back into her tight bun, and then she just started to talk.

'Long ago, before history began, before things had names, a Darkness walked the earth. And it fed on Fear and wherever it walked it spread terror and hatred and ignorance.'

She paused and listened, head tilted towards something she might have heard at the front of the house. After a moment she relaxed and carried on.

'And there was a Light that also walked the earth, spreading Life. And it couldn't bear to see its children live where terror and hatred spread pain and violence amongst them like a dark canker. And so it fought the Darkness and after a great struggle it won, and bound the Darkness deep in the rocky heart of the world, imprisoning the Evil in the stone below, so that it couldn't ever walk the earth again. And time passed and humankind, who are the sons and daughters of Life spread across the earth, and they built and lived and loved and laughed . . .'

The Blind Woman paused, caught out by her own words, as if she had only just remembered there were things like love and laughter outside the House of the Lost. Edie waited while she took a thin breath and then she resumed.

'And as well as building, they made things. At first the Makers – the artists and sculptors – worked with wood and clay, but their children began to dream of making things that wouldn't rot or perish with time. And they began to make out of stone and tried to work metal in the fire. But making sculptures out of stone and metal was much harder than working with wood and clay. And because they knew nothing hard can happen without tears and sacrifice, they began to believe that a sacrifice must be made to the stone they wished to use, to make it easier to work with.'

She looked blindly at Edie as if uncertain whether to go on.

'Although many ages had passed since Life had imprisoned the Evil in the rock, there were still people who had a memory that there was power in the stone. And these women – for they were women, the memory handed from mother to daughter – these women had the sense of the power and the memories that lived in the rock . . .'

'Women like us,' said Edie.

'Women like us.'

'Glints.'

'Glints.'

Edie wanted to scream at the woman. She wanted to ask how she could be so calm, so quiet, so evilly doing the Walker's bidding in this terrible house when she and Edie were, or had been, the same thing. She clenched her jaw and kept the scream inside. She wanted to know how the story ended.

The Blind Woman cleared her throat and continued.

'But time had made them forget that the power in the stone was dark.' And when the Makers came to the Glints, the women told them of the power, confirming that it was a living thing, and the Makers were happy, because they knew how to appease living things; they made a blood sacrifice.

'They drew lots and the Chief Maker's son lost, and he was taken to a stone that the Glints had chosen, and a stone knife was used. Now because these were children of Life, the blood sacrifice was to be just that: not a death; just a little finger nicked with a flint knife, the tiniest of wounds, and then the Makers would swear an oath to the Stone. The child might cry for a moment, but then it would be surrounded with flowers and laughter and celebration, and given the first of the food and the sweetest of the honey to make up for his short second of pain . . .'

Her hands fluttered up and passed over the stitches in her eyes. Edie knew that she was feeling the pain of her own sacrifice.

'And did it work?' she said.

'You know it did. The oath between Maker and Stone was that the Stone would not resist the Makers, and the Makers would use the power to work stone – to make, not mar. But the flint dagger betrayed them. Perhaps because it was a blade of stone and so had some of the evil pent hidden in it, it turned in the father's hand and the nick in the finger became a gash in the wrist, and before they could seal the wound the child was dead, and although it was an accident, his life's blood had run to the Stone, and the bond between Maker and Stone was sealed—'

'He killed his own son?' interrupted Edie.

The Blind Woman nodded.

'He killed his own son. By mistake, tricked by the Stone. And after the sadness and the wailing that came to the Master Maker's house, time passed. And the Makers made, and the Stone didn't resist, and what they made had power. They made idols and gods and devils and gargoyles for their temples and churches, and these, though the Makers didn't know it, were the first Servants of the Stone. They were made to frighten and to awe. And they were known as "taints" because wherever their shadow fell, the children of Light were tainted with fear.'

'But they made the spits too,' prompted Edie.

'They did – likenesses of living things, with a new intent, to represent people loved and admired, or even just for the sheer joy in recording that which the Makers found beautiful and pleasing.'

'And that's why spits aren't Servants of the Stone?'

'Yes, child. And they were called spits because they were made as a spirit and image of real men, and so had a sort of spirit inside them, that stood free of the Darkness and fear in the Stone.'

'And that's why the taints, the Servants of the Stone, hate them? Because they're free?'

'It's more than that. It's because the spits are the Makers' revenge on the Stone for taking the life of the innocent child. They found a way to banish a fragment of the Darkness and put a spark of Life back into the world with every spit they make. And . . .'

She stopped. And the dogs' ears pricked up. And then Edie heard the floorboard creak in the hall, and a voice she had hoped never to hear again, a thin, supercilious man's voice, ended the story.

'. . . and in this way the battle between Light and Darkness, between Fear and Joy, continues. And the Stone and the Darkness pent in it always waits for the Makers to tire, so it can return to the earth and rule again.'

The Walker appeared in the doorway, smiling humourlessly at Edie.

'And you know what? Fear always trumps Joy, and Darkness is so much more reliable than Light . . .'

He tapped the long shiny blade of his jewelled dagger on the door-frame.

There was a whimpering noise. Edie's first fear was that it was her. But it wasn't. It was the Blind Woman. She was bent straight forward over her knees, sobbing quietly. He turned and looked down at her.

Her hand reached out beseechingly, although she didn't look up. She had taken off the glove. Edie only just heard a single word sift through the sobs.

'*Please . . .*'

The Walker reached inside his long coat and pulled out a piece of sea-glass blazing a brilliant orange light, sending grotesque shadows around the room. It was on a chain. He dangled it into her hand.

The hand closed on it greedily, and the Blind Woman shuddered and sighed with relief.

Edie had survived by herself on the streets. She knew that shudder. She'd heard the junkie's sigh before. She knew how the Walker kept the Blind Woman just alive and hungry enough to do his bidding. He was using her heart stone like a drug to control her.

Edie's hand closed over her own stone, hidden in her pocket.

The Walker looked at her as if he could read her thoughts. He bared his teeth in a sneer.

'You're thinking you'd never be like her.'

Edie kept her face blank.

He jerked the glass out of the Blind Woman's grasp and caught it in his hand. She screamed. Despite herself Edie started towards her.

The dogs erupted into action and barked and snarled her back into her chair.

The Walker snapped his fingers. The dogs went silent and just stood there, looking at her.

'Stay calm. Stay still. I do not want to hurt you. I do not want to harm you. I do not, in fact, even want your warning stone. I do not want a thing about you except for your help in one small matter. I want you to use your gift for me.'

'How?' said Edie.

'I want you to test some stones. Just touch them and tell me what lies within. Do that and you may go free, unharmed and safe.'

'What kind of stones' said Edie, carefully, not believing a word about what he was saying about letting her go free.

'Ah' he grinned 'There's the catch. That's why you may keep your heart stone with you as you work. You will need all your strength.'

'What kind of stones?' she repeated, her voice snagging in her suddenly very dry throat.

He smiled wider.

'Dark stones. Very dark stones indeed . . .'

37

SUBSTITUTE

George ran behind the giant statue of Achilles, heading south. He was aware of the naked giant with a sword in one hand and a round shield held to the sky in the other, as if warding off an attack from above. He looked up in case something was howling in from the night sky, but his luck seemed to be holding. He ran across the level crossing on South Carriage Drive, through the left passage of the triple arch alongside Apsley House, and finally took a breath as he waited for the lights to change and allow him across the final road-width and on to the central island of Hyde Park Corner.

He could afford to allow himself this luxury, because right in front of him he could see the huge stone field-gun pointing to the sky, and two of the four bronze soldiers that stand, or in one case lie, on each side of the base. He couldn't see the Gunner's side, but he could see the soldier lying on a stretcher and the one facing into the centre of the grassy space, a bombardier, with two huge shell holsters hanging pendulously on the side of each leg.

The lights changed. And he ran. He felt the gravel spitting under his feet as he powered towards the huge memorial plinth. Then he was up on the surrounding dais, and ran round on to the Gunner's side, sure he was going to see Edie.

But there was no one there.

Where the Gunner usually stood was only a slab of bronze plinth and a blank wall of smooth-cut, weather-stained slabs, broken by the words RUSSIA – PALESTINE – CENTRAL ASIA.

George stopped dead, and bent over as if something had hit him. He braced himself with his hands on his knees. The truth was that now he had arrived and his run was over, he was finally letting his exhaustion catch up. He was disappointed too, no doubt, but he told himself it didn't matter. He'd find Edie later. Right now he had to stand on the Gunner's plinth. By the last clock he had past on Park Lane he had a good five minutes to spare.

As he looked down he saw the bronze helmet lying on the chest of the figure at his feet. The sculptor had made a body lying on its back, a coat thrown over his face. His booted legs stuck out from the covering, and the coat was thrown so casually that you could see a portion of the side of the face and a hint of hair, but not enough to get a good look. The boots were missing some of the hobnails, and showing signs of hard wear. He noticed that the laces in one boot had obviously snapped at the bottom, and had been quickly tied together in a rough and ready knot. Somehow this personal detail made the anonymity of the unknown soldier more poignant.

Having got enough oxygen back into his lungs, George looked at the Bombardier with the shell canisters on his legs.

'Excuse me,' he said, not knowing how else to begin a conversation with a statue that might not know that George could see him.

'Excuse me,' he repeated. 'I can see you. I know about spits and taints and everything. I'm a friend of the Gunner.'

The soldier didn't move a millimetre. George decided not to waste time. After all, he knew what he had to do.

'OK,' he said. 'I'm going to go on the other side and stand to for the Gunner. On his plinth. The Euston Mob told me about it.'

There was still no reaction, so he shrugged and hurried round to the Gunner's empty place. As he walked towards it he realized he was passing relief scenes of trench warfare carved into the white limestone of the memorial – men in shaggy sheepskin jerkins and tin hats wrestling weapons and shells and wounded bodies against a background of shattered trees and broken trenches. He saw a soldier struggling with a terrified team of horses, and then he was up on the Gunner's stand with the cold wall at his back. On the other side of the street a homeless man was pushing his belongings past in a tattered red-tartan wheeled shopping bag. His eyes weren't on the pavement in front of him. They were staring blankly across the traffic. They were black eyes with no hint of white.

The traffic was too loud for George to have heard him speak even if he had noticed him, which he didn't.

'One boy maker. Hyde Park Corner. On the War Memorial.'

George, oblivious to the eyes of the Tallyman across the road, wasn't sure what to do. Since it was nearly midnight, he leant back and spread his arms in the way he remembered first having seen the Gunner do. Something moved at his feet as he trod on it. He bent down and picked it up. It was a horse-whip. The Gunner had obviously left it here when he'd taken George under his wing and begun the first stage of the gauntlet George now suspected he had been running for ever.

He put down the hammer, picked up the whip and felt the solid heft of the thing in his hand. He noticed that once he took hold of it, the rigid bronze lash, casually wrapped round the haft, became flexible. It was as if the sculpted item was becoming real in his hand. He kept his feet on the plinth and shook out the lash. Somehow having something of the Gunner's in his hand made him feel more secure. He was going to be able to do this. How hard could it be? All he had to do was stand here until midnight was over, and then he'd have brought the Gunner another day.

'Hell do you think you're doing?'

The voice was tired and cultivated and mildly irritated, and it came from the left. George looked that way and saw the statue of the Officer from the other end of the monument standing there, looking at him as though his very presence was some kind of unforgivable insult. He wore a tin helmet and a pair of binoculars in a case high on his chest. Below that he held his hands together with a heavy greatcoat loosely folded over them.

'Er . . . I'm standing here . . .' he hesitantly replied.

There was a slight snapping noise as the Officer sucked his teeth in irritation. He had a small moustache neatly trimmed above his top lip, and it twitched as he looked at George.

'You're a boy,' he observed.

'I'm George.'

'Yes,' sighed the Officer, opening the lid on a wristwatch and then snapping it shut again. 'Yes, I'm afraid you are. You're the one got the Gunner-Driver gallivanting off his station in the first place. You know where I found him last night? Half melted by the Temple Bar bloody Dragon, face-down in a pond over there in St James' Park. Had half a mind to leave him there, but you know . . .'

He sucked and snapped his lips again.

'That's why I'm here!' said George. 'Exactly. He got taken by the Walker. He's not going to be here by turn o'day. So I'm going to take his place. Then we have another day to rescue him!'

'Poppycock!' exploded the Officer.

'It's not poppycock,' said George levelly. 'I'm going to do it.'

The Officer tipped the front of his tin helmet down and scratched the back of his neck in amazement.

'You're going to stand to, in his place?'

'Yes,' said George.

And as he said it he felt something shift and move on his arm. It was a ripping, burning sensation, as if his skin was splitting; and he doubled up, cradling the painful arm with his good one. The whip clattered to his feet.

The Officer lost his veneer of coldness as he dropped

his coat and darted over to George.

'What's wrong, boy?'

'My arm,' George gasped through clenched teeth.

The Officer checked his watch, sucked his teeth in worry and knelt by him.

'Quickly, boy. Show me.'

George held out his arm. The Officer took it with surprising gentleness and turned it over. Another tutting noise escaped his lips as he saw the scar of the Maker's Mark and the three lines spiralling down from it to where they disappeared into his cuff.

'Right. Jacket off. Look sharp.'

He helped George get his arm out of the double jacket he was wearing, and then rolled his shirt sleeve up to reveal the arm from shoulder to wrist.

'Not much of you under these layers,' he said under his breath, turning George's arm outwards in order to look at it better. A loud tut greeted the sight.

'Still, you're a plucky one, no doubt about that. You carry the mark of the Hard Way.'

George looked in horror at his arm. One of the flaws – the marble one – had suddenly lanced its way beyond his elbow and braided itself round his bicep so that the sharp, questing point of the fissure was now dangerously close to his armpit. The other two flaws were still twining below his elbow.

'That happened, the long one, just now?' asked the Officer.

George nodded, biting his lip, not trusting himself to speak steadily.

The Officer tapped the in-grooved vein. The sound of bronze tapping marble made George queasy. It was as if someone had reached inside him and tapped his bones. The Officer pulled his sleeve back down, hiding the arm. When he spoke he was all business, the veneer of mild irritation gone.

'Right. Cover up, jacket on, fast as you like. You're right, no question, you *definitely* have to stand now.'

George shrugged into the coats and fumbled with the buttons, happy not to be able to see his arm and the twining stone and metal veins that disfigured it.

'What . . .?' he asked.

'What what?' replied the Officer, eyes scanning the street in front of them.

'What changed your mind?' said George urgently.

The Officer looked into his eyes. Then he bent and picked up the whip and put it in George's hand.

'Because if you don't, that crack is going to continue up your arm and into your body and when it gets to your heart, I'm very sorry to say you'll be dead.'

He smiled encouragingly.

'*Nil desperandum*. It's not all gloomy. You take the

Gunner's place, like you said you would, stand to until stand down, and you should be right as rain.'

George understood what he was saying and suddenly discovered his mouth had gone dry.

'You mean this is one of the contests, one of the duels? But how does just standing here at midnight . . .'

Then he felt a sudden wash of relief.

'No, that's brilliant! I mean, that's great. Just stand here? That's easy – right?'

'Not *as such*. There's a little more to it than that, old son.'

He clapped George encouragingly on the shoulder and pushed him gently into place on the Gunner's plinth. George didn't like the smile on the Officer's face. It was the smile parents showed you as you were pushed inside the dentist's room to have something painful done to your teeth, only worse.

'What more?' he asked. 'Please, what exactly happens when you stand to?'

The Officer gestured to the tortured relief carvings ringing the monument.

'All that, I'm afraid. Carnage, slaughter, screaming fear, bloody waste of good men and horses. We stand to and relive it every night. It's who we are and it reminds us why we're here. It's the maker's purpose.'

He cleared his throat as if there was a great deal more

he would like to say about the maker and his purpose, but that good manners prevented him from doing so.

George found himself grasping at straws.

'But it can't be that bad – I mean, you know you're going to survive, right? I mean, you do it every night so . . .'

'Doesn't quite work like that, young 'un.' The Officer shook his head. 'Not like that at all. We don't relive it as statues. We relive it as the men we were made to represent. And while we're reliving it, it's real. We don't know that it happens every night. None of us do. Not even him, poor devil . . .'

He nodded at the dead soldier with the covered face at the end of the monument.

'Who is he?' said George.

'Depends who's asking,' he said, checking his watch. 'He's whoever people want him to be. He's the Unknown Soldier. That's why his face is covered, so the bereaved could come and imagine he was their lost loved one. Good idea, if you ask me. Jagger, the man who made us, knew a thing or two about loss. Mind you, he was a soldier too. Now, you're about to be one as well, if you're really going to do this?'

The way he made it a question offered George a way out.

'I'm doing it.'

He was doing it for a lot of reasons, but in the end they all boiled down into one simple one: he couldn't live with himself if he didn't. The Officer nodded.

'Good man. Be strong. Stiffen the sinews and all that . . .'

He gave George one final firm clap on the shoulder.

'Do it for yourself. Do it for the Gunner. Do it for whoever you like, but just do it. Don't step off the blasted plinth. You'll be tempted. And if you still believe in anything, pray to it.'

'Pray?' said George shakily, clenching the horse-whip. 'Why?'

The Officer checked his watch and moved back towards his own plinth, scooping up his coat as he went. He smoothed it over his arm and then looked at George before disappearing round the right angle in the stone.

'Because for the next hour, old son, you're going to be eye-deep in hell.'

38

HAPPY ENDING

'There are no happy endings,' said the Walker. 'But then I expect you already know that.'

Edie watched him place a scarf-wrapped bundle on the desk in the middle of the room and turn to smile balefully at her. All her muscles were tensed, ready to run or fight, but the fact that the door was now locked and the dogs were waiting outside severely limited the likelihood of success whichever of the two options she chose.

'Is that right?' she said, suppressing the tremor in her voice.

'It's a – in fact, *the* – fact of life,' he replied. 'Now please don't do anything sudden or stupid.'

He thunked the point of his dagger into the desk-top

and walked over to her. She stared at the jewelled handle and the long blade as it reflected the candle flame. She was remembering how he had been carrying it when she had glinted the scene on the frozen Thames, when she had seen him chasing the girl he had finally drowned in an ice-hole. The girl with her face. That had certainly not been a happy ending.

'That's good then,' she spat. 'That means no happy ending for you, either.'

She could feel his breath on her face as he leant in and laughed quietly, strapping her right hand to the chair-arm.

'Oh, there's an exception to every rule; and in my case, being cursed to walk for ever has the one advantage of also meaning I have no foreseeable end. So I'm sorry but I can't oblige you by fulfilling your kind wish.'

He took her left wrist and jerked the hand out of her pocket. She dropped the heart stone just in time as he quickly tied it to the arm of the chair with the efficiency of someone who'd done this many times.

All Edie had left was her feet.

'At this point,' he murmured, 'some of you decide that kicking me would be a heroic final gesture.'

He reached back without looking and pulled the dagger out of the desk-top. The blade flashed and he stabbed it into the arm of the chair.

'It's never particularly heroic, and I can always let the dogs back in. They're not nearly as understanding as I am.'

Edie relaxed her foot. Everything he said was a kind of threat. Even the gloating was a threat. Even the smile. It was all designed to make her scared. And suddenly she thought she knew why.

It was designed to stop her thinking. Fear can do that: make you freeze like a deer in the headlights of an oncoming car; it can dazzle you and take out your first line of defence, which is using your brain. So instead of coming up with a retort, she shut up and thought.

And as she thought she took an inventory of the room in the candlelight – the shelves, the stones on them, the desk, the leaded, unopenable windows, the piles of paper on the floor around the desk. And as she did so she forcibly shoved the fear to the back of her mind, in the same place she had earlier put the feeling that she was going mad when she had turned and found George had just vanished. She could always unpack the fear and the madness later. Right now she had to keep all her energy focused on there actually being a 'later' in the first place.

One thing mattered, and that was all she was going to focus on for now: she was going to do everything she could not to die in this dusty room.

The Walker was busying himself at his desk with the

bundle he'd brought from the British Museum.

'You want me to touch some of these stones,' she said, pointing with her chin at the shelves.

'You're a bright spark,' he said sarcastically, turning the wheeled chair so that it faced the desk.

'I'm a glint,' she replied. 'It's what we do, isn't it?'

'Indeed it is,' he smiled. He walked round to the opposite side of the desk and cleared a space amid the papers to make room to unwrap his bundle. Edie watched as he carefully laid out its contents. As he took the thick wax disks out they looked so like cheeses that she thought for an unsettling instant that he was unpacking a picnic, and then she saw the arcane magical symbols scratched all over them, and realized they were something else entirely.

'You'll forgive my good humour,' he said without looking up. 'But these are old friends, and I have waited a long time to retrieve them. And it is thanks to you and the boy that we have reason to be so happily reacquainted.'

He carefully placed the thin gold disk on top of the smaller of the circular wax tablets, taking great pains to align its design with the marks scratched on the surface. And then he placed the little crystal ball at the centre of it. Edie thought it must roll off, but there was an almost inaudible 'snik' as he let go, as if a magnet had been engaged, and it not only stayed in the dead centre of the arrangement, but rotated slowly as it did so.

The Walker exhaled in satisfaction, and turned his attention to the Black Mirror sandwiched between the two larger wax discs. He retrieved the gloves from his pockets and put them on. Then he lifted the top disk and placed it on the edge of the desk, close to Edie. And then he picked the mirror up from the other one, holding it gingerly by the handle, and placed it on top of the one that was centimetres from her bare hands.

She felt the black surface suck at her hand, so strongly that it began to move towards it without her thinking. And when she did think and tried to pull it back, it was with an effort that had her gritting her teeth at its intensity.

The Walker saw this and nodded.

'It's strong. Touch it.'

She shook her head, horrified at the way the shiny blackness was pulling at her hand.

The Walker came round the table and pushed her closer to the edge of the desk. The blackness dragged her hand across the rough wood towards it. She dug her fingernails in, but it did no good.

She had no idea what was in the stone, but its pull was far stronger than any other she'd ever glinted. She couldn't begin to imagine what kind of terror or pain she was about to experience when her hand completed its inexorable journey towards the mirrored surface, but she knew it would be worse than anything she had ever experienced.

With a final effort she threw her whole body-weight backwards, and her feet lashed out, sending a dusty pile of papers skittering over the floor. But it was no use. The Black Mirror suddenly seemed to exert a stronger pull in reaction, and her hand flipped back across the arm of the chair and slapped open-palmed across the centre of the mirror, splayed like a white starfish on a plate of ink.

The jolt of contact detonated through her body and out into the room – sending a silent shockwave through the layers of dust, blowing them into the air all round her. It blew out the candle too, and for an instant all was as black as the mirror. Then there was the scrape of a match and the Walker relit the candle and coughed at the airborne dust, and then Edie did too.

And as she did so she noticed an extraordinary thing.

She wasn't glinting.

Not as she had previously experienced glinting.

The past was not slicing into her in jagged shards of recorded pain.

Normally glinting tore at her and left no room for thought about itself until it was over. This was different and it didn't immediately hurt. She could still notice things – like it not hurting, for example.

The treacherous instant of surprise and relief lasted about as long as the match in the Walker's hand. And then she realized this was worse.

She wasn't feeling the past in the stone.

She was feeling nothing.

Absolutely nothing.

The stone was not a recorder of past pain. Whatever it had been used for, whatever it had witnessed had gone into it and out into a void beyond it, a void that Edie was touching. And touching that void was purely terrifying. It was as if Edie was touching the exact opposite of everything in the world around her, because everything around her was *something*; whereas everything at the end of her hand, sucking at her splayed fingers, was *nothing*.

It was such an alien feeling that given the choice between it and the foulest, most terrifying person that had ever lived, without a second's thought she'd have taken the side of the human monster and not what was touchable through the Mirror. The void stripped everything down to a very simple equation – human or inhuman.

What was at the end of her hand was a possibility of something so vastly, cosmically bad that she couldn't begin to get her head round it, and didn't want to.

'You feel it,' said the Walker.

'It's evil,' she whispered.

'It's just different,' he smiled. 'The world is full of people who brand what they are too stupid to understand with words like evil and unholy. It's a third thing, a way to power that only the cleverest and bravest can take. And it will set me free and let me rule . . .'

She gasped as something else edged into her consciousness.

'Can you feel them?' he asked.

And, horribly, she realized she could. The thing about an absence or a void is that it should, by its very nature, be empty. Edie was slowly becoming aware that all around the edges of this black hole at the end of her arm there were things like shadows in the dark, shifting and peering back at her over the rim of nothingness. She tried to see what they were, but every time she did so her mind and vision just slid off them as they ducked out of sight.

'Do you see the Presences?' he asked eagerly.

'No,' she gasped. 'But they're there . . .'

'Precisely,' he said exultantly. 'Don't worry. Not yet. They can't come here unless a gate is opened, and for that to happen we would need another Mirror to set up the reflections out of which they could step. I had the two Mirrors once, but a meddling fool stole one before

I had understood how to use them safely or work out how to contain the Presences within safe bounds on this side, once they emerged from the emptiness. He thought I was going to unleash the End of Days or some such nonsense.'

He scowled at the memory and pulled his dagger from the chair arm, looking at it before slipping it back in its scabbard on the back of his belt.

'I caught up with him and gutted him in a field outside the city but I have never found the twin Mirror again, and I have searched this metropolis from top to bottom ever since.'

He smiled suddenly. In many ways much worse than his scowl.

'And now I have a glint and an Ironhand at one and the same time, so I shall cut through the obstacle that has blocked me for three centuries and open the gates in the mirrors in one bold slash . . .'

And with that he jerked the gold disk out from under the crystal ball so quickly that it was left spinning furiously on the spot just above the wax surface of the protective tablet. In the same movement he sliced it under her hand, between it and the Black Mirror, and as it severed the connection between Edie and the void she felt a savage, blunt pain as if a limb had just been brutally chopped off, and then her hand was free and she jerked it off the gold disk with a sob.

She curled over the pain as her hand twitched on the chair arm like the jerking nerves of a dying fish.

'There,' he said. 'That wasn't too bad, was it?'

It had been *so* bad that touching the loathsome otherness in the Mirror left her feeling shocked to the core of her being. She had just touched something behind the scenes, something that humans were not designed to be conscious of, let alone contact. It hadn't been pain, but if her hand had been free she would have taken the dagger and killed him simply for making her touch it.

'It was worse,' she panted. 'It wasn't like glinting. It wasn't like touching a stone normally is.'

'Of course. And of course part of that is that the Mirror is not really stone. Scientists, these new magicians of your age, they say that it's not a stone at all. It's obsidian, which looks like a stone but is a kind of glass, a volcanic glass.'

'It's a glass. Like . . .'

'Like your precious heart stone, yes. Don't worry.' He smiled thinly. 'Keep it for the moment. You will need all your strength.'

He waved an arm at all the wrapped bundles of stone on the shelves.

'I will have you touch all of these pieces of black

stone. I have spent a lot of time collecting them, as you can see, in the hope that one day I would be lucky enough to find a Master Maker and a glint who can tell me which one of these rough items most closely matches the feel of the dark Mirror.'

It all came clear to her in one flash of understanding.

'You think George can make you a new Mirror?'

'I know he can.'

'He's not a stone mason, or anything. He's just a boy.'

'It's not a learnt skill. He will feel the shape of what is to be made in the obsidian you choose, and he will know how to bring it forth. It's not a skill. It's in his bloodline.'

She shook her head.

'No. He won't do it for you, even if he does have this skill you think he has. He just won't do it for you.'

'He will do it for you,' he said simply. 'He will do it to save you.'

And with a plummeting feeling inside her, she knew he was right.

He roughly freed her right arm and pointed to the shelves.

'I will unwrap these rocks. You will feel them. You will tell me which one feels most like the obsidian Mirror. You will glint for me . . .'

He looked at her. She was forcing the fear back and trying to think straight again.

'OK,' she said. It would buy her time. And now she had one hand free, even if the other was tightly tied to the heavy chair.

'I have freed your hand so you can reach all three levels of shelf. Do anything other than as I tell you and I will have the Blind Woman set the dogs on you. Understood?'

She heard the hungry snuffling of the two mastiffs under the door and nodded as if beaten. He started along the shelf away from her, unwrapping package after package, revealing black stones of every shape and size.

'Some of these are obsidian, some are flint. I did not know the difference when I began my collection. Don't worry about the flints. Just touch the black glass,' he said as he moved away.

It was the word 'flint' that made her know what she was going to have to do. She pulled against the strap pinning her to the chopping-board arms of the seat. The strap was only about a centimetre wide, but there was no question of breaking it. She would have to bide her time until it was time to move. It was all going to depend on him being in the right place.

'Go on then,' he said.

She took a breath and touched the nearest slab of rock. It was about the same size as a roughly-hewn telephone directory.

She jerked slightly as the memory in it flowed into her.

A weeping red-haired woman in a green coat sat in the chair Edie was sitting in.

She clutched a blazing heart stone that was pinned to her lapel as a brooch.

She had big hair, like an astronaut's wife in a 60s newsreel.

Her thick mascara was running.

She screamed as the Walker reached in and tore the heart stone out of her hand.

Edie convulsed as she felt the irreparable wave of anguish rip into the older woman as it was taken.

She heard the Walker say:

'Try another one, and you shall have your dainty back . . .'

And then the vision of the past was over, and it was herself who was strapped to the chair. She tried to understand what she had just seen.

'You have had other glints testing these rocks.'

He nodded.

'Ignore the memories of them. Their pain is . . . a minor distraction. Find me the rock with the possibility of a gate in it. Try them all.'

He tapped the dagger handle. 'Try and thwart me by choosing the wrong one, and I will open the boy in front of your eyes and you can watch his life puddle away through the cracks in these very floorboards.'

'But why do you need me if you've already had others test the stones?' she asked, in a final attempt to stave off the inevitable.

'Because the nature of the void in the Mirror changes in time. It's as if whatever is beyond the gate in the Mirror moves. As if it has been floating loose since it was separated from the second Mirror. Two of them together seemed to hold each other steady. The uncut stone that felt a match for the Mirror ten years ago won't be right now. That's why having a glint and a Master Maker on hand at the same time is so very fortuitous.'

And so she nodded, slowly turned and felt the next stone. And the one after.

And so began the longest hour of her life. Most of them held at least one anguish-soaked memory of an earlier glint, sometimes more than one. And she lost track of the pain and the faces in a mounting accretion of despair as she dragged her wheeled chair after her, trying stone after stone. The pain never made her numb. It just went on and on, wearing different faces that all blurred together. She began to feel she couldn't breathe, like she was drowning in a never-ending sea of tears.

Eventually she became so punch-drunk that she just assumed this was now going to go on for ever. Only the closeness of the heart stone in her pocket kept her going, because in her mind it was where she'd hidden her last hope, her one desperate plan for escape, a plan that could only happen when everyone was in the right place. And it was so unending, this onslaught of other women and girls' despair that when she came to the empty stone, she wept with relief.

He didn't have to ask her if it was the one. He just looked up from where he'd been bent over the desk, looking at the loose papers in the candlelight, and smiled.

'Good.'

Edie leant against the shelf as he reached past her and took the slab over to the table. As soon as he walked away her hand closed on the slab of obsidian next to the place where the empty one had been. She checked that he was still moving away. And when he was at the desk, carefully putting the empty stone on the surface next to the dark Mirror she took a fast deep breath and closed her eyes.

She lifted the heavy slab and smashed it down on the one on the shelf beneath it.

She heard a sharp cracking noise and felt chips of rock fly past her face.

Something stung her ear, but she ignored it and opened her eyes.

Sure enough, the obsidian had shattered, leaving fine shards all over the shelf.

'What are you doing?' the Walker shouted, and the noise started the dogs on the other side of the door barking furiously. Edie didn't spare a millisecond to see if he was going to get to her before she did what she had to do. If he was going to get to her before she did it she'd know soon enough. Her free hand darted into the stone debris and grabbed a long thin shard like a straight razor. It was the wrong way round, but she spun it in her hand in midair so the blade-edge faced out as she slashed it at her trapped wrist.

The obsidian blade, sharper than the sharpest scalpel, its edge a single molecule thick, seemed to whistle as it cut through the air and hit the taut strap, severing it almost as if it wasn't there at all.

Without pausing she kept the momentum of her slash going and rolled out of the chair, spinning to her feet and whirling the heavy wooden seat on its wheels so that it was between her and the incoming Walker.

He was diving forward and hit the solid lumber hard, knocking it off its wheels as he tangled in it and fell. Edie jumped out of the way as he and the chair crashed to the floor.

The candle on the table fell over with the impact, but it didn't go out. It rolled in amongst some of the loose sheets of paper that Edie had disturbed.

He managed to get one hand out and grab the edge of

her jacket. His normally sneering face was crimson with rage and pain.

'You will pay, you little hellcat!' he shouted in a voice like a thunderclap, dragging her towards him.

'You too,' said Edie calmly. 'And don't call me *little*.'

And with all the power and cold fury in her body she slashed the obsidian razor across his face.

She didn't wait to see why he screamed so loudly as his hands released her and flew to his eyes, she just vaulted over his hunched body, ran across the room, grabbed another big lump of stone from the nearest shelf, so heavy that she could hardly lift it, and with the last of her strength hurled it through the leaded diamonds of the window. The snow billowed into the room on a gust of breeze as she jumped out into the night without a second's hesitation.

The only thought she had time for as she fell through the air was that for all she knew she was going to break her neck, but anything was better than what was in that room, the void pulling at her from behind the Black Mirror.

39

CHIMES AT MIDNIGHT

George clenched the horse-whip in his hand and braced his back against the Portland Stone stacked massively behind him. He had a thousand questions that he wanted to ask the Officer, but before he could think which one to call out, he heard the sound of a deep familiar bell tolling, reverberating high in the night air.

It was the sound of Big Ben, marking the turn of the day from its position a hundred metres above the city. And though he was used to hearing the old bell on the radio, marking the hours before news broadcasts, now George heard it directly through the night air it felt like he was really hearing it for the first time.

He heard the warning carillion ring one, two, three, four times and then, after a pregnant pause, he heard the majestic lonely bongs of the great bell counting out the hours. And as he listened to them he thought of something his dad used to say when they'd returned home after an adventure or a treat of some kind. He'd look rueful and tousle George's hair and, no matter what time of day it actually was, say, 'Well we did that, didn't we? We heard the chimes at midnight.'

And then the memory faded as he became aware of something more present and increasingly insistent.

With each 'bong' he felt himself changing. And not only himself, but his surroundings. As the darkened city paled into a harsh winter light, he felt his body stiffen and become more ponderous. He wondered fleetingly if he was turning into a statue. His feet felt massy and increasingly clumsy, and his clothes seemed to become heavier. And then not only heavier, but less comfortable. They scratched and itched at him, and then he forgot his clothes and the heaviness growing on him as he focused on what was happening to the four-storey white stucco building opposite. With each sound of the bell it was fading, and in its place was a clear sky seen through a lattice of black and white silver birch trees. There were no leaves on the slender trunks and branches and he felt a chill breeze cut through him, and as he instinctively reached to fasten the plastic buttons on his reefer jacket his hands met stiff tarpaulin canvas and metal buttons and then leather straps, and he looked down in time to see the dark bronze rectangle of the plinth fade away and leave his boots standing on a muddy crisscross of wheel tracks, punctuated by hoof-marks.

Except they weren't his boots. They were the Gunner's boots, the Gunner's leather leg protector on one side and the tight twine of puttees on the other leg, although they weren't exactly the Gunner's, because the Gunner's had been bronze and these were real – leather boots, canvas puttees, woollen army britches, canvas and leather bags and holsters hanging off him, as real as the stiff crackle of the thick canvas groundsheet he was wearing as a cape. He looked down at his hands and saw they were flesh and blood, but not his hands: they were man's hands, perhaps the hands that his hands were going to be one day, but weren't yet – strong wide hands, grubby and calloused with work.

Somewhere at the back of his mind the sense that he was a boy of nearly thirteen standing on a traffic island in London was fading away like the vision of the bronze plinth at his feet, but before it retreated to a point where he couldn't connect with it any more, he was able to notice other changes as they happened.

His fingers rose to his face, and even without a mirror he could tell it wasn't George he was feeling: the chin was covered in a strange rough bristle, the nose was longer, and all the planes of the face were wider, flatter and wrong, the skin that covered them somehow felt thicker and more rubbery as he kneaded it against the bones of his skull. In fact his whole body just felt denser and blunter. It was as if his centre of gravity had moved lower, and as if the pull of that gravity had doubled. He no longer felt light on his feet, and it wasn't tiredness that made him feel that – it was a reconfiguration of his muscles and a thickening of his bones. He felt bulkier and stronger but he also felt, in a way that was as tinged with sadness as it was full of wonder, that he'd lost something irretrievable in this growth. Like something that you don't notice until it's gone, he was missing the green ease and lightness in his body. It didn't feel like a body that could just have run full tilt and without much thought all the way from St Pancras to Hyde Park any more, for example. His body had just fast-forwarded fifteen years. It felt blockier and more earthbound. It wasn't that he had become fat, it was that he had become strong, like the flexible tree sapling that grows into a solid trunk that can't bend as easily but carries more weight.

What he felt was simple age, and the inescapable weight of growing up.

He was also feeling an insistent itching, and he

realized he was scratching at those itches without thinking about it. He looked up at the bright winter sky through the birch branches and wondered at the brightness. He heard the wonder in a deep voice saying:

'I thought it would be midnight.'

And he realized that the voice had come out of his mouth. And as he heard it all the sounds of this new world dialled up around him and he heard a distant cracking and popping, and behind that an even fainter whine like an engine and then, much closer to he heard the rattle of harness and wheels and men moving and metal sliding against metal and the sound of someone coughing his guts up close by, and then he heard the Officer's voice right beside him saying:

'Thought what would be midnight, Gunner?'

And he looked down from the delicate fretwork of birch branches against the pale winter sky and saw the world he had fallen into and realized that he was, as advertised, eye-deep in hell.

A horse's body hung upside down from a tree, frozen and unmoving on the sharp stump it had been blown on to, its legs pointing skywards in an obscene imitation of the branches it had replaced. The other trees around it looked as if they had been hacked and slashed at by some wayward giant, their randomly splintered and shattered trunks jagging up out of the plashed earth at crazy angles.

Below it the earth itself was torn up in senseless ridges and random shell holes, strewn with barbed wire and the smashed detritus of war.

The Officer was standing in front of him, still carrying his greatcoat, and he too was now flesh and blood, no longer a statue.

'Nothing, sir. Sorry, sir – daydreaming.'

The words came out of his mouth as if he was partly on autopilot. It certainly hadn't occurred to him to call this man 'sir' on a conscious level.

'Well, snap to and get those nags into some kind of cover before that spotter plane gees Fritz into lobbing a wake-up call our way.'

He looked at the horizon, and George saw a tiny twin-winged plane moving slowly against the light, like a paper cut-out. He realized that was the source of the distant whine.

'Sir,' he heard himself say, and he saw his hand rise to the overhang of his tin helmet in a sketchy salute. Again he hadn't thought of doing it, but the conscious part of him seemed like a passenger without control of the body he was in. He didn't feel detached from it, just not wholly at one with what it did. It was the same feeling when he reached back over his shoulder and found himself patting the muzzle of a horse that the part of him that was George hadn't known was there.

'Come on, then,' he heard himself say. 'Let's find a better 'ole.'

He turned and gathered two leading reins in his hand. A pair of chestnut coloured horses stood there, and behind him he could see a pair of field guns being set up for action by teams of gunners working fast to manhandle them into position just behind the lip of a shallow ridge. Some wore greatcoats and mufflers, others wore shaggy sheepskin jerkins, but all wore tin helmets and looks of fierce determination as if they were working against the clock.

George could feel his heart thudding with adrenaline. He realized there was a huge sense of apprehension churning in his gut, as if something very very bad was about to happen. He could see from the tight faces around him that everyone else felt the same. It was as if someone was playing a single unending high note on a violin string, a note so high that you almost couldn't hear it, but just audible enough for it to be painful in its persistence, in the way it underpinned everything. His mouth was dry and he felt he would murder someone for a cup of tea. Which was strange, because George – normal George – didn't much like tea at all.

Two artillery spotters were receiving orders from the Officer. One carried a trench periscope strapped to his back. They nodded and set off over the lip of the ridge, keeping low. They held a spool of telephone cable on a bobbin between them that unspooled as they ran. Then one stumbled and fell and lay still. The other man kept hold of the bobbin and carried on running until he disappeared over the ridge.

The Officer swore and trained his binoculars on the fallen man.

George felt the horses pull against the reins and found himself jogging away from the guns, leading them towards a dip in the landscape that had two walls of a ruined farmhouse at the bottom of it. He ducked them under a low arch and wasn't surprised to find two more horses already hobbled and waiting, faces obscured by nosebags, contentedly chomping away at the contents. Except for the lack of a roof the protective walls of the ruin made good cover. High above them George heard the distant engine whine getting louder.

There was another soldier crouched by a wall, trying to get a fire going under a large, blackened tea-kettle. His helmet lay on the ground beside him, and he was wearing one of the shaggy sheepskin jerkins.

'Char'll be up in half a mo'. Tell them to keep their hair on,' he said.

George found he was hobbling his horses as if he'd been doing it all his life, but the watching part of himself in the back of his mind was looking at the shoulders and hair of the soldier hunkered down in front of the small fire. He had a cigarette parked in the side of his face, and George could hear the pop and suck of him smoking without using his hands as he squatted before the meagre blaze, looking at something held in front of him.

Maybe because he was trying not to think too hard about why the man carrying one end of the bobbin of telephone wire had not got up when he had stumbled and fallen, George concentrated on the back of the man's head.

He had dark hair, the same colour as George's, cropped short on the back and sides. When he swept his hand back through the unruly longer hair on top, George felt something tug at him in the pit of his stomach at the familiarity of the gesture. He suddenly and fiercely wanted this moment to freeze. He didn't want whatever was going to happen next to happen, because whatever was actually going to happen wasn't going to be the thing that tug had so treacherously hinted at, because that was impossible.

Then the man picked the ragged stub of his cigarette out of the side of his mouth and spun it into the fire and stood up, stretched and turned.

And George's heart stopped.

Any heart would stop if it saw the impossible happen.

Any body would forget to breathe.

Any throat would choke up so tight that there was only room for one small word to escape.

A word as small as:

'Dad?'

And the eyes that he knew so well, the eyes he'd known he'd never see again crinkled at him, and one brow rose higher than the other in an expression he not only remembered, but had himself practised to death in front of the bathroom mirror in the weeks after the funeral so he would not ever forget. And the doors of his heart burst open and he felt light again and he started to run towards him.

'Who you calling dad, mate?' The soldier laughed. 'I reckon I'm younger than you . . .'

And George stopped dead as he realized that though the eyes were smiling good-naturedly, there wasn't a hint of answering recognition in them.

And then the ground skipped beneath his boots as the first bomb hit.

40

THE GUNNER'S
LAST LAUGH

The Gunner was up to his neck in the water filling the hole he had dug in the gravel spit. And now he had moved the skeleton of the girl from where it had been blocking the outflow at the base of the water tank, he was definitely feeling a small current moving past his ankles.

He held his breath and submerged himself. Sure enough, water was moving through a low arch that came up to just below his knees. He closed his hands on the flaking bars that blocked it. They moved. He stood up and hacked at them with his boots. He kicked and kicked at the ancient metalwork. As he did so he thought of the Walker's sneering face and imagined his boot was pounding into the centre of it. It allowed him to rise above the exhaustion that was sucking at him just long enough to make a space he could possibly crawl through. He reached down again and confirmed that this was so.

Then he scrambled carefully to the top of his hole and pulled the bundle of heart stones wrapped in his cape into his hand. He took out his matchbox and lit a final match. The skeleton of the young girl gleamed whitely back at him. He had arranged the scraps of dress over her as decently as he could, and he had covered her face. He looked at the long hair and thought of Edie. He remembered how pale and shaky she had been when she was separated from her heart stone, how the life seemed to drain from her and be replaced by an enormous, all-pervasive fear. And then the match guttered out and he thought how scared Edie would be if she was left in a dark place like this without even her warning stone for comfort.

And so he paused for a moment to reach into the scrabble of sea-glass in the bundle and pick one at random, and then he felt for the skeleton and found a shred of dress by touch alone. He tore it off and wrapped the heart stone tightly inside it, so no light would blaze out of it if the Walker was to appear. He wrapped it in several layers, because the main point of all the digging he'd done was to make sure that if the Walker used his mirrors to come back here, the absence of warning lights might make it impossible for him to ever get out again by using the mirrors. The Gunner reckoned if he couldn't see into them, he might just be stuck here for ever.

He reached into the skeleton and placed the tight parcel of cloth where he thought her small heart would once have beaten.

'Sleep easy, little 'un,' he said. 'He can't hurt you no more.'

And then he grasped the bundle and dropped back into the hole with a splash. Even though he knew he could move underwater without needing to breathe, he didn't actually feel that he could. He knew this was because there was a gap between what he was – a bronze statue – and what he had been made to represent – a man. The man side that had been instilled by the maker would go through all the agonies of drowning, even though he – as a statue – wouldn't die. Although since he was sure it was nearly midnight, that was going to be something of a technicality, because he was about to die as a statue for entirely different reasons.

He was going to do it anyway, he decided, since the point was to get the heart stones that the Walker so clearly valued out of his clutches for ever.

'He who laughs last, mate,' he said into the darkness. 'He who laughs bloody last . . .'

And then he grasped his helmet in one hand, the

bundle of heart stones in the other, and took a deep breath, and ducked below the surge and pushed himself into the narrow water duct.

He kept his eyes open but he might as well have closed them. The jagged shards of bar he had kicked out from the crumbling stonework rasped against the gravel in the pipe, and then as he pushed himself deeper into the passage, the gravel-spill thinned out and he was crawling over a water-smoothed layer of slime on top of something that gave as he moved on it.

As he pushed forward he felt the acid burn of oxygen starvation scorching up from his lungs and tightening across his throat and gullet. His eyes bulged and his mouth began to strain against itself, the automatic reflex to breathe fighting the willpower he was using not to do so.

His teeth ground together as he fought the reflex and he pushed blindly on. He knew in the part of his brain that was not occupied by horror at the searing lack of oxygen that he was crawling away to die. The fact that he was hiding the Walker's precious stash of glass gave the otherwise futile gesture a point, and he held on to that point as his willpower finally gave in to the inevitable and he reflexively opened his mouth and breathed in the water.

And as he did so he squirmed round and made his screaming body face the unseen sky above the ground, so that he would not die face down, but looking upwards. After all, since this was the last choice he was going to make, he wanted to look towards a place where maybe happier endings than the lonely death that would come for him at midnight were possible.

41

THE BROKEN LACE

The ground jumped as the bomb hit. George was knocked on to one knee, and then the horses were pulling and bucking at their restraints and the soldier with his dad's face was running across the ruined space swearing as he looked up into the sky. He grabbed the Lewis gun set up on a stand against the low wall and squinted through its sights as he knelt beneath it and aimed it almost completely vertically.

As he opened fire George found he was grabbing the horses' bridles and pulling their heads together and automatically stroking and shushing them. His calming noises were drowned in the chuntering rip of heavy-calibre gunfire as the Lewis gun rattled through the bullets held in the circular drum mounted on top of it.

George looked up and saw a yellow and black biplane turning overhead, so low that he could clearly see the goggled face of the spotter sitting behind the pilot as he leant out and dropped a bomb by hand.

He had a sickening sense of the world going slow as the tiny bomb seemed to fall straight towards him; but slow as it felt, he didn't seem to have time to run. Or maybe it was something else, maybe it was the impulse in the body that was not his, the Gunner's instinct driving his movements: whatever it was he found that instead he was turning his back to the blast and protecting the horses' heads with his outstretched arms.

The second bomb fell somewhere beyond the walls of the ruin, and though something smacked into the other side of the wall and made the dust bounce out of the cracks between the bricks, George and the horses were unhurt. The Lewis gun was suddenly silent. George looked over and saw with relief that the soldier was still in one piece, just trying to snap on a new drum of ammunition.

'Bloody spotter plane,' he swore. 'We'll be in for a pasting now.'

He stared after the aircraft that was already a diminishing shape heading for the horizon and shook his head, sick at himself for missing.

'I don't know why they let me waste rounds with this

thing. Couldn't hit a bloody barn if they locked me inside and made me let rip with a full drum of ammo.'

He locked off the weapon and turned to George with a rueful smile. George realized he had been right. He was impossibly younger than he was. It was his father's face, but it was the face from the photographs from before George could really remember, from before he was born and when he was a baby.

The soldier saw something on the ground between them and bent to pick it up from where he had dropped it on his run to the Lewis gun. It was a thin, pocket-sized book with a scuffed red-leather binding from which several black and white photographs had strewn themselves across the floor. George picked up the ones nearest him before the restless horses could mash a hoof on them. One picture showed a bright eyed girl in a wide hat smiling coyly out of the frame, showing a lot of teeth and neck and shoulders in front of a potted aspidistra plant. And the other picture showed the same girl sitting on a chaise longue in front of a painted back-drop of trellised roses, holding a tightly wrapped bundle on her knees, and rather awkwardly tilting it forward so that the camera could catch the bug-eyed outrage of the small baby being shown to the world.

'You see the horse in the tree?' asked the soldier.

George nodded, not trusting himself to speak.

'Bloody shame, that. I mean, I've seen some things out here, but animals? I don't know. This isn't their fight, is it?'

George shook his head, and then realized that the soldier was holding his hands out for the photographs he had retrieved.

'Sorry,' he grunted and held them out. The soldier took them and looked at them. He grinned ruefully.

'The wife.'

'Very pretty.' George swallowed.

The other man beamed proudly.

'She should be. She's on the stage.'

'Right.'

George was somehow limiting himself to short words for fear that he might betray himself if he allowed himself anything as complicated as an actual sentence.

'She's a sing-a-bit, dance-a-bit girl really. She's different, you know.'

The face that was impossibly his dad's face crinkled in thought for a moment, and George saw something raw and vulnerable in it that he wasn't used to seeing.

'I mean, I got pals think she's a bit flighty, but they don't know her. She just . . . likes attention. No harm in that.'

George realized that he was asking for reassurance, and he felt embarrassed at the vulnerability being shown in the very face that he had been used to going to for comfort.

'No.' He shrugged, out of his depth. The other man looked at the picture with the baby. He coasted his thumb over the grimacing little face. He looked up into the sky.

'Maybe the nipper'll be enough. Maybe slow her down a bit.'

'Maybe not.'

The words came out of George's mouth before he could stop them. They sounded flat and rank and bitter.

'Yeah well. If not, it doesn't matter. We'll have something good to show for it, eh?'

He waved the picture of the baby, and then slid the pictures back between the printed pages of his book.

George nodded. His dad's eye found his.

'You got nippers, chum?'

The question took George by surprise.

'Course not . . .'

'Takes you funny it does. By surprise. It's like this.' He waved the small much-thumbed novel over his shoulder before pocketing it as he went back to crouch over the kettle that was now coming steamily to the boil. He carried on speaking without looking round. 'It's like a book isn't it – one minute you're the hero of your own story, and then your girl produces this little atom and, even though he's ever so tiny, everything moves a bit and you see you got it all wrong, you ain't the hero of the story at all. And what you took for the centre of your own stage isn't the centre of any stage, it's just a space on the edge of a much bigger place that was there all the time only you didn't see it . . .'

His voice tailed off in wonderment, and for a while all that George heard was him tinkering with tin cups and the kettle and billy-cans, and then he turned with a face that was brightly smiling and so obviously trying not to be scared that it hurt George to look at it.

'But it's all right, it's good. It makes all this easier. I mean it makes it lots worse too, worrying and all, but you know even if some bloody whizz-bang's got your number on it, at least you had a speck of a hand in something that carries on, right?'

He held out a steaming tin cup to George. George took it and nodded. He took a swig and gasped as the liquid burned his mouth. The other soldier seemed not to notice as he continued earnestly.

'I mean I ain't ever seen the little mite, not to hold, but if I was to stop one and never get back to Blighty, she'd tell him all about me, right? I mean he'd know that I . . . you know, how much I . . .?'

A giant sledgehammer slammed into the earth with an impact that knocked them off their feet, and the shockwave made George's ears go momentarily deaf to anything except the sudden panicked pounding of the blood in his head.

His hands scrabbled down his body, and he was appalled to find wetness all over it. He waited for the pain of the gushing wound to hit him, but all that happened was his hearing slowly returned and he saw his father's face looming over him as it fumbled on a tin helmet.

'Waste of good tea, chum.' He smiled and reached a hand down. George let himself be pulled back to his feet and looked down to discover no red pumping horror disfiguring his torso and legs, just the dripping contents of his tin mug.

Another slamming impact hit the ground, this time farther away on the other side of the ruin. The soldier grimaced. It was such a heartbreakingly familiar expression that George couldn't help believing that this was his father in front of him. It was deeper than thought, it was flesh calling to flesh and recognizing itself.

'Ranging shots. Fritz has got us bloody bracketed. This is going to get hotter before it gets better.'

Astonishingly, now that they were in action George saw that all the doubt and vulnerability had gone from his father's eyes. He looked solid again, more like the dad George remembered. And then his body took over and he was being a soldier, not a boy caught in a good dream about to go bad, and he was busy comforting his horses as a new series of explosions began.

'That's our mob hitting back. We'll have to see if we can't hit them before they plaster us!' his father shouted, ducking as something whirred past his head. 'Call them artillery duels – duel, as in the way posh gents used to resolve arguments. But I'll tell you what, there's nothing gentlemanly about them, it's kill or be killed and devil take the hindmost or the one whose gun-layer can't cut the mustard.'

BOOM. A shell clipped some of the remaining thatch off the top of the wall and left them ducking reflexively under a hail of dry rushes and plaster dust.

'And a happy Christmas to you too, Fritz.' His father grinned, a fierce light in his eyes.

The horses were bucking and pulling at their hobbles in terror and then there was a sharp crack and a whump as something hit nearby, and something flew past George's head, and something else glanced off the leather protector on his leg, kicking him hard. He had to hold on to one of the horse's tack to keep his feet, and then the horse was neighing and shaking and trying to wrench itself free, and when George looked down he saw something smoking sticking out of its leg.

And the sight of the blood and the rising thunder of the barrage and nearness of the miss jolted him and somewhere at the back of his mind he remembered that he could end all this by just stepping off a plinth in a city far, far away. It was a strong temptation, an instant ticket home.

He felt the shocked quivering of the horse's nose, soft as down beneath his hand. He didn't think as he dropped into a crouch, fumbling at one of the bags hanging off his belt for a field dressing.

'Here, give me a hand!' he heard himself yell. 'Grab his head!'

And the soldier with his dad's face grasped the horse's head and started trying to calm it, and George saw himself reach down and grab the red-hot shard of metal protruding from the horse without a second's hesitation, and he felt the shock of his fingers burning as he gripped on to it and yanked it out of the shaking leg muscle, and as the redness gushed from the wound he jammed the thick pad of field dressing over it and pushed down hard to stop the bleeding. With his other hand he shook free the bandage and looped it round the leg, cinching the free end snug against itself as he did so.

And then he ignored the fact that the ground was bucking and heaving around himself and wound the bandage tight over the dressing pad, passing the roll to himself on either side of the leg until he ran out. As his hands worked he noticed how very white the bandage was, and how well it looked against the deep chestnut of the leg. He also inhaled the clean healthy smell of the wood smoke from the fire. He'd never smelt anything so good before. Then he leant down and tore the end of the bandage against his teeth, and twisted the double end he'd made back on itself and tied it off securely.

The horse's leg was shaking, but he was pleased to see the blood wasn't yet leeching through the gauze.

'Good job,' said the soldier. George saw him smiling grimly down at him from where he was holding on to the bit below the horse's widely dilated nostrils.

He stood up and put his arm round the horse's neck, stroking and calming it.

And suddenly there was a hole in the thunder and they stood there on either side of the horse's neck, still and waiting. And George saw the horse's eye with extraordinary clarity, and thought he'd never seen such a deep and beautiful brown. And then his eye was distracted by something red, and his focus shifted to a ladybird calmly walking up the leather of the bridle towards his father's hand resting between the horse's ears, and beyond the ears he saw the sky, and he realized that it was not a pale white sky as he'd first thought, but a delicate blue that had an exquisite green tinge to it. It was as if the moment of silence and the fact that death could come smashing in from that sky at any moment was making him see everything more intensely.

He suddenly knew, in a kind of extension of this heightened awareness, that this was an extraordinarily precious moment, and that he had to take advantage of it before it was eviscerated by the next salvo of shells. He had something to say to this soldier who was and was not his father, more than a once in a lifetime opportunity, a never-in-a-lifetime chance that he mustn't squander.

He turned to look into his father's eyes, his mouth opening to say it, but the horse's neck obscured his father's face and all he could see was the untidy tuft curling up and off the front of his head, and as he moved to make eye-contact there was another explosion, not too close, but enough to make them both duck their heads. And then the shells began dropping all round them and the day split open and hell blasted out in a thunderous series of hammer blows that slammed into the ground and seemed to suck the air out of their lungs as they clung on to the horses' neck and kept their heads down as flying shrapnel and earth and stones blew past them.

And this time there was no more silence, just incessant noise and a relentless pounding that made the hard earth beneath their feet buck and roll like a ship's deck in high seas.

George never saw much of the barrage they were stuck in the middle of. Every time there was an explosion his head was ducked down, and when he opened his eyes all there was to see was the air full of dirt flying around. All he could do was bury his face in the horses' necks, both hands rhythmically stroking the two animals as he heard his voice saying:

'Easy now, easy now.'

The bombardment was shaking more than the foundations of the earth on which he was standing. It was shaking his grasp on everything. Every time he heard an explosion he flinched and he knew the next one would be the one that blew him apart, and when it wasn't the anticipation of the following one made him wish it had been.

Some distant memory of a plinth and the fact it would just take one step to free him from this hell again tried to make itself heard in the back of his mind as the endlessness of the horror took his legs out from under him, but he closed his ears to it.

He realized that it was only the other soldier's arm gripping his over the top of the injured horse's neck that was keeping him upright. He tried to brace his boots and set his legs, but it was like trying to stack jelly. He gritted his teeth, and then he heard his father's voice saying:

'Good boy, good boy, you're going to be fine.'

And even though the soldier was saying it to calm the horse, he was also gripping George's arm as he did so, and George's heart opened again, despite the cacophony of the world coming to an end all around him, and he found the iron in his soul and made his shaking legs do their job, and as he looked down and saw them braced and supporting him, he noticed the thing, the last bad thing just before it happened.

His father's boots were like his.

The only difference was that he had broken a lace and had hurriedly mended it by knotting it at the toe end.

George knew what was going to happen even as his hand clenched on his father's sleeve and he started shouting—

'No! Dad! Listen, please, I didn't . . .'

The soldier's head jerked up and met his eyes across the horse's neck. He was smiling.

'It's OK—'

The wall came in as if another giant had just booted it down. The horses kicked sideways and they both flinched and then George found the hand that had been gripping his over the injured horse's neck go limp, and suddenly it was his turn to be supporting the whole weight of the man on the other side. Then both horses tumbled over as a gout of flame rolled over them.

George never let go of the arm, even though they were suddenly enveloped in a cloud of dust and smoke that it was impossible to see through. He felt the horses' hooves lashing about in panic and heard their screaming neighs, and with his free hand he found the hobbles and released them and then the horses were gone and he pulled his father's limp heavy body on to his shoulders and staggered out of the burning debris into the open.

He shouted for help, but none came and so he staggered forward, up the hill, the weight on his back heavier with each step, and he heard himself sobbing and then the wind whipped away the smoke and the barrage stopped and he saw the hill ahead of him and he dropped to one knee at the horror it revealed.

The two guns were destroyed. One was pointing crazily to the sky, the other was just not there. In its place was a crater with the gun team neatly splayed around the rim like petals on a flower. There were bodies blown into the barbed wire, some of which were not moving. Something was trying to crawl out of a shell hole. The impaled horse was gone, as were most of the birch trees.

His scream for help turned into a question, and he heard the word 'Why?' convulse repeatedly out of his throat. And all the time he clutched his father's dead arm tighter and tighter as he felt the weight of the body buckle his legs and start to drive him into the ground.

And then something clattered to his feet and he saw it was a stretcher, and he looked up and saw the Officer and the Bombardier looking at him with infinite sadness in their eyes, and heard the Officer say:

'Put him down, Gunner.'

He shook his head and tried to straighten his legs, despite the crushing downward force on his shoulders.

'Can't carry him for ever. Put him down.'

Again George shook his head and clenched on to the arm all the more tightly.

He heard himself say:

'It's my dad.'

And one of his hands twined fingers into the dead hand's fingers and he held on for all he was worth, but there was no answering flicker of life. Then the hand seemed to grow bigger in his and his fingers slipped out of it and he heard the fast percussive wah-wah of a police car roaring past, the rumble of London's traffic dialled back up as the sky dimmed. His knees gave way and he fell off the bronze plinth at his feet and felt himself caught in two bronze arms. He hung there, looking down at the Officer's boots and then the light continued dimming down to black and he let it close over his head like the sea.

42

GUNNER'S END

The Gunner lay in the dark water waiting for death. The human part of him was numb with the constrictive horror of drowning, the pounding claustrophobia of the pipe, the terrible impossibility of taking a last breath and the choking wrongness of it all.

The statue part of him knew that turn o'day was upon him, and that his death as a spit was coming. He had spent his whole existence marking midnight and standing to, and as with any habit the rhythm and timing of it was hard-wired into his body clock.

He would cease to walk, or talk, and just become an inanimate lump of metal. Somehow dawn would see him winnowed to the elements and reconstituted on his plinth, never to move again. He had often wondered if the spits who had died were dead inside, or merely unable to move or express themselves. He hoped they were dead. Otherwise it would be like being buried alive for ever, with a tiny window to view the passing world by, but no way to communicate with it other than an unending scream that only sounded inside your own head.

Death, he hoped, would be just nothing. A big blank, a full stop, a balance where the absence of life and hope was counterweighed by the absence of pain and despair, a final equation where nothing equalled nothing and all calculation ceased.

And then he managed to squeeze his arms so that his hands could lie calmly across his chest, and closed his eyes and composed himself as he waited for oblivion.

The trouble was he didn't feel composed inside, and as the seconds ticked away he couldn't help thinking that the whole oblivion thing was an easy way out. George and Edie would still be in danger, no matter whether or not he was conscious of it, and that felt bad. He grimaced as he realized he was not going to go gentle into any good night, rather he was going to go feeling like he'd betrayed them by checking out early.

His eyes snapped open in the blackness.

'Well,' he said to himself, 'Forget this composing yourself lark. Go down fighting.'

So he kicked his heels in and started pushing himself further into the pipe. And as he did so a savage smile played on his lips. He was smiling because he knew this was a doubly futile gesture, first because he was soon going to be dead and second because no one would ever know he had made the gesture. He was smiling because he was just doing it for himself. He was going to die living his last moment being exactly who he was and not a damn thing less.

It was a good plan. It was tough, it was valiant and it was, in the finest tradition of all good plans, destined to fail.

He didn't die fighting.

He didn't die being who he was meant to be.

He didn't die at all.

Somehow in the middle of kicking and pushing his way along the narrow pipe, shoving the bundle of heart-stones ahead of him, he realized that he knew the day had turned, midnight passed, and he was, unexpectedly and extraordinarily, not dead.

He didn't know that this was because George had stood his watch and kept his place on his plinth alive, he just knew that not only was he not dead, but that he was feeling stronger with every foot that he moved along the narrow pipe.

And the pipe was narrow. It was getting definitely smaller as the debris on the floor got thicker and the

Gunner's nose began to scrape along the roof.

And then the pipe came to an abrupt end. He was reaching ahead of himself to push the bundle onwards when it met an obstruction and all progress ceased.

The fact that his vigour and strength was unaccountably returning had the contrary effect of making his predicament feel much worse. When he'd been winding down into what he thought was an inevitable death his weakness had enabled him to ignore the claustrophobia. Now he was strengthening, the fact that all his energy was being crammed into a blank pipe-end buried under who knew how much city earth was insupportable. The pressure building up in his head and body made him want to scream and kick, but you can't scream under water and there wasn't really room to kick. So instead he tried to ignore the fact that he had been worming his way forward only to jam himself into a coffin of his own making, and think clearly. He had got into this pipe because there was a small but definite whisper of a current running through it. If there was a current it meant the pipe was not a dead end. So he reached ahead of himself and ran his hands over the roof. He felt nothing but stone. He moved the bundle and his hands felt the sidewalls. And there it was – a void. It wasn't a dead end, but an angle. He squirmed until he could get his arm further into the angle and was amazed to find he could feel nothing but water, no sides at all.

He realized that the narrow duct he was in must be a side tributary to a bigger underground stream, and in this he was right. The underground water-tank was an ancient spur of the Tyburn, diverted for the very purpose of providing an underground reservoir. The water he was feeling moving against his fingertips was the flow of the main channel of the stream itself.

He shoved the bundle of sea-glass ahead of him and wrenched himself round on to his side. He couldn't quite get his body round the angle, but because he was gaining strength and because when you get a second chance at life you grab it with both hands, he wrenched away the crumbling corner stone and pulled himself into the wider stream.

He felt the pull of the water tugging at him. He could easily have gone with it and seen where it took him. But something pulled him the other way. He scrabbled for the bundle, took a firm grip on it, and pushed his way against the mild current. It was a contrary thing to do, but if anyone had been able to see his smile in the black tunnel, they would have seen it was not only contrary but obstinate and fierce and somehow exulting.

If he wasn't going to die he was certainly going to live, and live *his* way – and he was not going to do that by taking it easy and going with any damn flow.

43

UNQUIET DEATH
AT GHASTLY GRIM

Edie fell one short storey and was saved by a combination of thick snow and a hen-house.

At least she imagined it was a hen-house, because it squawked alarmingly when she hit it and rolled off into the alleyway.

It was still clucking in outrage as she ignored the fact she was winded and her shoulder felt dislocated and ran off into the snow that was still falling. Somewhere in the distance a barrel organ was playing and a church bell was cheerily tolling the hour as she thudded through the snow, George's jacket flapping wildly behind her as she tried to put as much distance as she could between herself and the House of the Lost.

The street was dimly lit by occasional oil-lamps

and she ran from pool of light to pool of light, checking behind her as she did so. The houses hunched over the street with drooping eaves and upper floors that overhung the narrow thoroughfare as if ready to pounce.

She was very conscious that her footsteps were the only ones in the virgin snow. She wasn't going to be hard to find. And then she ran out into a wider street whose surface was churned up by the passage of carts and cabs, and she ran in the middle of the road, hoping her footprints would be hidden in the general confusion.

She didn't, however, want to run in the middle of any street for long because she was too visible. She also had a strong sense that she was being watched, but when she whirled to look behind her she saw no one in the road, and only blackness stippled with falling snow above her. The sense of being observed became like an unbearable itch that needed to be scratched, so when she saw a chance she leapt across the strip of virgin snow and into a narrow alley, hopefully leaving no clue as to where she'd left the general melee in the middle of the street.

She looked back and noted, with satisfaction, that she'd left no trace at all. She ran along the side of the alley, keeping in the shadows, turned a sharp corner — only to come to an even sharper halt.

Straight across the street was a church, and beside it a small churchyard. The high wall surrounding it was topped with ornate multi-barbed spikes that poked through the soft topping of snow like a thorn-bush. There was an arched stone gateway, also topped with spikes, above a black iron gate that stood ajar.

Edie normally stayed well clear of churchyards, but there were two reasons that she started across the street, heading for the gate. The first was that there was a mash of footprints and wheel-tracks leading into it, so her footprints would be lost among them. And secondly she heard the chilling noise of dogs baying behind her, coming closer. Her plan was to get through those metal gates, close them, and wait behind their safety for her pursuers to pass. She knew without a doubt that the barking came from the mastiffs from the House of the Lost.

As she approached the gate she looked up and saw that it was decorated with stone skulls. There were two on each side, buried to the eye-sockets in the snow, impaled on the savage barbs; and there were three in the centre of the arch, resting on some bones. The central skull wore a laurel wreath like an Ancient Roman, which made him look even more ominous, like the Emperor of Death.

It was too late for her to stop now, because the baying was closing in and there was nowhere else to hide. She ducked into the gate and pushed it shut. The latch clunked to but there was, she noted, no way to lock it. She griped the obsidian blade and listened, ready to fight.

The dogs were suddenly silent now. She hoped this was because they had taken a wrong turn and run on. She crouched in the shadows of the wall and looked at the graveyard behind her. It was a cramped space, hemmed in by the blind-eyed backs of houses on two sides, and by the square tower and side of the church on the other. It was a mad jumble of snow-capped gravestones, as if the bodies beneath were stacked four or five deep. The spaces between the stones were far too short to leave room for the full length of a coffin between them.

There were no lights in the houses, but there was a dim flicker from within the church. She saw a narrow door in the base of the tower. Without thinking she slipped through the close-stacked ranks of gravestones.

And then she heard a voice and froze.

'What a busy night.'

'A busy night indeed, Majesty.'

The voices had a hollow, doomy quality to them. They sounded dry, and they were accompanied by a bony clacking as they talked.

'One goes out, one goes in.'

'No rest for the wicked, Majesty.'

'No rest for the good either. Not with the resurrection men abroad in the night.'

She realized with a chilling certainty that she was hearing the skulls talking to each other on the other side of the arch. The three central ones on the outside face of the stonework were of course invisible to her, but the two skulls on top of the wall were outlined against the night sky. And she knew what 'resurrection men' were. She'd always listened in school, even when making it look like she wasn't. Resurrection men used to dig up dead bodies and sell them to surgeons to cut up.

She looked down and realized that the muddy footsteps and wheel-tracks in the snow were just the kind to have been made by people digging and wheeling something away in a barrow. That explained why there was such a churn of markings leading into a graveyard at night.

One of the end-skulls swivelled on its impaling barb and looked at her.

'She's listening, Majesty.'

'Impossible. Unless . . .'

'Exactly.'

'Ask her.'

'Are you a glint, girl?' said the skull that she could see.

She nodded.

'She says yes, Majesty.'

'I didn't hear her.'

'She nodded. She's hiding.'

'Tell her there is much hidden in the boneyard of

Ghastly Grim, but that none of it is alive. Tell her to go.'

'You must go,' said the skull.

'Please stop talking!' she said urgently, ears straining for the sound of hounds or footsteps beyond the prattling chatter of the skulls.

'What does she say?'

'She's arguing, Majesty.'

'She can't argue with me.'

'You can't argue with the Majesty.'

'I'm not arguing. I'm asking.'

This was the noisiest deserted churchyard Edie had ever been in. She backed up to the narrow door and tried it. It was locked.

'She's trying to get in the church.'

'Will you please be quiet,' she hissed again, stepping round a newly opened grave. She hunkered down behind a gravestone. She noted the name carved across it. It read *Aemilia Bowles*. 'Please stop talking.'

'No. We always have the last word.'

She was really regretting her decision to seek refuge in this unquiet 'quiet' graveyard.

'OK,' she said urgently. 'Have it. Just be quiet.'

'She says have it, Majesty.'

'Tell her we don't need her permission to have it. We have it by right, for we are Death!'

Edie boiled over.

'You're not Death,' she said. 'You're a bunch of chattering stone skulls who can't keep their mouths shut!'

'She says—'

'SHUT UP. You are not Death . . .'

There was silence. Then another voice said quietly,

'No. But I am.'

It was the Walker. And she could see the two dogs silently pawing the other side of the gate.

Only now did she remember to look down at her hand, holding the heart stone. She had been gripping it so tightly that she hadn't seen the warning light blazing from it.

And then something large leapt to the top of the wall and crouched there, and where the dogs were panting, this thing was breathing in short choppy shrieks of hunger. It clapped its stubby wings together in excitement over the hunched mass of its torturously enclosed body.

It was the Icarus.

And all the energy seemed to drain from her as she slid down behind the grave-marker, realizing that now the Walker had her and would have George, and the Gunner was probably dead and that it was all over. And even though she knew she was done for, she used the last piece of her energy to scrabble away the snow and mud at the foot of the gravestone she was hiding behind and jammed her heart stone deep into the earth.

And then she stood up and kicked the earth in on top of it and stamped it down, hoping her legs were hidden as she did so.

And she saw the Walker come through the gate, knife in one hand, the other one covering one of his eyes.

And she dropped her head and closed both of hers.

44

HOW TO FALL OUT
OF A RIVER

A s the Gunner crawled his way against the flow, he felt life returning to his body in more ways than just the renewed strength. His hands felt like his hands again, not clumsy obstacles at the end of his arms. He could think straighter too, as if layers of thick cloth had been lifted from his brain.

He wondered if this miraculous increase in wellbeing extended to a lifting of the Walker's power over his ability to dig his way to the upper air. He flexed his muscles and reached for the roof of the pipe. Somehow the instructions were blocked between his head and his arms, which just stayed where they were and didn't attack the roof as he had told them to do.

He ignored the disappointment and pushed on.

The dark water-filled pipe just seemed to continue for ever, and the absence of any visual clues made it even harder to bear. Some of the time he hallucinated that he had become weightless and was crawling on the ceiling of the pipe, other times it seemed as if the pipe was moving past him and he was keeping still.

He realized he could fight these disorienting feelings if he concentrated on what his hands were touching on the wall of the tunnel as he went forward, because the texture beneath his fingertips was the one thing that did change. Some of the time it was bricks, some of the time it was long curves of stone or concrete piping. At one stage it appeared to be just clay, and he felt his fingertips leaving a groove as he squirmed forward. He imagined the cloudy trail his hand must be leaving in the clear water, invisible in the darkness.

He had been feeling a brick side to the tunnel for quite a long time, and had just wondered if he could work out how far he was going by counting bricks as his fingers moved from gap to gap, when he felt a new texture.

It was unbroken by any mortar cracks, so his first thought was that it was more concrete piping, but he quickly realized that it was different. It was metal.

He rapped his knuckles against it, and the answering vibration confirmed his first impression. He moved on for a few paces, and then the implication of that answering vibration hit him: a metal pipe, bedded in the clay of London would be deadened and sound-damped by the surrounding earth. There would be no answering vibration.

The implication was that he was in a metal pipe, and that there was air, not clay on the other side of it. His first instinct was to hit the roof of the pipe, but his hands wouldn't obey his commands. He kicked the floor of the pipe in frustration.

His boots definitely set off a bigger vibration. He did it again, harder. And then he smiled.

'Didn't say anything about digging *down* did he?'

And he turned on his back and hacked the metal-shod heels of his ammo boots on to the floor of the pipe. He sledge-hammered them down again and again, and every time he felt the answering vibration in the wall through his braced fingertips. Every kick of his boots got the same result, and then suddenly the vibration wasn't there but a sharp single shock shuddered through the pipe, and he had no idea what it meant, but he stomped down one last time with all the power in his body, and instead of the jarring impact of his boots, there was a slight resistance, and then his feet continued downwards, out through the bottom of the pipe and he was suddenly falling . . .

The Tyburn is one of London's hidden rivers. But it does show itself in one place, and that's where the

Gunner was: it crosses over the Regent's Canal in an aqueduct disguised as a footbridge, close to London Zoo, and it was out of the bottom of that aqueduct that the Gunner tumbled, in his own personal waterfall.

He experienced a moment of elation as he felt the air and then a jolt of surprise as he depth-charged into the water of the canal. The surprise was, in the circumstances, understandable: not many people fall out of a river, and even fewer fall out of one river into another.

He pushed off the muddy bottom of the canal and breathed in the night air. He looked back at the bridge out of which he had just tumbled, and the liberated Tyburn pouring out of it into the water below. He realized what must have happened, and grinned. Then he lofted the bundle of heart stones on to the towpath and pulled himself out. He paused only to put his helmet on, and then he picked up the bundle and vaulted a fence into Regent's Park and started running south east.

He knew it was after turn o'day and that he should be dead. If he wasn't, it meant someone had stood his watch, and he wasn't going to waste a minute getting back to Hyde Park Corner to see who it was.

He smiled as he ran.

Because of course his gut told him exactly who it must have been, and where George was would also be his best chance of finding Edie before the Walker got to her.

The glasses chinking in the bundle as he ran were all the evidence he needed to know that once a glint was in the Walker's grasp, there was no escape.

45

IN THE WALKER'S GRASP

The Icarus stood in the middle of the dusty library, its cropped wings brushing the roof as it loomed over Edie panting short angry screams out of the curved hull hiding its torso and head.

Edie turned her face away.

'If you find it worrying you shouldn't have broken the window,' said the Walker. 'It would never have been able to get in here without an opening that size.'

Edie looked at the Walker's face. There was no blood where she had slashed him, but an impossibly healed white scar cut across his face, below one eye, taking a nick out of the bridge of his nose, and ending in the other eye. That eye was now dead, clouded a pinky white, with no iris or pupil to be seen.

'And if you didn't want it angry with you, you should never have killed its brother.'

'I didn't kill its brother,' said Edie quietly.

'The Minotaur was its brother. Not an actual brother, but a brother in that they were the creations of the same maker, the same sculptor. They had much in common as a result.'

Edie didn't need to look to confirm the truth of that. The Icarus had the same powerful legs and body, the same sense of dark energy bunched and ready to erupt.

The Walker stood up and looked down at her.

Far off in another part of the house Edie could hear the despairing sobs of the Blind Woman. The Walker noticed her listening. He smiled and snapped his fingers. The Raven flew in the window and settled on his shoulder.

'You're wondering why she is crying so heartbreakingly.'

Edie didn't say anything. The Walker's hand traced the scar across his face.

'You're wondering what I am going to do to you. For what you have done to me.'

He was right, but she wasn't going to give him the satisfaction of letting him know it. She was unnerved by how calm he had been ever since finding her at the churchyard. He had almost been polite as the Icarus had trapped her and they had led her away.

He smiled without a shred of humour, and started writing on a sheet of paper. His voice was quiet, conversational – almost warm.

'I am doomed to walk the city until the Stone releases me. And so I cannot die. I heal, as you can see, prodigiously well. But in four hundred years no one has done what you have done . . .'

And here he looked up from the writing and fixed his one good eye on her and then pointed to the blind, pinky-white eyeball next to it.

'Now, because of you, I must walk the world one-eyed. Be sure that this is a wound and an affront that requires a magnificently well thought-out punishment. I shall not deny myself the pleasure of planning the gradual stages of your end by rashly killing you now in anger. For despite what foolish men say, revenge is not a dish best served cold: to my taste it is a dish best cooked after exquisitely detailed preparation, and enjoyed at blood temperature.'

He finished off his note. Edie found that the more he tried to frighten her, the angrier she got. And the angrier she got, the stronger she felt. Unfortunately it was also true that the more he tried to frighten her, the more frightened she got too.

She tried to suppress the mind-killing fear and watch what he was doing as he folded the note and then produced the two interlocked circular mirrors from his pocket. She watched as he unsnapped them and then took each one in his hands and unsnapped it again, revealing a second set of mirrors clipped inside the first. He then took one set of mirrors and carefully adjusted a tiny bezel running round the edge.

'That will bring them straight back to where I shall be,' he said to himself, then noticed her listening.

'We shall meet in an open space. That way if he brings help I shall see them and you will suffer the consequences . . .'

He reached over to the table. Edie saw that he had sandwiched the Black Mirror between the two wax discs, and tied them in place. He had also knotted a leather thong through the hole in the mirror's handle. He put the thong round his neck so that the heavy package hung on his front like a giant medallion. Then he pushed it inside his sweatshirt and buttoned his coat over it.

He pulled his dagger out from behind him and turned back to her. As he moved he revealed a woman's cloak and a bonnet on the desk behind him. She had seen them before. She had seen the bonnet tangled round her own face as the Walker drowned it. In the open spaces of the ice-covered Thames. At the Frost Fair.

Despite herself she shrank back in the chair. He waved the knife, imagining that it was what was causing her to flinch.

'Now. Do scream if you like. The Icarus will enjoy it. But I do need just one thing from you before we go.'

46

THE CHALLENGE

'Here he comes,' said the Officer's voice.

George swam slowly upwards out of the dark pool of sad dreams as if he was made of lead. It was hard for him to leave unconsciousness, and it was a huge effort just to open his eyes.

When he did, there were two pairs of bronze boots in front of his nose. He was lying beneath a heavy greatcoat that was somehow warm and supple as wool, despite being made of the same bronze as the boots.

One pair of riding boots was the Officer's. The other pair were heavier and more workmanlike, laced boots topped off by mismatched leggings, one a set of puttees, the other armoured with a calf protector.

George knew those boots.

He scrambled to a sitting position and looked up.

The Gunner smiled down at him.

'Hey,' he said.

'Hey,' said George.

'You OK?'

George thought about it for a moment.

'Not really.'

'Good enough,' grunted the Gunner, and he squatted down in front of him, eye to eye. 'There'd be something really wrong with you if you done what you done and felt all tickety-boo about it.'

George suddenly had to get the great thing rising in his throat out before it choked him.

'I saw my dad.'

'Yeah,' nodded the Gunner. 'You would.'

After a beat he pointed over his shoulder at the body lying at the north end of the monument.

'It's him, isn't it. The Unknown Soldier. That's why his face was made covered, so he could be everyone's lost one. So. You just made him your dad . . .'

George nodded and put on a tight smile. He didn't want anyone to know that somewhere inside there was a well of sadness that he had been drowning in. He didn't trust himself to speak.

'Must have been rough,' said the Gunner.

And he put his hand on George's shoulder and looked

away.

George took a series of long deep breaths, getting himself back together.

'You want to let it out, son. No one here's gonna think any the worse of you.'

'Absolutely not,' said the Officer, busy looking with great interest anywhere but George. 'Couldn't think more highly of you, as it happens.'

He coughed in embarrassment and lowered his voice a little.

'And for what it's worth, I blubbed like a baby all the way through my first bombardment . . .'

Maybe because they gave him permission, maybe because they understood, George didn't need to let it out. He swallowed it and found it went back inside and didn't seem so terrible.

'I'm OK.'

The Gunner turned back and looked at him with a raised eyebrow.

'. . . in a not entirely OK way,' finished George.

'Look at your arm,' said the Officer.

George had forgotten about the marble groove jagging its way towards his armpit and the heart beyond. He tore at his shirt, and looked.

The entire flaw had disappeared, leaving only a faint red mark, like a scar well on the way to healing.

'It's gone!' he said.

'A duel is a duel, I'd say,' said the Officer, smiling. 'Whether it's fought with duelling pistols, rapiers or great big hulking artillery pieces like that one . . .'

He nodded up at the huge stone gun topping the monument.

'And you certainly stood your ground. I'd say that's one down, two to go.'

George smiled and felt the other two grooves still twining below his forearm, the gritty stone one and the smooth brass one.

'I'd say.' The Gunner grinned and gripped his shoulder. 'And by the by: thank you.'

He held his big hand out. George took it. The Gunner grasped it firmly.

'Saved my bacon, no mistake. And if you don't mind me saying, I reckon your dad would have been proud of you.'

'Yes,' said George.

And the truth of it was suddenly there inside him. And it was as if it had always been there, but that he hadn't noticed it because he'd always been looking the wrong way, staring at the pool of sadness. Maybe it was like what the soldier that had worn his dad's face had said, maybe it was like imagining you were in the centre of a stage, and then realizing you weren't when you turned round and saw you were just on the edge of something much bigger instead. Whatever it was, he realized that a very big pain in his heart had gone simply because he had stopped concentrating on it.

'Yes. I reckon he would have been. I reckon he was.'

It was as if by not crying on the outside, all the tears had fallen down inside and left him feeling washed and clean. And clear-headed.

He got to his feet in one lithe move.

'Edie,' he said decisively. 'We need to find her.'

'No question,' said the Gunner. 'The Walker's after her, and he's after you.'

And he told George what the Walker had told him about the Black Mirror. And then George told him all that had happened to him, and just as he got to the bit about the Euston Mob the Officer tapped the Gunner on the shoulder and pointed at a dark shape gliding in from the east.

The two soldiers unholstered their guns and aimed at the Raven as it coasted in towards them. George picked up his hammer.

'It's got something in its beak,' said the Officer.

The Raven landed calmly on the white stone in front of them and gently laid the two mirrors on the ground. Then it stepped back. It wasn't going to make any fast moves with two revolvers trained on it, but it also had too much self-respect to look interested in what might or might not happen to it.

'There's a note tied on it,' said the Officer.

'Last pair of mirrors I saw like that was in the Walker's hands,' said the Gunner.

George darted forward and slid the note out. It was a simple message.

Come to me. Beneath the main banner at the Frost Fair. Step into the mirrors and they will bring you. Come now, or the girl dies.

The Gunner and the Officer read it over his shoulder.

'He could be bluffing.'

'He lies like the rest of us breathe,' said the Officer.

'No,' said George. 'He's not lying.'

And he gently lifted the cord that had been used to attach the note to the mirrors. It was not quite black. It was a dark, almost aubergine colour.

'It's her hair.'

The Gunner swore under his breath. Then he aimed his gun at the Raven.

The Raven wasn't surprised. It knew what was going to happen next. In its experience people had always shot the messengers when they brought bad news.

What did surprise it was that it wasn't a bullet in the chest-bone that sent it to hell again. It was a spear, thrown with great force and accuracy from the opposite direction.

George and the Gunner and the Officer looked at the sudden explosion of shocked black feathers, and then across the grass to where the spear had come from.

There was a parked chariot, and a very businesslike Queen striding over the grass towards them to retrieve her weapon.

'What are you men all staring at?' she said. 'It sounds like we have a girl to rescue.'

'I think we can manage, thank you ma'am,' said the Officer, stiffly.

'No we can't,' said George sharply. 'We'll take all the help we can get.'

And he picked the spear out of the pile of feathers that was already being winnowed into the night air and handed it to the Queen.

'Thank you, boy. Now, what I suggest is—'

'You don't suggest anything. If you want to help, you listen, because Edie told me about this. She glinted it, and it ended badly . . .'

The unmistakable crack of authority in his voice made the spits look at him in surprise. The Queen swelled in indignation.

'Why, I will not—'

'Yeah, you will,' the Gunner interrupted. 'If you want to help the girl, listen in. The boy knows what he's talking about.'

And the Queen bit her lip and kept quiet as George quickly told them how Edie had glinted the Frost Fair and seen herself chased by the Walker and drowned in an ice-hole. He told them every detail he could remember her telling him.

'And I don't know if it really was herself that she saw being drowned, and if it was I don't know if you can change the past. All I know is she saw it and I'm going into those mirrors to do everything I can to stop it happening.'

There was a beat of silence.

'I could do with a hand; but either way, I'm going.'

He turned and retrieved the lump-hammer from where he had leant it before standing to. The weight felt right as he hefted it in his hand.

The spits looked at each other. The Queen turned and snapped her fingers at her daughters behind her.

'Girls,' she said. 'Come and hold the mirrors. It's going to take very careful riding to get the chariot through in one piece.'

47

FROST FAIR

You can't change the past. Even if it hasn't happened yet.

This was the thought going round and round in Edie's head as the Walker led her from the House of the Lost towards the frozen Thames. She scarcely noticed anything except the snow in front of her and the strap binding her wrists together. Her vision was restricted sideways by the edges of the bonnet the Walker had tied round her head. Her bound hands were hidden in a muff, a roll of padded cotton and rabbit fur that hung from the front of what she assumed was the Blind Woman's cloak.

She knew what the Frost Fair would look like when they escaped the narrow warren of snow-deadened streets leading down to the river's edge. She'd seen it all before when she had glinted her own death.

You can't change the past. Even if it hasn't happened yet.

The thought kept whirring round and round. If she was going to be able to escape, then she wouldn't have seen herself in the ice-hole. If she wasn't going to be able to stop this happening, why try and escape? But if she didn't try and escape, how could she stop this happening?

Edie was a fighter. She knew one of the reasons she was beginning to spin loose in her mind was that she didn't have her heart-stone any more. But neither did the Walker. That was something. It probably wasn't enough to keep her alive by itself, but it was enough of a spark to keep her trying to figure out how to.

'Cheer up, girl. This is a sight rarely seen . . .'

If she hadn't already glinted it, the sight that met her eyes as the Walker led her over a plank that spanned a narrow open channel of icy water to the frozen surface of the river would certainly have amazed her. Having previously seen it as a background for her own murder took the edge off it somehow. But it was an extraordinary sight.

Below the looming span of Blackfriars Bridge the entire width of the Thames was iced over and covered in snow. The night was banished by the light of hundreds of lanterns and flaming torches that illuminated the ramshackle street of makeshift tents and shelters set up down the centre of the river. There was music and laughter and the sounds of a holiday crowd enjoying itself, mingling with the smell of roasting meat and wood smoke. London's tavern owners and cooks had taken to the ice, selling their wares from hurriedly built temporary premises decorated with garish signs and billboards. And it wasn't only food and drink that were for sale.

There were souvenir stands and portrait painters, there were jugglers and acrobats, there were fairground games and a huge swing-boat full of shrieking men and women of all ages. There was even a printing press being cranked by hand, next to a man with a monkey and a barrel organ. A huge painted banner straddled the street, reading 'FROST FAIR – COME ONE COME ALL!' and from the numbers thronging the ice, it would seem all London had responded to the invitation.

Again, if Edie hadn't already seen all this before, she would have been captivated by the magic of the sight. As it was, seeing it all – especially the monkey and the barrel organ – just terrified her. She remembered all of this, but the monkey and the organ were a very specific part of what she had glinted. She had seen and heard them and then noticed how their music had been drowned by an approaching sound of bagpipes as a parade moved down the ice street, leading a white elephant that had stolen everybody's attention.

On cue, Edie heard the warning rattle of snare-drums as a pipe band skirled into life in the distance.

The Walker was pushing her ahead of him, one hand firmly on her shoulder.

She needed to stop her mind unravelling. She knew she needed to think fast and move before everything closed in on her and her diminishing series of options disappeared altogether, leaving her nothing. She needed to choose something, and she needed to do it now. Even if it didn't work she would go down fighting.

The flash of a knife blade caught her attention and gave her something to focus on. A cook was serving slices of beef from a joint turning on a spit in the mouth of a booth just ahead. He had stabbed the blade into the wooden carving block as he took a customer's money.

The sharp steel blade was her way out. In the absence of any other options, this was the one she was going to choose.

She pushed the muff awkwardly up one arm, shoving it against her stomach and disguising the wriggle with a cough. The Walker just shoved her forward, not noticing that she had exposed her wrists to the cold night air and the cruel blade beckoning just a few short steps away.

She held her breath and then, when the knife was in

reach, she threw herself forward. Her hands chopped through the air on either side of the blade, slamming on to the red juices covering the carving surface. The blade was not as sharp as the obsidian razor she had used to slash the Walker but it was sharp enough to give her the escape she wanted.

It cut through the strap binding her wrists together, and as soon as she felt the constraint part she pulled her hands back up and grabbed the handle of the knife, yanking it out of the wooden block.

And as the Walker grabbed for her, she ducked and spun. His arm swung over her head, just missing and knocking the bonnet awry, and she kept spinning and slashed the carving knife into his leg, catching him behind the knee.

She heard a yell of pain and fury and left the knife in his leg. As he buckled forward clutching at his leg, Edie saw the bright blaze of the Blind Woman's heart stone in the chest pocket of his coat. Without thinking she plunged her hand in, grabbed it, and just ran, cannoning off people, heading for the open ice.

As she ran she remembered that when she had glinted this scene before she had seen the bonnet fall in front of her face as she tried to escape, and that that had been the thing that had done for her, because she had run blindly into an ice-hole, where the Walker had caught up with her. So as she ran her first thought was to get rid of the stupid bonnet before it killed her.

Her fingers fumbled at the ribbons, which was a good idea but a bad mistake: because fumbling at full tilt, trying to get the bonnet off, turned out to be the very thing that made it fall in front of her face and blind her in the first place.

You can't change the past.

Even if it hasn't happened yet.

48

LAST DITCH

'How's this going to work?' said George.

It working didn't seem likely from where he was standing. Mind you he was standing in a pretty unlikely place – in a chariot being driven by a Queen of the Ancient Britons, next to a World War One Gunner, cantering towards two small mirrors being held parallel to each other by the Queen's daughters.

'I touch the mirrors as we pass and we will go through,' said the Queen, lowering her spear.

The mirrors seemed impossibly tiny, and then they were right on them, and the Queen jabbed with her spear point . . . and missed.

'OK,' said George, looking across at the Gunner and the Officer. 'We don't have time for target practice.'

The Queen circled the chariot so tightly that it made the turn on one wheel, and for a moment George and the Gunner could do nothing except hold on to avoid being spun out on to the grass. Then the wheel landed with a thump, and the Queen raced back at the mirrors.

'Just getting her eye in,' said the Gunner.

The mirrors approached again, and the daughters didn't flinch as the whirring blades on the wheels whipped past centimetres from their knees and the Queen jabbed her spear – and missed again.

'Third time's the charm,' she said, reining the horses into another tight turn.

'There's no time for this!' said George, and leapt clear of the chariot. He heard the Gunner shout after him, but he ignored it and just ran towards the Queen's daughters.

They looked at him in shock.

'How does it work?' he said, hand grasping the hammer tightly.

'Just step in,' said the daughter to his right. 'Either mirror. The Walker has set them to bring you right to him.'

It didn't seem likely to George that this was going to work either, but he remembered how he'd seen the Walker step into the mirrors and pull the Gunner with him, and he thought of Edie, and the urgency of that thought made him reach into the mirror and step impossibly into it.

And he felt the surface tension give and then he was falling through layers of blackness that strobed at him, making him feel suddenly nauseous with plunging vertigo – and then the fall ended abruptly and he was face down on the ice with a mouthful of snow.

He looked up and saw the louring black wall of a barge in front of him, a boat that had been frozen in the ice. And then he turned round and saw, a hundred metres away, the lantern-lit carnival of the Frost Fair, and a parade with a white elephant at the centre of it wending through the tented street.

He had dropped the hammer as he landed, and he scrabbled in the snow for it. He'd just found it when there was a popping noise from behind him, and the Gunner tumbled out of nowhere. He looked at George with a short grin.

'She's going to take for ever getting through.'

'We don't have for ever,' said George, getting to his feet and pointing. 'The elephant's already here.'

And he started to move forward. The Gunner's hand stopped him.

'George. Thought just hit me. I broke my oath. The Walker's got power over me. He used it. Couldn't control my arms.'

'What?' said George, eyes raking the distant crowd for signs of Edie.

'I'm thinking if he sees me, he could make me do something bad . . .'

The Gunner looked shamefaced. 'Should have let the Officer come instead.'

'No,' said George decisively. 'Someone had to stay behind and watch for us coming back in case the Walker's on our tail when we do. Someone's got to be ready to shoot him down.'

'Yeah but—'

'No buts,' said George, kicking into a sprint.

He'd seen Edie.

'Just don't let him see you first,' he called back to the Gunner.

And then he was just tearing across the expanse of snow-covered ice towards Edie who was running away from the crowd at an angle. He yelled as he ran, trying to cut her off.

'Edie! Over here!'

She didn't seem to hear him. Maybe because she was fumbling at a bonnet someone had made her wear.

The Gunner started running too. He saw the Walker break out of the crowd at a fast hobble. He saw him turn and shout at something in the darkness on the other side of the river. Heard the words.

'Get the girl! Icarus! Where's the Bull? Get the bloody girl!'

The Gunner saw what was going to happen before George did. He stopped heading for Edie and ran towards the side of the river, where the Thames watermen had cut a wide channel between the shore and the ice so that they could still charge people for crossing over on planks they had erected. He saw a portly father quibbling about the fee, while his beribboned daughter jumped excitedly up and down at his side and pointed to the ice beyond. Her voice was sharp enough to cut straight through the sound of bagpipes and drums and into the Gunner's ears.

'Oh Daddy, no Daddy, please, pay the little man! It's there and we're missing it! The elephant . . .'

And George heard the voice and remembered Edie saying she'd missed seeing something because of the elephant, and he raised his hands like a megaphone and yelled at Edie, who hadn't seen him yet.

'Edie – don't look at the elephant!'

And then he hit an ice hummock and tripped.

But not before Edie saw him. And as she was about to shout back the Walker hit her from behind and they fell to the ice. Edie kicked and hit and bit like a wildcat, without thought, as furiously brutal as any wild animal fighting for its life. She smashed the Blind Woman's blazing heart-stone clenched in her fist into the Walker's one good eye. He managed to close his eyes and duck his head away just in time, but the searing light did temporarily blind him.

'Now you die, girl!' he screamed.

And she booted him in the chin and tumbled backwards on to her feet and ran, while he swiped at her through his stone-dazzled vision.

He pulled the long dagger from inside his coat and ran after her.

Edie was struggling with the bonnet that had been mashed forward over her face in the struggle.

She was still so pumped by the adrenaline of the fight that she forgot to look out for the metre-wide hole full of freezing water right in front of her.

Her foot hit water instead of hard ice and she plunged forward, straight into the hole, and the shock of the cold and the water in her mouth hit her simultaneously. She scrambled up through the icy Thames and her fingers clawed on to the edge of the ice as she tried to pull herself out of the hole. Her face broke into the air, her hair covering it like a thick flap of sea-weed, and she remembered that she must be watching this happening as she glinted this past death in a future and far away London. She screamed a warning to herself as she tried to scramble out of the water's icy grasp.

'Edie. The Friar's OK! Don't trust Little Tragedy! He's not what he seems! Tell George! Walker's trying to open evil . . .'

And then a rescuing hand reached over and grabbed her hair, only it wasn't rescuing at all. It was pushing her back under and all there was were bubbles and splashing and black water and then she broke free for an instant and fishmouthed for air and used her last words to try and complete her warning.

'. . . gates in the mirrors . . .'

And then the Walker's hand grabbed the bonnet and plunged her spluttering face under the water for the last time, and she carried on shouting as her lungs filled with water and the last thing she saw as she sank into the inky blackness was the Walker's face, lit red by the distant lanterns, grinning down at her through the floating tangle of her own hair.

And in that terrible last moment she wanted everything. As she started to fade the years of her life peeled away and she became younger and younger, all the layers of toughness she had had to put on to survive dropping off and leaving her feeling helpless and young and tiny. As she hurtled towards the full stop of her life she felt outrage that this should be so. She just wanted to start everything again. She wanted her mother before she changed, before she went strange, before she went mad, before she just went and never came back . . .

. . . and more than anything she wanted that child's first and best sanctuary, the heart's last ditch – the warm embrace of her mother telling her it would be all right, that today's pain would fade and tomorrow the sun would shine.

But her final thought was the desperate despair of knowing it wouldn't, as her eyes dimmed and the freezing blackness took her, alone and in the dark.

And then Edie died.

49

IRONHAND

George hit the Walker at full speed, every ounce of power and rage in his body powering him into the larger man like a runaway train.

He knew he was too late. He knew Edie was dead. He knew it was his fault.

The impact cartwheeled the two of them back in a cloud of snow.

George swung the heavy hammer in his fist right at the Walker's body, as if he could stop the black heart in one massive blow.

The hammer slammed into something the Walker was wearing under his sweatshirt, something thick that gave and cracked at the same time.

The Walker gasped as the air was pile-driven out of

him, but his left hand clawed out and gripped George by the hair and ear. The two of them staggered to their feet, eye to eye. The Walker got a breath and snarled at George, his one good eye blazing.

'Are you going to try and fight me, boy?'

'No.' gritted George. 'I'm going to kill you.'

And as he accepted the challenge he felt a ripping pain in his arm, jagging towards his armpit, and he knew without being able or needing to look that the twisting channel of bronze in his arm had ripped forward, heading for his heart.

He knew this was the second contest; this brutal tussle in the snow and ice was the next duel, the moment he would live or die by.

And he didn't care.

Because there was no way on earth that he wasn't going to make good on his word.

The Walker was a dead man.

'It's a waste, boy. But I have all the time in the world . . .'

And time went slow for George and he saw the flash of the knife as the Walker pulled it back and then slashed it up towards his belly in a cruel, gutting, killing blow.

And George's hand was moving before conscious thought kicked in, and this time it didn't flinch. It closed round the sharp blade and held it tight, stopping it a finger's width from his belly.

The Walker's eye widened in shock at the strength of the smaller boy. And what the Walker saw made him step back half a pace.

The boy's eyes were hard and unforgiving as stone.

'I don't think so,' said George.

And he jerked his hand sharply, and snapped the blade clean from the haft.

Then he pulled his hand back behind his shoulder and when the Walker let go of his hair and tried to get away he gripped the Walker's hand and held him as he stabbed the blade down into the Walker's heart.

The blade hit something hard and skittered sideways, but with all the cold rage George had put into the blow it still buried itself in the Walker's shoulder, so deep that George couldn't pull it out.

He let go and took a microsecond to notice that his hand wasn't cut at all, despite the fact he'd gripped the double edged blade like a vice.

The Walker stared at the broken blade buried in his shoulder, and then howled in fury.

George had time to look down at the black hole in the ice. Edie was long gone. He quickly stooped and picked up the blazing piece of sea-glass she'd dropped in her struggle. He could see it wasn't hers, being the wrong shape and colour, but he knew it for what it was, and without thinking he dropped it into the water. If she was alone and dead in the inky blackness, somehow the least he could do was leave the light on.

He turned back to the howling Walker, stepped across the gap between them and punched him in the face. The Walker went silent in shock at the force of the blow.

In the distance there was the approaching sound of something screaming in short excited bursts of noise. But George ignored it and kept on coming. He hit the Walker with a straight punch that knocked him flat on his back. Only then did George step back, in order to pick up his hammer and stand over him.

There was a thunder of hooves, and the Walker's eyes flicked left. He sneered up at George through a bloody mouth.

'Now you die, boy.'

George turned his head and saw the Bull thundering across the ice at him.

'Maybe,' said George. 'But you die first.'

He raised the hammer.

'I'll deal with your bull after that.'

'It's not the bull,' smiled the Walker, his eyes flicking upwards.

The Icarus hit him like an airborne sledgehammer.

50

UNDER THE ICE

The Gunner hit the narrow channel of water between the ice and the riverbank like a depth charge.

He'd seen Edie go under for the last time, and he'd seen that neither he nor George would get there in time to save her. So he did the only thing that remained, which was to go under the ice.

Tons of bronze don't swim too well, so he hit the bed of the Thames and did the best he could do to plough through the blackness towards the spot where he estimated the hole in the ice was. The human part of him went through the searing, drowning pain of oxygen starvation, but he was so driven that he didn't bother trying to hold his breath and put it off – he just sucked in water and got on with it.

He couldn't see a thing and surged forward by instinct alone. The snow-covered ice made a perfect roof over the river, blocking out all light. And as he moved ahead he realized he wasn't going to be able to see the hole either, since looking straight up was only going to bring a dark view of the night sky, which would be indistinguishable from the impenetrable murk surrounding him.

He flailed around with his arms as he went, hoping that if he couldn't see Edie's body he might at least touch it by chance. But as he stared blindly he realized it was a forlorn hope.

The girl was gone.

And then an orange light dropped out of the ice-roof overhead, and he looked up, and he caught a brief glimpse of the world above through the ice-hole, with George staring sightlessly downwards, his face momentarily up-lit by the falling heart-stone before he jerked away from the hole.

The Gunner reached out his hand and caught the stone on its chain and held it high, like a lantern in the storm. And the orange light shone so brightly that the turbid river-water flowing past became somehow less opaque – and that's when the Gunner saw the body, its foot caught in a broken cart-wheel half buried in the ooze, its hair lifelessly going with the flow, pointing to the sea.

He freed her foot and grabbed her, surging towards the riverbank. As he powered forward he looked down at her pale dead face, and looped the heart stone round her neck so he could get a better grip on her. He hugged her tightly, as if he could force some of the life within him into her dead body.

And of course you can't cry underwater, so the stinging in his eyes must just have been the Thames resisting his attempt to run through it.

He scrambled up the slope towards the torchlit strip of light, and pulled himself up and out of the water. He felt Edie's body flop against him as he coughed his way to his feet. He was about to start pumping the water out of her, when he heard the ice scrabble and the angry snorting that heralded the approaching Bull. He scooped her up and ran.

George saw the Gunner emerge from the ice out of the corner of his eye as the Icarus flew him away from the Walker, who was busy lying on his back and tugging at his clothes, trying urgently to get something out of his sweatshirt.

The Icarus screamed at George who reflexively looked into the blind curve of the creature's breastplate: somewhere inside the intricate structure a mouth was shrieking anger at him.

The Icarus was a worse flyer than Spout. George was

only about five metres off the ice, being flown jerkily away from the Gunner and Edie's body, unable to see what the Walker was doing, when he saw something pop into existence and gallop across the ice beneath him, heading for the Gunner, the whirling blades on its chariot-wheels twisting ice-devils out of the snow as it thundered beneath him.

George still had the hammer in his hand.

'One chance,' he said to whatever was behind the jutting hull in front of him. 'Put me down.'

The Icarus howled and shook him angrily. When George looked down he realized that the thing was gripping him with human feet its toes crushing him like sinewy talons.

'Fine,' he said.

And he smashed the hammer into the hull. He hit it again and again, and as he did so the Icarus shrieked and lurched in the sky, and then there was a crack and the breastwork gave away and George was staring into the mad eyes of the Icarus.

The Icarus was a contorted man jammed into the narrow space of the basketwork hull. His arms and hands were folded in on themselves and his mouth and lower face were bound with some kind of webbing – but not obscured so much that George couldn't see the hostile insanity snarling out of the face.

'Put me *down*,' said George.

The feet tore at him angrily and the eyes burned brighter. The head shook violently back and forth in an unmistakable 'No'.

'Then I'm sorry,' he said, and whacked the hammer dead centre on the straining forehead. The mad eyes rolled back and the Icarus plummeted, unconscious and – for the first time – silent.

George had time to see that they were going to land in open water, just beyond the point where the ice began. He booted himself free of the Icarus's limp feet in the instant before they hit the river.

The Icarus hit the water and kept going down. George kicked for the surface and gasped air, and then turned in time to see the jumbled edge of the ice approaching as the current pulled him towards it. The edge was a confusion of trapped driftwood and branches, and he had a horror-struck premonition that he was about to be sucked beneath the ice. He grabbed at the edge as he reached it, but the ice bobbled away beneath his fingers and he was pulled under.

On the surface of the ice the Gunner had seen the Bull just in time. He grabbed Edie's body and leapt clear as the sharp horns thundered in. The Bull tried to hook him, but its momentum made it overshoot and it crashed into the snow piled on the riverbank.

The Gunner heard his name being called, and whirled to see the Queen approaching across the flat ice-field, her horses straining against their harness, their feet kicking up great divots of impacted snow as they raced to the rescue. There was another figure on the chariot, and because he was hatless it took the Gunner an instant to realize it was the Officer.

He sped towards the incoming chariot, cradling the dead body as he ran. He heard a snort and the drumming of hooves behind him, and knew that the Bull had turned and was now thundering after him.

As the chariot approached without slowing, the gap behind him closed almost as fast.

He saw the Officer pointing urgently straight down and shout something.

'Mind the wheels!'

And then the Officer snapped his arm out, leaning so wide over the spinning blades that the Queen had to lean far out on the opposite side to stop the chariot tipping. Then time went very quickly as they closed on the Gunner at breathtaking speed, and he felt the Bull's breath on his back and a light tug as it tried to hook him again, but he had no time to think about how close the creature must be because he had to concentrate on the spinning blades whirling in towards his knees, and he stuck his arm out as if he was signalling a turn and hurdled the blades as they swept in under him. His open hand slapped on to the Officer's reaching forearm and gripped it at the same time the Officer gripped his arm.

And then the momentum swung him up and round as the Officer anchored himself on the chariot rail, and he was on board.

The Bull had no time to slow his headlong pursuit, and the spinning blades opened him up like a giant can opener, splashing twisting curls of bright bronze in its wake. The Bull pitched forward, its horns digging into the ice and throwing it into a slamming somersault where it lay still, upended and wreathed in its bronze entrails.

The Queen looked back.

'*He* won't be killing any more women.'

The Gunner dropped Edie to the bucking floor of the chariot and started trying to pump the water out of her. It was like trying to work on the pitching deck of a ship.

'Help me,' he said.

The Officer grabbed him and held him steady.

The Queen was turning the chariot.

'Hold on,' she shouted. The Officer looked up and saw she was racing towards her two daughters, who were holding the mirrors up.

'George,' shouted the Gunner as he futilely pumped water from the dead girl.

'*You* hold on,' shouted the Officer. And as the Queen

hit the mirrors first time with the tip of her spear, the Officer let go of the Gunner and leapt off the back of the chariot. There was a pop and the chariot disappeared. The Officer scrambled to his feet.

'Stay there,' he said to the girls, and ran away from the lights of the Frost Fair towards the dark end of the ice.

51

HEART-STONE

'She's dead,' said the Gunner as the Queen reined the horses in and brought the chariot to a sliding halt in front of the Artillery Memorial. The Queen dropped to her knees next to where he was pumping at her chest with the heel of his hand.

'Then why are you still doing that?' she asked as she moved round to Edie's head.

'Because I don't know what else to bloody do,' he said.

And she looked up at him and saw the big tears rolling out of his eyes.

She bent over Edie's open mouth, tilted the head back and pinched her nose. And then she took a breath and blew it into the waterlogged lungs. Then she did it again.

And then she listened. And when there was no answering breath she did it again. And for a while the two of them tried to revive the small dead body, refusing to accept the truth that she had gone.

Eventually the Gunner looked at the Queen in between breaths. His eyes had emptied and were now deserts of dry despair.

'Why are you doing this?'

She wiped her eye and the Gunner saw an echo of the dead girl beneath his hands in the way her jaw came stubbornly forward.

'Because I don't know what else to do either. Except keep fighting.'

'Fair enough.'

He pumped Edie's chest.

'Neither did she.'

And he thumped his fist into Edie's breastbone in frustration and grief, and Edie threw up a great lungful of river water and then convulsed in a terrible coughing spasm.

Her eyes flickered open, and then closed again as she passed out. The Gunner felt her heart. It was beating faintly. He stared at her in disbelief. Then he looked at the Queen. He'd never seen her smile before, but now her face shone back at him.

'Neither *has* she, I think you mean,' said the Queen.

He beamed back at her.

'If you wasn't a bloody Queen I'd kiss you.'

'If I wasn't a bloody Queen I might well let you.'

Then her face snapped back to its normal businesslike demeanour.

'She's not out of the woods yet. She's still likely to die of cold. We need a fire.'

'We haven't got a fire.'

The Queen was unfastening her cloak.

'Get a coat or something. We need to warm her up.'

He held Edie's wrist.

'Her pulse is hardly there at all.'

'Well get a move on then!' she snapped, and started stripping the wet clothes from Edie's body.

The Gunner ran over to the monument where he saw the Officer's coat and hat sitting next to the wet bundle of heart stones he had brought from the underground tank. As he picked up the Officer's coat he noticed the bundle was steaming.

'Hurry up!' shouted the Queen. 'We've got to get her into something warm. She's slipping away again.'

'Hold up,' he said as he threw the coat over his shoulder and untied the bundle. Light blazed at him. He quickly looked round to see if there was a taint or the Walker creeping up on them. But then he noticed something about the light. The glass stones he had put in here had all been of different colours, but now they were glowing with the same warm hue, like the orange at the heart of a well banked-up fire.

'Gunner!' shouted the Queen. 'We're losing her.'

She looked up in surprise as the Gunner dumped the heart stones next to her.

'Heart stones. The bloody Walker kept them as trophies of all the glints he'd culled.'

Like him, she looked round, searching for danger.

'No,' he said, as he started placing the stones round Edie. 'They're not warning us. I think they feel her. I think it's the spark of all them troubled girls kindling one last time. I think it's them having a last laugh at the Walker.'

The Queen watched him carefully place a stone over Edie's heart, and then she dug her hands into the blazing stone pile and helped him surround Edie with the warmth, then wrapped it in with her with her cloak and the Officer's coat.

And in the end it wasn't just the fact that the Gunner and the Queen wouldn't let her die that saved her. It was as the Gunner thought: it was all the lost girls and the lonely girls, all the odd women who thought they might be a bit mad because they didn't understand that their glinting could be a gift and not a curse, it was all of them who surrounded this last lost lonely girl and gave her the final warm sparks that their lives had stored in their stones, so that she could go on and live for them.

And because the Queen knew this was so, she wept as she watched the colour return to Edie's face and her eyes flicker open again.

Her small hand twitched where it lay in the Gunner's big bronze palm. He closed his hand gently on it. And then her eyes focused on him, and as she recognised him she gripped his hand fiercely, and he again saw the rare small miracle of her smile break across her face like sunshine.

'It's all right.' he said gruffly. 'I've got you. You were too tough for the Walker to kill. And you were too bloody tough for the river to kill, and all. You're safe.'

Edie nodded and coughed harshly.

'Where's George?'

52

ICE DEVIL

The Officer didn't find George at the ice edge. He found his hammer, caught in a branch. And when he pulled it he found George's hand still attached to it through the thong. And then he pulled on the hand and that's when he found George and pulled him spluttering and shivering out of the river and on to the ice.

'W-where's Edie?' was the first thing he said. He'd seen the Gunner dragging something out of the river as he flew over, and he hoped with an intensity that hurt worse than the cold that it had been her.

'I'm afraid she's dead, old man,' said the Officer. 'They've already taken her through the mirrors. Can you run?'

George looked terrible as he stood there trembling,

teeth chattering, fist clenched on the hammer.

'Yeah,' he said, staring across the ice.

In fact he looked like murder. Because he was staring at the hunched figure of the Walker, who was bent over something on the ice, scratching marks all round himself in the snow.

'Good,' said the Officer, taking his shoulder, 'because the real trick's going to be to get to those girls over there, the ones with the mirrors, without him seeing us.'

George shook the Officer's hand off his shoulder.

'No,' he said, hefting the hammer. 'That's not the bloody trick at all.'

And he began to walk determinedly towards the Walker.

The Walker was oblivious. He was so fired up that he could barely breathe, and the reasons for that were in two pieces in the snow in front of him.

When George had hit him in the chest, the blow hadn't stopped his heart. He had been protected by the two wax disks surrounding the Mirror. And whereas the disks were there to protect him from unintended contact with the Mirror, they had failed to protect the Mirror itself.

George had broken the Black Mirror in two.

And the reason the Walker was so fired up was that he

realized he had, in front of him, the solution to only having one Black Mirror. It had never occurred to him in all the centuries of searching for the lost second mirror that he could simply take the one mirror and split it.

The marks he was scratching in the snow were a pentacle of protection.

George had just broken into a trot, the Officer on his heels, when there was a pop from behind him and the Chariot appeared.

'Boy!' yelled the Queen. 'Get over here!'

George kept going towards the Walker.

'I'm going to finish him,' he shouted.

'No George,' she shouted. 'The girl is alive!'

George stopped dead in his tracks.

'What?'

She reined in next to him.

'Jump on. She's badly shaken and very miserable, but she's going to be fine, and she's asking for you. Come, quickly, we should hurry and get out of here.'

The Officer grabbed George and dumped him in the chariot and jumped on after him.

'Home James, and don't spare the horses,' he grinned.

George and the Queen were both looking at the Walker and the intensity of his activity in the snow. They looked at each other.

'What?' said the Officer.

'On the other hand, why not?' said the Queen, and George grinned through his shivering teeth as she clicked her tongue and urged the horses forward into a gallop.

'Oh, hell,' said the Officer, unbuttoning his holster. 'He doesn't stay dead long you know . . .'

'Every little helps,' said the Queen, snapping the reins and smiling fiercely as her hair flew out behind her in the wind. 'Every little helps.'

The Walker was so intent on lining up the two broken halves of the Black Mirror to face each other in the snow that he didn't look up until the first shot kicked ice into his face.

What he saw were horses careering towards him at full gallop, with the Queen hefting her spear, the Officer firing at him and George leaning out of the side of the chariot with a hammer held ready above whirling scimitars attached to the wheel.

'Fools!' he screamed.

They were going to run him down. There was nowhere for him to get away. So instead of standing up he crouched down with his nose on the snow, making sure that the two dark Mirror surfaces were facing each other exactly.

He knew he had it set up right, because there was a burst of heat and steam as snow began to melt under each Mirror edge.

Without a microsecond to spare he muttered something

under his breath and reached into the dark Mirror.

As the whirring blades tore through the space where he had just been, the mirror pulled him in and out of the way.

And as they rode over him the Queen leant over the back of the chariot and stabbed her spear through the ice in the very spot where he should have been. And George looked down and saw he'd disappeared and saw that they were riding through the pentagram of protection, obliterating the boundaries he had scratched in the snow. And as the Queen wheeled the chariot in a fast U-turn they saw something else.

The Black Mirror halves melted their way straight down through the ice and disappeared. But before they had quite vanished something escaped through the door that the Walker had opened in them.

And because that something was made of nothing, it needed substance if it was to survive in this world, and the first thing it encountered in the empty air were the ice devils kicked up by the spinning blades of the chariot as they raced over the pentagram. The Queen leant out and retrieved her spear from the ice. And then they were hurtling back to the Queen's daughters, and the safety beckoning in the silver mirrors they were holding.

And as George looked back he saw the ice crystals in

the air whirl into a body shape that suddenly grew and crashed after them.

'Faster!' he shouted. 'Go faster!'

The ice devil grew bigger as it gained on them, impossibly fast, and then the Queen twitched the reins and the lead horse hit the mirror and there was a pop and for a beat they all fell through layers of black. And as they did so they all had the sense of something flying past them, something very cold and alien indeed, like a blast of otherworldly frost –

53

CRACKSTONE

The London Stone sat behind its protective grille, in its usual niche on the side of Cannon Street.

Nobody noticed it, nobody stopped as they passed. Nobody felt the dark hum of power it throbbed through the city, connecting its streets and its buildings and the stone creatures that peopled its landscape.

But something noticed it. It noticed it the moment it arrived and the moment it noticed it, it went to it, faster than thought.

And there was no movement in the Stone, but suddenly it was covered with an intense white frost that was so cold that it cracked.

It was only a small fissure.

But it was enough.

54

LAST STOP IS NOWHERE

– and then the chariot bumped on to the grass, and the Queen pulled the horses to a halt. She turned in time to make sure her daughters reappeared behind them. They nodded at her, and all three shared the same fierce grin.

'Did you feel it?' said the Officer.

'Feel what?' said the Gunner, looking up from where he sat next to Edie, a red-faced, warm-looking Edie, swaddled in the Queen's cloak and the Officer's coat.

'Something followed us back,' said George, jumping out of the chariot and racing towards Edie. She grinned at him but threw up a warning hand—

'Mind the stones!'

All the warning stones were spread out on the ground around them, and all were now dull. Except for a small blue one clasped in Edie's hands, a blue the exact same colour of the bonnet a duck had worn in a story she'd been read as a child. A small blue warning stone that had been made into an earring.

George stepped carefully over to her, and not knowing what to do, punched her on the shoulder. She smiled up at him and punched him on the leg. And that seemed to be OK for both of them.

In the distance he heard the strangely comforting resonance of Big Ben sounding the hour.

'Get the boy that blanket,' said the Queen, pointing at the Unknown Soldier's draped body.

'But—' said the Gunner.

'No buts,' said the Queen. 'Boy's catching his death, he's already half dead.'

George put down his hammer and started unbuttoning his soaking coat with fingers like frozen sausages.

'Nice hammer,' said Edie, a small hint of mockery at the back of her voice.

'Nice earring,' he replied, equally unimpressed.

'Yeah,' she said. 'It's my mum's.'

'What was it doing in there with the rest of— oh,' said the Gunner.

'She went mad,' said Edie. 'That's what they said. That's why she got taken away . . .'

She looked at the earring.

'No question about why she was mad I guess . . .'

'She was a glint too,' said George.

'Yup,' she replied. 'Only nobody told her.'

'The question,' said the Queen, 'is why all the other stones have faded but it keeps blazing.'

The Gunner cleared his throat.

'Those stones belonged to glints the Walker killed or sent off to die mad and alone . . .' He looked at the Queen. She nodded. He went on. 'Maybe it's still alight, because she is too.'

'Alight?' said George.

'Alive,' said the Queen.

Edie looked down at the ground. She couldn't speak. George looked at his arm. The second flaw that he had felt jagging up his arm when he'd accepted the Walker's challenge had gone as he knew it would.

He caught the Officer noticing it too. The Officer smiled. Held up three fingers, then folded two down.

'One to go, boy. Good man.'

In the background George could see a police motorcycle flashing its blue lights as it roared down Piccadilly and leant into the curve that would take it round Hyde Park Corner.

George looked at the last flaw, still circling his arm in a tight spiral as if it was waiting for the Knight to reappear and finish the duel he had begun.

He wrapped himself in the blanket the Officer handed him, deciding to worry about the final duel with the Last Knight later.

'My mum could be anywhere,' said Edie in a very small flat voice.

'Budge up,' said George and sat down next to Edie. 'The Gunner could have been anywhere too. And so could you. But we got ourselves back together, didn't we?'

She nodded.

'There may be a bigger problem,' said the Officer.

They all looked at him.

'Can't you hear it?'

They listened; there was only silence. And silence, in London, doesn't ever happen – even at night.

'The city's gone very still, and the clock just struck thirteen.'

They all stood up slowly and looked around them.

The city *was* still. Unnaturally still. So still that nothing moved.

There was no breeze.

No noise.

No people.

The few cars on the street had stopped dead.

George walked to the edge of the road.

The police motorcycle was frozen leaning into the curve. There was no rider.

He looked up at the familiar red mass of a night-bus. There were no passengers, and no driver.

The others slowly walked out into the street, seeing what George was seeing. Edie peered into an empty taxi and stared at George.

'Where have all the people gone?'

He shrugged, turning in a slow circle, looking for signs of life.

'And why has everything just stopped?'

The only thing moving in the whole city was the thick snow that had begun to fall silently around them.

The five spits and the two children stood in the rapidly whitening road and stared about them as the shock of what they were seeing slowly dawned on them.

'Whatever we brought back with us,' said the Officer slowly, 'I don't think it's good.'

And – unconsciously – they all moved a little closer to each other, each one feeling strangely alone in the silence as they peered down the unmoving streets, too caught up in what was happening around them to notice what was happening above them.

Which was a shame. Because what was above was definitely noticing them.

The stone gargoyle was perched on the very tip of the giant stone field gun on the top of the Artillery Memorial.

The Gunner saw it first.

He stepped in front of Edie and George, fumbling for his pistol.

'Look out, here we go!'

Everyone turned suddenly.

George's hand shot out and he pulled the Gunner's hand down hard.

'Wha—' began the Gunner.

'It's OK!' said George. 'It's OK.'

'Gack?' said the gargoyle.

George grinned.

'He's one of us.'

And they all looked at Spout. And then at George. And then back at the gargoyle.

The Gunner put his revolver away. The Officer gave him a cigarette which he lit, and they all stood there looking at the grinning gargoyle through the cigarette smoke and the heavily falling snow.

'Blimey,' said the Gunner. 'If he's one of us . . . we're really in trouble.'

THE END

ACKNOWLEDGEMENTS

It's hard to write in a vacuum, and talking to other writers seems to ease things along on the tough days – especially when you have to raise your game to keep up with them. Thanks to the game-raisers for the help, provocation and support over the years and across the disciplines – Alex 'Nander' Cary, Fergus Fleming, Jonathan Darby, Al Whiting, Katie Pearson, Patrick Harbinson, Robert Harris, Amanda Silver, Rick Jaffa, Kate Bucknell, Rose Baring, Mary Miers, Barnaby Rogerson, and Mary and Philip Contini. Special thanks to my family, *consiglieri* and other secret readers for all the help and support in getting *Ironhand* on the page – Kate Jones, Ron Bernstein at ICM, Michael McCoy at ITG, Jack, Ariadne, Zillah More Gordon, Finn Younger and Charlie Harris. Much belated gratitude to the photographer Andrew Errington for taking a fantastic portfolio of images of London statues to get me going, and apologies to my dad for the bits where the Gunner was trapped underground – I forgot about the claustrophobia. Honest . . .

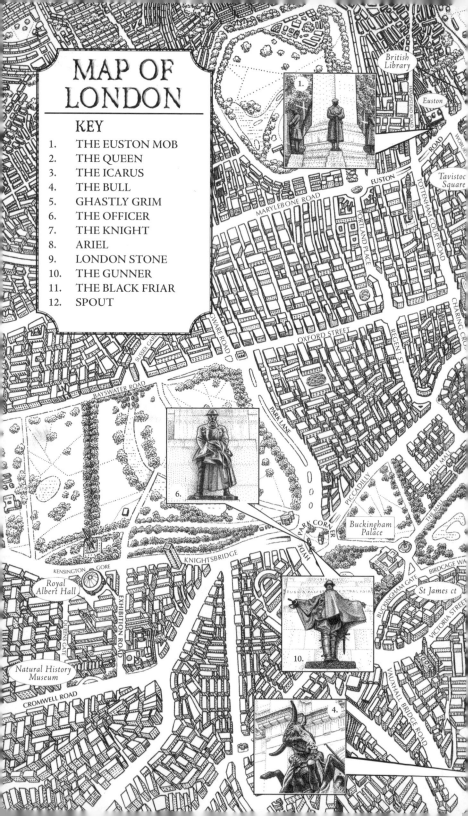

MAP OF LONDON

KEY

1. THE EUSTON MOB
2. THE QUEEN
3. THE ICARUS
4. THE BULL
5. GHASTLY GRIM
6. THE OFFICER
7. THE KNIGHT
8. ARIEL
9. LONDON STONE
10. THE GUNNER
11. THE BLACK FRIAR
12. SPOUT